the shadows in my mind

Printed in Australia
First Printing: October 2022
Shawline Publishing Group Pty Ltd
www.shawlinepublishing.com.au

Paperback ISBN 978-1-9228-5063-8
eBook ISBN 978-1-9228-5072-0

 A catalogue record for this
work is available from the
National Library of Australia

the shadows in my mind

KELLY WILSON

Dedication

To Brei, my forever Aanya.

Acknowledgements

I would like to thank my family, you are always so supportive of my writing journey, and encouraging me when the doubts creep in. To my amazing mum Joan. You are so encouraging and supportive. Thanks for reading my manuscript patiently, offering advice and helping to design the amazing front cover of this book. To my beautiful mother-in-law Jill. I cherish the many hours we spend revising, editing and brainstorming each time a new novel is in progress. You are a wealth of knowledge.

Thanks to the many people I was able to interview and source information from to ensure my facts were correct. I was able to create characters true to life and a thrilling storyline through the many personal experiences of very brave people. Thanks once again to my editing team Darren Lines and Kristy Pate. Your experience and dedication are very valued. Darren, I also need to acknowledge your constant support, advice and ideas for helping me navigate this new publishing world.

Lastly to the incredibly supportive, patient, and highly skilled team at Shawline Publishing. I am so grateful for every one of you, and your guidance and nurturing throughout this process.

Aanya

India, 2009

The little girl was a shadow of what she should have been in the physical sense.

Yet her spirit was strong, that of a lioness, despite it all.

She was brave and headstrong; the traits perhaps that had kept her alive.

Her clothes were soiled and ragged; her young skin rough and bruised.

The long rope tied to her wrist dragged a dirty water bucket, causing dust to swirl behind her like a cape.

Every movement forward was an effort.

Her frame was slight. She was starving.

She wondered why her latest punishment had been far worse than any before.

What exactly had she done wrong?

Her dark eyes were wary, but glazed over.

At the tender age of just 10, she remembered nothing of her parents nor the village she was born into.

But she knew she would never forget the strangers.

For as long as she could remember, they had moved her from place to place, forcing her to work like a man.

She was unsure which town she resided in now, but knew she was trapped.

Captive in a life that was very different from the one in her dreams.

It was her imagination that kept her alive.

They could never take that from her.

Her fingers and toes were scorched and blistered. Her master's tasks were brutal and endless, yet they were better than the alternative.

She hated the dark, damp cage he would throw her in as punishment.

The rats inside tried to gnaw through her skin. Their vermillion eyes watched her from the shadows until fatigue got the better of her. Then they would crawl silently onto her shivering body. It hurt when their bites penetrated.

Reaching the river's edge now, she could see her reflection in the fast flowing, dirty water.

It made her cringe. A single tear slipped hesitantly down her cheek.

The cut on her neck was infected. She could smell it.

He never tired of leaving his mark.

What had she done to deserve a life like this?

If she slipped into the water, maybe God's angels would save her.

If the swirling water engulfed her pain and fear, could its rush wash it all away?

She knew death was her only escape, but she also knew she needed to remain here. It was her job to protect the only thing that mattered.

Staring back at her reflection, she wondered where her spirit would go if she died?

He had said it many times.

'You are nothing. Pure evil. Some people matter and some people don't.'

Rahul

India, 2013

The man stormed ahead, fueled by his untamed rage. His fury was clearly exposed by his blackened eyes and clenched jaw. Angry at himself for letting his guard down, he was even further enraged that the girls had been daring enough to attempt escape. Had they not learned from last time?

He dragged a little girl behind him, unconscious and severely injured. Even if she died before he got her home, he cared little. Over the last couple of years, the girls had become more trouble than their worth. Her skin scraped along the jagged ground, yet she made not a sound. Oblivious to the further torture. Blood streamed from a cut above her left eye, covering most of her tiny, ashen face. This time things would be different, thought the man with contempt. He would make sure.

Unlike the last time, he'd returned with just one girl. Striding toward home, he was almost amused they had made it as far as they did. Through the darkened streets, like wild, scared animals, they had scurried no doubt. Running for their lives, desperate to escape the only life they knew. The only life he believed they deserved.

But he had found them. Stupid little bitches. They could not even do that right. Did they really think they could ever outsmart him? His evil laugh penetrated through the blackness, becoming lost in the sounds of the traffic and chaos beyond. His rage again returned, magnified. Everyone in his home would pay the price for this latest episode. He knew he must regain his power, ensure no one else would dare try such an escape.

The other little girl he had left behind was dead. His beating had ensured that. One less to cause him trouble. Her twin would surely learn from witnessing her killing. He made sure she had stayed conscious just long enough to see her sister's last pitiful breath. The man had tossed her useless corpse into the bushes beside the river. No one would ever trace her back to him if they found her. She was scum, meant nothing to no one.

Some people mattered and some did not.

He had told her that on a daily basis.

She would be easily replaced. Girls like her were ripe for the picking.

Aanya

Australia, 2018

I needed them to stop. The images racing through my mind, made no sense. I couldn't escape them. It was like staring into an old-fashioned projector screen. The pictures were random, out of order, distorted.

Why were they coming in such rapid succession?

And the voice. I needed those deep raspy utterances out of my head.

Had I known the man they belonged to? Or was this just an auditory hallucination?

I will find you again, Aanya, and when I do, you will pay.

Confusion reigned. The images made me dizzy. I felt like I was falling, swirling through time.

Yet from the outside looking in, I knew I had moved not a muscle.

Maybe it was the drugs they had given me.

Or maybe this was how it felt to lose your mind.

I always sensed it was a strong possibility that someday I would.

༄

I didn't want to wake up this time. I couldn't face the pain, not again.

'Aanya, honey, I need to take your vitals. Can you try to sit up for me a bit more, please?'

I remained still under the cold sheet, pretending I hadn't heard.

I hugged myself into a tighter ball. I wanted the harsh lights, the unplaced white noise, to dissolve.

And them, I wished for all of them, whoever they were this time, to leave me be.

They couldn't help me, no one could.

The pains, they just kept coming, different every time.

I felt a hand on my shoulder. It was gentle, warm, trying to coax me to respond.

I couldn't, or maybe I just wouldn't.

'Aanya, there is someone here to see you"

Somewhere in the distance, I heard the booming speaker interrupt the already loud room. It had been a constant disturbance throughout the night. This time, a male voice alerted the staff of a Code Blue in Ward Two.

Maybe now they would leave me alone. Let me sleep and disappear from this reality.

'Hi Aanya, I'm Doctor Ruby Belshar. You can just call me Ruby if you like. I'm here to see if we can sort out these mystery pains of yours.'

Her voice was smooth, reminding me of honey dripping onto a slice of toast. Somehow, its tone calmed me, and momentarily, the images ceased running through my addled brain. The pain however, remained constant and throbbing. I gingerly rolled over, rubbing my eyes as I adjusted to the harsh lighting in this prison.

As I focused, I saw her smile. It was a kind and knowing gesture, which seemed to light up her face. She reached for my hand.

Could this finally be someone who would understand? And answer the mysteries which had eluded me for so long?

I stared into her imploring green eyes.

'Am I going crazy?'

My voice sounded weak, husky. Tears escaped without warning from the corners of my eyes. My body was exhausted.

She squeezed my hand tighter and smiled again. Her eyes

seemed to glisten as she intently focused on me, wiping a tear from my cheek.

'No, Aanya, I promise you that, but will you let me help you?"

And there it was again; I'd been here so many times before. No one could help me.

You are not worth it Aanya, some people count, some don't.

I grabbed at my head. Shut up. Stop talking to me. I screamed silently back at the intruder in my mind. He was becoming more frequent.

This time, I just wanted to die.

❧

'How long are you going to feel sorry for yourself this time? You are stronger than this Aanya.'

I knew her sassy voice too well. I smiled.

'Well? It's not easy for me to get into this place, you know. The least you can do is turn that pretty face of yours away from the wall and look at me, girl.'

How did she do it?

How did she always seem positive, when she had little to justify the emotion?

As Tilly always said, positivity was a choice.

'Hey Tilly. I just want to go home.'

My groggy voice was so unlike my own; tears once again flooded my cheeks.

'Well, did the docs say you could? Let's go then, I need you to push this wheelchair for me anyway. I'm tired today.'

Without lifting my head, I rolled over and faced my best friend. I simply loved this girl more than life itself. She could always make sense of my disjointed reality. Tilly saw the world in a different way from most. Beaming at me now, she laced my hands in hers, pulling me closer. Our faces were only inches apart. She was so beautiful. Her red curls cascaded around her tiny frame. Her blue eyes seemed extra bright today, not reflecting the tiredness she had spoken of. Her freckled cheeks seemed flushed, and I could smell the strawberry scent of her lip gloss. Unless she had been eating lollies again; she always had a stash somewhere.

As I looked at her smiling face, I felt a little ashamed of my self pity. After all, she was the one in a wheelchair, and her prognosis was not good. We'd met when we were both 14, in this same hospital, both so frightened. Yet our stories were far from similar.

'Finally, you're awake! I won't be bringing you a mirror,' she'd said. 'You look bloody awful...I'm Tilly, I am your roommate. You took your bloody time!'

They'd been her first words to me. The first conscious sounds I remember. Those and her laugh. The sound had almost seemed too big to come from her small body.

That was how my induced coma had ended.

So, there was Tilly, a complete stranger at the time. She'd sat casually on my hospital bed, prattling on, as I struggled to comprehend where I was.

Nothing made sense.

Little did I know in that moment, it would be a long while before anything would be plausible.

I had arrived after a 10-hour flight only a week earlier, too injured to comprehend or remember. That moment, when Tilly was suddenly in my face, was my first conscious experience of Australia.

'You look pretty shit yourself' I'd managed to whisper back in a husky tone, razor sharp pains piercing my throat. It was as if I hadn't spoken for weeks. The effort was enormous.

How long had I been mute? I'd wondered.

I will never forget the overwhelming confusion in that moment. To have no idea where I was, what day or even month I was in, was paralysing, to say the least. But mostly I remember feeling a kind of inner panic. Because, no matter how hard I searched the depths of my mind, I could not remember my life before now.

Inside my head, it was like everything had been erased. I was searching a blank canvas for answers, yet could see nothing but emptiness. I knew at that moment it was more than just forgetfulness. Something was blocking me from remembering anything at all.

I was frightened. The physical injuries I would deal with, but what if my mind never recovered?

Who was I?

Where had I come from?

'We will be best friends, I can tell.' Tilly had laughed in her robust, warm way, gently squeezing my non bandaged hand. Somehow, the small gesture had made me feel she was right. I'll never forget the yellow beanie she had worn or the colourful cardigan draped over her hospital gown. She looked so out of place.

The only indication she was unwell at all were the black circles under her eyes and the restrictive tubes attached to her forearm.

The room had become a frenzy of people and noise, as nurses and doctors flooded in. I searched for Tilly, but could no longer see her. She had disappeared behind the sudden crowd. I felt like a little bird in a nest. Wild predators moved all around me, waiting for their moment to pounce.

My waking up was a big deal, apparently. Question was, what had I woken from? Where had I been?

That was 5 years ago now. To this moment, I still do not know the Aanya who existed before. How could the years just be extinguished like a candle? My light had become dark.

And here I was again, back in the same hospital.

My visits were becoming more frequent. This time mum had called an ambulance.

'The pain came again Tilly. This time around my neck, like I was being choked. I swear I couldn't breathe. I still have excruciating pain in my shoulder and my ribs, and one of my wrists. But there is nothing, no bruises, nothing to explain what the hell is happening.'

Hot tears of frustration welled again.

'You know I believe you Aanya. It's real. I just wish we knew why.'

'Be honest with me, do you think I'm going crazy? The doctors have done tests and scans just like last time and all the times before that. Apart from the injuries I came to Australia with, they can't see any reason for this pain. What if it's all in my head? Maybe I was a crazy person before...It is possible you know.'

'Aanya, shut up. You are not crazy, okay! Bloody weird, no question, but that's normal for you.'

Her laughter filled the room, but caused her to cough profusely. She took a moment to steady herself and catch her breath. Tilly reached for her Ventolin from the crochet bag hanging on her wheelchair.

'Somewhere, someone will be able to figure you out. I just know it. But Aanya, we made a pact remember, not to get down on ourselves. We can't. We have to stay strong, to fight our demons. Don't forget our mission. You will get well, and we will work out who you were before, while I still have time.'

I wanted so desperately to believe her.

⅋

Like every other time after an episode, my life got pretty much back to normal.

Well. My kind of normal.

Except the voice. I hated everything about its tone, its relentless threats. I had told no one about it, for fear they would think me insane. I remained determined to block it, block *him*. But so often felt powerless against its inflection.

Again, I was sent home from hospital.

It seemed it was an expectation I'd pick up where I left off. Maybe it was just one I had of myself. I found coping easier this way.

I resumed my hours at Uni, went back to my part-time job at the bakery and did my best to appear interested in being social, when I could muster the energy. But this time, I was finding it harder. The battle within my restless mind was becoming more intense, as much as I was trying to block this reality. Flashes of images I had no understanding of flickered in my mind. Again, I questioned, was this the beginning of insanity?

⁊⁊

I'd been so embarrassed earlier this week at Uni. My wider friendship group knew little of my real story. This included the most popular of them all, Bec. I never actively hid my past from people, but just wasn't one to blab on about it all unless asked. Bec, like the others, was far too into herself anyway to really care. As we had sat around the café, I'd honestly not heard my name being called. Bec had asked me something about whether I was going to the planned party this weekend.

How had I not heard her voice?

My awareness at that moment, had once again been drowned out by the chaos and distractions my ruminations caused. Tilly had poked me hard enough to make me flinch, spilling my latte over my jeans, Bec had been staring at me like I had two heads. Her smile seemed as insincere as her fake lashes and over tanned skin.

'You dreaming about that boy who keeps giving you the eye in class, hey Aanya? You should definitely hook up with him, tell him to introduce us to his boys.'

In that moment, I had felt further detached from my normal life, than ever before. But why?

Then there was the episode hanging out with Tilly and another friend of ours Tamsin. We had been wandering aimlessly through the clothes shops. I was doing my best to smile and nod in all the right places as we tried on outfits, tested make up and hair products and checked out any passing talent.

I felt grateful I could grip onto Tilly's wheelchair pushing her along from behind. I'd had the strangest sensation that given the chance, my body would have floated away. I'd imagined myself hovering above the scene, like I didn't really belong.

Did I?

I'd hooked up with a few boys in the last few years, partied like my friends, gotten myself drunk or stoned, but now, there was no denying, something had shifted deep within.

The problem was, I didn't know whether I welcomed the deviation. It scared me. I just wanted to stay in the now. I wanted to be normal. Just fit in with my friends. Get my nursing qualifications. Stay busy. Go under the radar. Just be 19.

My stupid bloody brain seemed to have other ideas.

⁂

This morning was chilly as mum and I headed into the Queen Victoria Market. It was a ritual we had enjoyed for a long time. Once a week we would pick our fruit and veggies, eat market food, drink exotic tea and hang out. I loved this time with her. Even though many of my Uni friends cared little about their olds, it was not like that for me. My parents were the centre of my life.

Admittedly though, my life was different to most.

Mum and dad had given up their roles as missionaries overseas, to adopt me at 14. When we had returned to their hometown in Australia, I was just an injured, confused, mere stranger to them. Yet not once did I feel like anything but family.

It had been easy getting to know mum and dad. They were open books, patient and kind. Always giving me the space I needed to recover. Never once did they pressure me. I felt strangely comfortable with them from the moment we had officially met.

Despite the confusion my past inflicted on me, I knew I was one of the lucky ones. But lately, I've been more consumed than

I wanted to be with my past. Up until now, I'd managed to quash these feelings, believing there was no point in rehashing something so dark. It annoyed me that I couldn't seem to let it go anymore, and switch off from the unknown.. I always had been able to before. What had changed?

It had to be the increase of spasmodic images. Were they memories? And the body pains? What the hell were they about?

Did this happen to other victims of trauma amnesia?

I'd been told early on, when I was first recovering, about the possibility of memory resurfacing. Each case was different, and it was up to our subconscious to decide when a person was ready, if ever, to discover the truth.

I'd rather not know. Or until now that had been my way. I would ever consider myself a victim. To me, that mentality was weak. I was headstrong enough to believe my past didn't matter. Nothing was going to hold me back from achieving anything and everything I wanted.

Recently, in the middle of one of my Uni rounds at the hospital, I had stood staring at the babies through the nursery window. I was captivated, trying to imagine myself as a little baby.

Had my real mum and dad held me in their arms?

Had my parents whispered promises they would always take care of me?

It's not like I was actively 'searching' for answers as to who I was before, or where I'd come from. But certainly, an unsettling, heavy fog had set in. Five years was a long time to have no memory of anything much before I'd woken next to Tilly and her yellow beanie in an Australian hospital.

Had I asked to come to Australia?

Was there no one in India who had fought for me to stay?

How did I even really know the minimal personal details I had been told about myself were correct?

I'd woken in hospital to a new reality. Suddenly, I was facing a long recovery and rehabilitation from serious bodily harm.

What had I done to deserve such a torturous beating and from whom? I had thought I'd never want to know, but something deep inside was stirring the pot of intrigue.

'You look a million miles away today, Aanya. What's going on in that pretty little head of yours, my love?'

I smiled at Mum as she fumbled with the controls on the dash. Our car was fogging up as we drove. Elvis was belting out a melody on the radio. Our dog, Rhubarb, was panting excitedly out the back window. He loved a car trip. His red shaggy coat was almost dancing with the magic of what adventure may lie ahead. Melbourne was always so cold. Today the wind was howling, the last of the autumn leaves swirled on the pavement.

'Was it cold in India, Mum?'

She laughed, turning the heater up a notch. It began blasting into the compartment, causing me to sneeze.

'So that's where you are, hey? Back in India. It's hot and humid there, for most of the year. Not like the unpredictable seasonal changes Melbourne can present in just a day, that's for sure. When we lived there, we acclimatised eventually.'

I wish I could remember. I glanced over at her. Mum flashed me one of her reassuring smiles.

'Can you drop me at the library after the market? I really want to check out a few things for Uni.'

'Sure hon. You know, it is more than okay to delve back into the past if that's what you need to do. All I ask is that you don't shut us out.'

The comfortable vibe between us seemed to shift slightly, and I watched mum's hands as they gripped the steering wheel with a little more intensity. She cleared her throat.

'As we have discussed, we know very little of your situation before we found you by the river. But as you know, whatever you had been through was brutal. I just need you to be ready to face that.'

Mum reached for my hand now, yet her eyes never left the road. 'You're strong enough Aanya. You have been from the moment we met.'

Typical mum, she always saw me so differently than I did myself.

'So, you need never feel you are alone if you want to start investigating your life before Australia, okay hun. Honestly, I would be the same. It has surprised your dad and me you have never wanted to know much. But we always knew one day you would. We still have many good contacts in India to help. You just have to say the word.'

I smiled across at her as she met my gaze nodding. Her smile was broad, yet I could see a slight tension in her eyes

Despite being in her mid 50s, her vibrancy made my mum appear much younger. Mum was lean and strong, full of energy. Her calming, knowing way had made me feel loved and protected from the very beginning. She always had my back. Her inner strength made me feel safe. From the first moment we met, I had thought her so beautiful. Mum had cried the first time she saw me awake in the hospital. Apparently, they had kept a bedside vigil for weeks.

'My brave, fearless girl. Welcome back.' Those were her first words to me, as she had gently cupped my face and stroked the hair from my eyes. I have never forgotten because I always wondered, was she right?

As I began to get to know her, I realised her real beauty was within. She was wise, and tenacious and hard to ruffle. Her hair was still naturally blonde, cut bluntly at her shoulders. And her complexion was fair, almost milky white. So different from my own dark locks and rich olive skin. Nancy's eyes were hazel, mine almost black. She was tall and lanky; I was petite, with a fine frame. But as different as we looked on the outside, over our years together, we had grown alike. We shared many similar values and life aspirations. Mum was such an inspiration. She grounded me, taught me how to remain strong. Best of all, mum showed me the importance in believing I was valued and loved, despite not knowing who I was before.

It was now that mattered.

Reflecting in this moment as we drove silently together, I realised most of who I am, is nothing more than a made up narrative. The fictional story which changed as often in my mind, as did my moods.

Maybe this was how I coped.

My response came slowly today. Another thing I loved about my mum was she never rushed my thinking, or demanded answers. Dad was the same.

I studied my hands absentmindedly. They wore many deep, ugly scars. Missing was the very tip of my little finger on my left hand. I had no idea how that came to be.

I shook off my pensive mood, replacing it with a well-worn smile. Be present in today only, Aanya.

'I'm good, Mum. I just wish I could understand these pains that come and go. They were so intense last week. My wrist, it felt exactly like the time I broke it when I was 16, yet there was nothing to show for it! If I could just rationalise the pain, it would help me believe I'm not going crazy.'

'Oh, Aanya, you are certainly not going mad. But I agree, they are disrupting your life too much. Listen, I have found someone I think just might be able to help you. I hope you will agree to see her. Think on it for me, will you?'

Within a few days, I found myself in the waiting room of the same hospital I detested so much. A different building this time. Today, it was the Specialist Centre. As I looked around at the posters on the wall, I watched the other patients waiting restlessly. The hospital staff were buzzing around like they were the busiest people on earth. All knew their purpose. Did I?

The feeling was back, like I didn't really belong; an imposter in this world. Something about the smell assaulting my senses seemed to unsettle my head. Why exactly, I couldn't place.

Tilly's text had coerced me out of the car just moments earlier. I'd text her from the hospital parking lot, looking for reassurance.

Don't make me come down there, Aanya. Get your arse inside. Better to know what you are dealing with so you can get on with it. Her words had nearly leapt from the screen.

'Alright!!!!!' had been my reply.

ॐ

'Aanya, nice to see you again! Come with me, honey.'

It was the doctor from my last visit here. Ruby, she had said her name was. She had seemed very interested in helping me that day, before abruptly being called away to an emergency.

Wasn't my situation an emergency?

Here we go again. I seemed to weigh a ton as I forced myself to stand and walk behind her. She smelled like lemongrass and I could hear her dress swishing against the movement of her voluptuous frame. As she walked, she hummed a tune I did not recognise.

Why was I even here? Maybe this was a mistake?

You are not worth it, Aanya. You are nothing.

What the hell? I shook off the intrusive inner voice. Reluctantly, I picked up my pace behind her.

Dr Belshar's office was bright and cheerful. I had to assume that was deliberate, aiming to help her patients relax. I felt anything but. Pictures of peaceful ocean scenes, rainforests and snow topped mountains filled the walls. Fresh flowers were on her desk. She gestured with a wide smile for me to sit on a burnt orange couch in the left corner of the room. This was not like any doctor's office I had seen before.

Like the last time I had seen her, she wore vibrant colours. Ruby was short in stature, but well-rounded one would say. She had an attractive demeanour, a strong energy. I wondered how long she had spent on her hair and makeup this morning. Her lips were a little too red, just like I remember from the hospital. Her hair stiff and pinned in its carefully placed bun. Studying her as I sat in silence, she appeared confident and deliberate in her actions. Strategic was a word that came to mind. I tried to imagine feeling that sure of myself. Maybe it would come with age. I certainly wasn't unsure of myself, but this woman was next level.

Despite this, I found it hard to get a read on her personality as she shuffled through the papers on her desk. Was all the surrounding brightness real, or just a facade?

Time would tell. She seemed nice enough, I suppose.

My silent alarm bells were already gonging in my head, my stomach was doing flips. I tried to push these reactions down.

She deserved a chance, my mum had said.

So did I.

'Thanks for coming in, Aanya. I'd like to get to know you a bit, and perhaps see if I can help you. As a psychologist, I specialise in trauma amnesia. So, you can see why you are of great interest to me. But at the end of the day, what happens next is completely up to you, of course. You are an adult and in complete control of your choices.'

She flicked through my file, moving her fingers from page to page as fast as she spoke. The movement caused the huge pink diamond on her finger to glisten as it caught the speckled sun entering through the window.

'Oh, you are studying to be in the medical profession yourself I see. That's really great. Perhaps you can join me here at the Royal Melbourne one day?' she said.

I wondered what exactly was in my file. It sure was thick enough.

Suddenly, I felt overwhelmed. A little claustrophobic. I just needed a moment. I stood, then sat quickly again. My body felt agitated, and my legs were jittery. As much as I wanted to discover why the excruciating pain kept recurring in my body, I felt skeptical it was in any way related to my past.

Why would it be?

'Are our sessions private? I just don't know if I am comfortable with strangers unpicking me from the inside out.'

Ruby looked up sharply from the folder she was thumbing through. She studied me silently without responding. I looked away, feeling my face reddening. I didn't mean for my words to be as abrupt as they did in that moment. I had always been fiercely protective of myself, especially if I felt I could not control an outcome.

She smiled. Placing my folder down and giving me her complete attention, she moved to sit beside me on the couch.

'Yes, Aanya, strictly between you and me. Unless, of course, I feel you are in danger at any point.'

'Danger? Of what?'

'Maybe yourself, or maybe your past. But I am sure we have nothing to worry about.'

She nodded, continuously smiling as her lime green glasses slid down her nose. Her red lips seemed even more prominent and glossy as she reached over and patted my arm.

I wanted to run. But I knew I needed to stay.

Maybe she could help me.

That would be worth being brave for.

Then again, if I hadn't remembered in all this time, could anyone help me?

I agreed to see her a couple of times a week. Just to chat, so she could, 'get to know me,' she said. I almost laughed. That wouldn't take long, after all, I only 'knew me' after the age of 14.

The following week, the rain was again pouring outside. It was only the beginning of winter in Melbourne, yet already icy. Her office was becoming strangely comforting, and her coffee tasted excellent.

'So, tell me about Tilly. I had the pleasure of meeting her on your last admission here. She certainly is full of life. How did you become friends? Obviously, you are very close.'

If this was going to help me, I needed to be open and tell her the facts.

'Well, I met Tilly when I first came to Australia at 14. When I woke in hospital, there she was, just sitting on the end of my bed. She is my rock. I owe so much to her.'

Even talking about Tilly made me smile. I hoped our friendship would last forever, even though I knew it was near impossible we would be able to grow old together. I found myself shifting uneasily on the couch at the thought.

'Tilly was in hospital at the time, too. This was when she was first diagnosed with MS. It's bloody unfair. She deserves so much more than being trapped by that horrible illness. We were both scared and confused about what was happening in our lives. We have such different backgrounds, yet the bond was instant. It felt like us against the world. We've helped each other ever since, neither path has been easy.'

I looked up at Ruby, she offered very little expression, somewhat deep in thought herself.

'Seems your worlds were meant to collide that day Aanya. It's amazing how the universe always gives us exactly what we need to proceed. Never ceases to amaze me.'

I couldn't argue with that.

'We have been through so many ups and downs, faced each new challenge head on, together. Tilly is the bravest, happiest person I know. Even when she feels shit, she picks herself up and makes the best of the day. I try to be like that too. But I'm not.'

'We are all different Aanya, there is nothing amiss with that.'

'She inspires me greatly, but she is also such a dag, you know.

Tilly likes to keep things real.'

I shook my head, my smile telling of my love. Ruby got up and headed over to sit beside me on the couch. She sat heavily almost spilling her coffee.

'Sounds like you are both lucky to have each other. So, she lives near you then?'

'Yes, as it turned out, in the very next street to my home. She's in a wheelchair now, as you saw her health has deteriorated rapidly. But that never stops us. I drive her around, or walk with her, whatever, as long as we can catch up. She is also studying to be a nurse.'

The room stilled, Ruby faced me directly, putting her hand on my knee. For a fleeting second, I felt like bolting.

'And what does she make of the body pains you keep getting Aanya?'

I hesitated, looking away at the ground. I didn't really want Tilly to be right on this one. Something always held me back from being brave enough to go back beyond the point my memory would allow. I took a long slow breath.

'She thinks they are related to my past, 100%. We just haven't figured out how.'

'And you? What do you think, Aanya?'

'Well, up 'til now, I have tried just to focus on my present life. I decided from the beginning not to allow my mind to get blurred and tormented by a past I can do nothing more than speculate about. Obviously, whatever happened was not ideal. But lately, I will admit, I am getting curious'.

I felt a surge of energy through my veins.

'Actually, that's wrong, it's more than that. I feel like something inside is willing me to go back there, almost pulling me back into my past I mean. I know that sounds crazy Ruby. I'm not going crazy am I?'

I met Ruby's eyes. Her stare was intense but knowing.

'You are far from crazy Aanya, as I have said before. But to put it bluntly, I do believe part of your mind is reaching out to you if you will, perhaps trying to help you understand. You are curious, that's only natural. I know you don't want to believe it, but I think your mystery pains are related without question.'

I stared at her for what seemed like forever. What could that mean? It was a lot to process?

'You are the first doctor to say that to me, Dr Belshar.'

'You know what else I think, Aanya?'

She leaned close, almost too close, but I dared not move as I wanted to hear her take.

'Somewhere, buried deep within you, is the knowledge you need to understand who you really are. I like to call them shadows of the mind. Soon, when you are ready to fully receive them, these adumbrations are going to come into the light.'

Becoming quickly exhausted, I was keen to leave her office. I barely registered the lights and sounds of the hospital as I exited. I was swirling on the inside. Deep in thought, I remained in my car for some time in the parking lot. Something about her words confronted me on many levels. She really believed she could help me. No one had ever put it quite like that.

'The shadows in my mind.'

I visualised nasty creatures lurking in the darkness, clawing to get out of their hidden space. And me, pushing the door tightly shut, willing them to stay away, stay hidden just a little while longer. Dr Belshar had said often trauma amnesia never rectifies itself, and until the subconscious is ready to release the memories, our brains work feverishly to protect us.

Did I really want to know?

After all, my life was pretty great now. Apart from the debilitating pain that randomly struck me, time and time again. And then there was the voice, or the thoughts, or whatever it was that lately had been plaguing my mind. These brief, personal attacks, were unnerving. I'd read only last night about 'auditory hallucinations.'

What the hell did all this mean?

Was *he,* the mysterious voice, actually real? Was he the shadow I had been protecting myself from?

Did I really want Dr Belshar to take my mind back there?

⚹

Some hours later, I headed up the familiar path toward the leafy entrance of my home. Where had the time gone? I could smell the delicious aroma of curry long before I opened our front door. Pausing, I reflected on the bright yellow of the entrance. I smiled at the memory. When I had first come home from hospital, my folks had asked me what colour I would like to paint the door. Yellow. I didn't know why, but I was certain it had to be yellow. It was the smallest of gestures from my mum and dad, yet it instantly made me feel like I belonged.

Wednesday night was always curry night. Mum had learnt to cook well in her years spent in India. Tilly was talking at the speed of light as I pushed her toward the house. She joined us most Wednesdays. I found my mind wandering back to my appointment with Dr Belshar. At this stage, however, I would keep the sessions to myself. My processing time needed to be private.

I shook my head and willed myself to stay in the present. Tilly was talking about our Uni sessions today. She was the keenest student I knew. I desperately hoped the world would be kind enough to allow her to realise her dream of becoming a nurse. Tilly would simply be brilliant in the role. Few understood pain and suffering like she did. It killed me to watch her health regress so significantly in the years I had known her. Not that we ever said it out loud.

'Howdy girls, how was your day?'

'Hey Papa Jeff! Smells good in here. Mama Nancy Pancy been cooking up a storm again, so my nostrils tell me?'

Tilly loved the nicknames she had fondly given my parents. Only she could get away with it. Secretly, I think they loved it.

My dad met us in the entrance hall, helping me to get Tilly inside. His smile beamed through his grey beard, and I fell into the arms of my very own gentle giant, for a bear hug. He kissed my cheek, his facial hair scratching like a wire brush. This man was the calmest soul I knew. Instantly, I felt better. Nothing much phased him. Even the way he looked. 'If it feels good, wear it' was his saying. Today he wore Indian patterned loose pants with a green poncho. Tilly and I stole a glance at each other. Stifling a laugh, it was obvious we were thinking the same thing.

Dad worked in mental health now as a social worker. I could just imagine how much his clients would love him. He had a genuine ability to make everybody feel like they were the most important person in the world.

'Tilly, how's tricks my favourite friend? You are looking particularly glamorous this evening. Is that a new diamond wheelchair you are driving?'

'Good evening my second favourite dad, and no, I sparkle enough thank you very much, without a blinged up vehicle.'

His laugh filled our small entrance room.

'Too right you do Tilly.'

He kissed her warmly on the head before we ventured toward the source of the aroma. I linked my arm in his.

Why would I want to risk changing my life right now?

My shadows were there for a reason. I was safe in the light. Right?

❦

The day had exhausted me. I felt relieved to be jumping into bed, despite it only being 10pm. Tabitha was curled at the end of my throw rug. She sleepily opened one eye and meowed as I peeled my doona back to slip underneath. Reaching toward my bedside table to plug my phone into the charger, I felt a pang of guilt. Yet again, there sat my unopened nursing textbook. Tomorrow, I promised myself, I would get this week's reading done. I couldn't risk falling behind in class. Anatomy was tough enough as it is.

It was then my eye caught a glimpse of something else.

A letter.

The envelope looked quite thick, with many different stamps and markings on the front.

Mum hadn't mentioned a letter. I rarely received actual mail. Everyone was online these days. Intrigued, I sat back up, grabbing the envelope. The postage markings revealed it had come from overseas, India no less. Strange. I had never had any correspondence before. I noted no return address or name on the back. The black inked handwriting on the front seemed almost childlike in its font. I lifted it to my nose. A mixture of incense and spice filled my senses immediately. My brain registered them at once. Somehow, I knew these smells were not foreign to me.

Welcome home, Aanya. I am waiting for you.

The voice again. I pushed it down, physically shaking my head to clear my mind.

The bulk of the envelope suggested its contents were more than just a letter. Tabitha swaggered up the bed to investigate. Her sniffing resulted in a sneeze. My laughter eased some of the nervous tension I was unaware had been building within. Shaking off the weird unease, I convinced myself it possibly was just from the missionary organisation mum and dad were linked with. Or perhaps even the orphanage I had originally been placed at in Nepal.

Momentarily, I closed my eyes, trying to visualise the orphanage in my mind. Nothing came.

Had I cried the day I had been placed there?

Why was there no one else to take me in?

Did that mean I was the sole survivor in my family?

Surely mum would have mentioned a letter? Dad must have

collected the mail today. He was far more absentminded than her when it came to giving me messages.

Tabitha curled up in a ball on top of the envelope now resting in my lap. She stretched out her ginger paw and began grooming herself. I couldn't help but smile. Cats never failed to sit exactly where you needed them least. Mostly, she sat on the keyboard of my laptop as I tried to work. I stroked her long fur, finding comfort in the soft purr. She had been with me from the start. Here to greet me the first day I had walked into my new life in this home.

Did I have a pet when I was in India?

A brief vision momentarily consumed me. Rats running over my skin, tearing at my flesh.

What the hell?

Tabitha was very intuitive; I had come to know this over time. For a fleeting second, I wondered if she were trying to protect me from something tonight.

'It can wait till the morning, hey Tabby.' I placed the envelope back on my bedside table and turned off my lamp. 'It will be just some sort of marketing or charity thing.'

Deep down I sensed I was being a coward, but self-preservation in this moment was paramount.

You always were, Aanya. That's why you ran away.

I willed my mind to stop racing, just forget the letter and switch off for sleep. I was restless, tossing and turning in frustration. Trying to sleep was pointless. I was aware my body felt strange, tingly, as I became conscious of my surroundings again. Tabitha had left and was curled up on my chair across the room. As my eyes adjusted to the minimal light, I sat up, annoyed I could not settle. Tabby's eyes were penetrating and seemed to glow back at me in the moonlight.

Was she judging me because I had been too scared to open the letter?

Stupid. I shook off the idiocy as I got up and pulled my curtains shut.

Switching on my lamp, I sat heavily on the side of my bed, staring at the package. No question, it was causing me unease. Tilly would have long since cracked it, had she seen my procrastination. She was one to stare the unknown right in the face and welcome its challenge.

'Better to know what you are dealing with so you can get on with it'

I quoted her famous line to Tabitha. Tilly was so brave.

But you are so weak Aanya.

The fleeting voice in my head was enough to spring me into action. It didn't scare me as much as annoy me. Mum and dad had instilled in me a great confidence. I believed in who I was, and the strength I had. Was this voice trying to break my self-assurance? Why was his venomous tone becoming more frequent?

I carefully pulled the envelope apart, wanting to preserve it as much as possible. Or maybe I was just wasting more time. The thought made me smile. Tilly would have ripped it wide open by now.

My hands were trembling.

Dr Belshar's words swirled in my mind. 'The subconscious always knows before the conscious mind does. Most people just don't hear the whisper of warning.'

Maybe I should've waited until Tilly was with me, or mum?

I'm so pathetic at times, I thought.

'No!' I spoke into the room. 'I am not.'

Peeking into the envelope, the first thing I saw were some photos. Perhaps had I known what was about to reveal itself, I never would have proceeded on my own. The evidence was clear. Staring back at me, was my own face.

I must have been about 11 or 12. I felt a shockwave, followed by sharp pain run through the length of my body.

Somebody had known me.

Why did they let me go?

Was I in India when this was taken? I had to assume so.

I silently traced the outline of the figure. The anticipation of what was to come was causing my pulse to pound not only in my chest, but throughout my entire body.

The haunted expression dominating my fine features was unmistakable. I was skin and bones, my cheeks hollow. My dark hair was limp, cut short, my clothes disheveled and soiled My feet were bare.

Was that bruising around my ankles?

I searched for a background to try to site the photo. I could see I was in some sort of house, or shed maybe? A dirty apron was tied around my waist.

You were born to serve me, Aanya, and you couldn't even do that.

Like always, any memory of that time was completely dark to me. This photo made no sense at all.

Turning it over, I felt all the air leave my lungs, no breath would come and a haze set in confusing my senses

'Jiera. 2010. India. What the hell? Did I have another name? So, I was 11, as this was taken 8 years ago. But where in India exactly?'

Tilly so often teased me about talking aloud to myself, but this was how I processed best. I wanted to call her. I needed her.

I ran my finger again over the image. Maybe this wasn't me?

I felt sick even looking at the poverty-stricken child, this shadow of myself. Reaching for my phone, I knew I couldn't call. It was after 1am.

More photos remained in the envelope. I had to know, but at the same time, I was terrified. For so long, it's been the hardest thing to come to terms with, not actually remembering my past. Right now, I sat in one of those moments that might just turn out to be the link that re connects me.

Was that a good thing or bad?

Bracing myself, I pulled out the remaining photos. The next

image showed me sitting on the floor of a big building. It was quite a dark photo, but I could see once again I looked unkept and malnourished. I wore a blue oversized shirt and shorts. I could see the bruises up my legs and circling my wrists. It looked as though I also had a nasty gash under my left eye. I felt for the scar that still remained. It was one of many on my body. Tools and boxes surrounded me. Flipping the photo over, it too had writing on the back.

'Aanya, 2011 India. 12 years old. At least they got my name right this time. So, this was me, two years before I lost my memory. Who had I lived with? Surely I hadn't lived there by choice?'

When I pulled out the third photo, I couldn't comprehend what I was looking at.

The pulsing in my body throbbed in my ears, drowning out any present sounds. My vision momentarily became a little blurry. I forced myself to focus.

Was this some sort of joke?

Grabbing at the envelope again, I searched for clues of its sender. The folded letter inside remained untouched. Maybe that would bring some clarity, yet I hesitated. My hands shook now, and although a rarity for me, in this moment I was overcome with anxiety. I sat further upright, and rubbed my eyes again, just to be sure. How did I really know this wasn't a dream? I stood, ripping open my blinds. Dreams were not unusual for me.

The moon was dull, hidden behind the clouds. I opened my French doors, just for a moment, as the blast of cold night air quickly became too much. Again, I stared into my own eyes in the third photo I clutched.

How could this be?

There were two of me?

Both girls in the photograph looked exactly alike. They sat with their tiny frames entwined. One girl was slightly behind the other, resting her head on her companion's shoulder. Both looked frightened and unsettled, their black eyes wide with terror.

The scrawled writing on the back of the photo had been blurred over time, perhaps by moisture, but it was still readable.

'Aanya and Jiera 2011. India.'

Frantically, I searched the image for an explanation. Some evidence that these two little girls did not look exactly alike. I felt hot and cold all at the same moment. Clammy and unsteady.

How could there be someone identical to me? I couldn't even tell which one I was.

I still had another unseen photo.

You left her, you ran away to save yourself.

The voice made me sick with confusion. Why had I opened this on my own? I desperately didn't want to be alone right now.

The minute I looked at the last photo, its image blurred as tears filled my eyes. My breathing was rapid and shallow, yet it seemed beyond my control.

I fell to the floor.

I was overcome with nausea.

Then confusion and fear, like I could never recall feeling.

'Aanya and Jiera. Nepal orphanage 2001. 2 years old. Parents deceased.'

The shock of my spoken words caused me to dry retch. Scrambling to my feet, I only just made it to my bathroom. I desperately tried to steady myself as I fought the dizziness and stumbled back toward the letter still sitting on my bed. Drenched with sweat, my palpitating heart felt like it was fluttering and skipping beats.

What the hell was going on?

I tried to warn you, Aanya. You will never escape me.

This time, without warning, the inner voice was partnered by an unsettling image in my mind. I saw a little girl staggering through a rubbish filled street. She tried to call out, but no one could hear her. Falling, she stilled on the rough ground, blood trickled from her head. Her arm reached out in front of her, as if willing someone to come. I could see the tattoo clearly on her forearm. It was the numeral 2. This reality I was not ready for, the surge of adrenalin almost too much. I grabbed at my own forearm now. So many times, I had tried to scratch or rub this marking off. Never had I understood why or when I had been branded this way.

I had no choice. I had to know, and suddenly I felt anger rise. The hate. For whom, I was still unsure. Did I have a sister? How dare someone do this to me, to us. We were just innocent children.

Weren't we?

Gathering myself, I carefully opened the sharply folded paper. The same black writing greeted my eyes. I forced myself to take a deep breath, all the while becoming more aware of my strong gut feeling.

I knew this letter was going to change my life, whether I wanted it to or not.

I knew the shadows were being exposed.

Dear Aanya,

My name is Ami,

I am the housekeeper at the estate you were sold to in outer Eastern Delhi, India. You came here in the year 2008. You were just 9 years old. I did my very best to keep you safe from when you first arrived. Many times, I failed you. It saddens me deeply to think of the conditions in which you lived and the torture you endured. No child should be kept in the manner you were.

I pray my dear girl my correspondence finds you safe and well. God knows you deserve it. Please forgive me for not contacting you sooner. I am ashamed to say fear prevented me. Should I be found out, I will certainly be killed.

I was pleased to discover you found refuge in Australia. I'd heard whispers you were still alive but had to know for myself. My master was adamant he had killed you all that time ago.

After pleading my case, I was able to get your contact details through the missionary institution in which your parents worked. They were also able to update me on your present condition and well-being. I am so grateful you are alive. I learnt you have no memory of your time here, and perhaps that is for the best.

Your disappearance was a mystery and of great concern to me. Our master was not pleased and his anger was felt far and wide for many weeks. No one in the house was spared his wrath.

I ask you not to attempt to return mail to me, or contact me in any way. Our safety depends on it. However, I could not bear the pending situation. It is my last wish that I can try to help you understand.

Dearest Aanya, despite the shock my revelation will bring, you need the truth. You have a twin sister and time is running out for her. I understand both you and your adoptive parents have no knowledge of Jiera. I have provided the only photos I could find to try to prove my word. You were both sold to our master, into slavery. Bought and smuggled across the border from Nepal. On the night you disappeared, in 2013, you had been beaten within an inch of your life. You were caught stealing some broth for Jiera. She had a fever and you were simply trying to help her get well. She was feebler than you. Despite your size, you would always fight to protect her at any cost. Somehow you got away from him and disappeared into the city streets. That was the last time we ever saw you.

Your sister was told that he had drowned you in the river. Jiera was informed the same punishment would apply to her, should she try to escape. I regret to inform you; it has recently been arranged for Jiera to be sold on. She is to reside and work in a brothel on GB Road. She will become a forced sex worker in Delhi. Jiera is very distressed and I fear will try to end her own life. If there is any way you can help your sister, I implore you to do so. She too, needs to be rescued from a very dark and dangerous world. I have not told her you are still alive, as I do not want to give her false hope.

God speed my child. Please forgive me, I could not protect you both.

With faith and gratitude,

Ami.

The letter fluttered to the floor; I barely registered my body crashing down heavily soon after. The silence that had surrounded me in the dead of night shattered as I began to scream. My own sound was foreign, primal like. Curling into a ball, I began pulling at my hair, scratching at my face. Anything to keep me in the present.

My terror was real.

My confusion was all consuming.

More graphic images came, racing through my head. Were they memories? They remained clear despite jamming my eyes tightly shut, hitting my own head repetitively in an attempt to gain relief.

The images were lurking out from the dark place; the one I'd always refused existence.

The shadows of my mind were real.

I could smell their evil stench, hear their wicked laughter.

They were coming and I couldn't stop them.

※

'Aanya, Aanya, you need to wake up now. Come on, you can do it.'

Someone was squeezing my hands. It was annoying.

I blinked rapidly, adjusting to the light. I had no clue where

I was. Suddenly, like a rush of icy air hitting me in the face, I remembered.

I wish I hadn't. I tried to recoil back into my slumber, but I knew it was too late.

The letter.

The photos.

Jiera.

I sat up too quickly and was overcome with dizziness. Immediately, I fell back down into the pillows.

'Steady on there, Aanya. It's okay hon, you are safe here. You are back in hospital, just so I could check you out. But everything looks good. You just had a fair fright I'd say.'

I felt heavy and groggy, like I'd been asleep too long after a big night out. I wish it were that simple

My face stung, and I remembered clawing at my skin and pulling at my hair. I could see the scratches down my arms. Had I done that to myself too? Taking a deep breath, I desperately tried to gather myself. Where was Tilly? I needed her. Dr Belshar smiled down at me, chart in hand.

'Take it slowly, Aanya, everything is going to be okay.'

No, she was wrong, nothing was okay. Everything had changed.

'I'm sorry for the trouble, Dr Belshar. If it's alright, I want to go home now. I have no pain. I need to see my parents. It's really important, urgent actually. It's kind of hard to explain. I could hear myself rambling. I felt better lying flat again, the spinning room was slowing.

I noticed my body was hooked up to a few different monitors and wondered why.

'You had an episode at home. Do you remember?'

An episode? That's what they were calling it?

Her words almost made me laugh.

How could I not remember?

The letter.

The words had been etched into my very core.

The images of the little faces.

The confusion of knowing the stranger staring back from the photos, was me.

The guilt, knowing I had left my sister behind.

How could that be true?

One single envelope which in an instant had changed my life's course forever.

How did I even begin to explain?

'Yes, I remember last night. I have a twin, Dr Belshar, and she needs me.'

I tried to sit up again, intending to leave, but the woozy feeling returned and the room spun around me.

'Aanya, it was not last night. We have been unable to wake you for two days now. That is not unusual when a trauma victim receives such a shock. The human body is very good at protecting itself when need be. But you need to take things slowly now. You are just fine, but we need your body to know that too, okay?'

'Two days! But what if it's too late. I need to help my sister, Jiera. Where is my mum? Does she know about the letter?'

Tears flowed freely now. Frustration swirled around the confusion within, like a hurricane.

'Aanya, take a breath. Stay still for a minute. Your parents have seen the letter and photos. They have had a phone meeting with the missionary centre in India already. The authorities have also been contacted in Delhi. Everything possible is being done to help Jiera. But first, there are a number of checks being done to make sure this is not some sort of scam.'

It was not a scam. That, I already knew for certain.

Somehow, I could feel her. Deep inside my being, she was there.

Why had I not felt her before?

Or had I?

As I showered in the small cubicle the hospital provided, the hot water stung the scratches and bruises on my body. I cringed at the thought they had all been self-inflicted. The steam seemed to make it hard to breathe. My eyes burned. Every one of my senses felt like they were on high alert.

My mind raced as my heart continued to beat like it was about to leap from my body.

A sister.

I have a sister.

How could this possibly be?

All my life, or what I could remember of it, I'd thought I was alone, assuming I was the only survivor of my family, yet now everything was different. I knew I wanted to know her, to find her. These feelings made me addled and completely bewildered.

Jiera was my blood, yet in essence a stranger.

My emotions raced as quickly as my thoughts.

Obviously, I loved her once?

She is my twin, We had survived the unthinkable together. How had we become separated?

Did she love me back?

I slid down the wall of the shower, the water still hitting my back as I rocked in a ball at its base.

Stinging pain and a strange kind of guilt further assaulted my consciousness. Why had I escaped, but she had not?

Should I be ashamed? Was she angry I'd left her?

Then the heaviness of desperation set in: What if I were too late? I grabbed at my head in an attempt to slow my thoughts.

Inadequacy: how could I possibly pull off this rescue mission? I knew so little of India, or anywhere other than Melbourne. Confusion: how had I forgotten my sister, the one I should love the most.

Anger: how could life be so cruel? How could child trafficking and slavery possibly exist in today's world?

Disgust and hatred: for the man who held us captive and treated us worse than animals.

Then, just like that, I felt it.

Courage.

I knew what I must do.

⚘

I was cleared to go home that afternoon, and it couldn't come quickly enough. Dr Belshar had arranged to catch up with me later in the week. We would talk then about repression of memory, so she had said. I was barely listening. That's something to look forward to, I thought sarcastically.

I studied myself in the mirror. What a mess.

How could I unlock what I needed to save my sister?

What the hell was I supposed to do now? I could see where I had ripped chunks of hair from the side of my head. The scratches down my face. That must have been scary for mum and dad to witness. I felt ashamed of what I was putting them through, yet at the same time, I knew most of it was beyond my control Then I thought of Jiera, trying desperately to imagine what she looked like now, who she was deep inside. Was she like me?

I knew nothing more than the information Ami had written, but the photos told me more than her words. She was the one I had seen in my dreams.

I felt sick to my stomach again at the thought of abandoning my sister. Had it happened that way?

She must hate me.

'I didn't know. I don't understand it, but I promise I didn't Jiera. I am so sorry,' I whispered into the mirror, consumed by my confusion, white as a ghost.

My eyes were wild, black, and intense.

My image seemed as much a stranger to me at this moment, as my twin.

ॐ

It felt good to be home. There was so much to do, I barely could focus on where to start. Wandering down to the kitchen, I could hear mum and dad talking in hushed tones. Obviously, both had taken the day off work. I was a little annoyed at myself to be missing Uni again. But nothing had ever seemed important right now as finding Jiera.

'Hey beautiful, come and join us. You have been through a lot in the last 48 hours. Eat with us honey.'

I smiled at mum. She rose and began re heating the pancakes she'd obviously made earlier. Mum knew nothing made me feel better than her blueberry pancakes. But right now, I wondered if I would ever be able to eat again.

Had Jiera eaten today?

I could see the letter and photos placed to the side of the table. Dad pulled me into a hug before encouraging me to sit. He heavily sugared a black cup of tea, and placed it in front of me. Its blackness reminded me of the bruises I had seen on the skin on the little girls. Jiera and me.

'This is obviously a huge shock, Aanya, to all of us. We promise you honey, that we never ever would have taken you back to Australia, had we known.'

I was staring at the steaming liquid and twirling my hair through my finger, when the crack in his voice caused me to look up at him. It was the first time I had ever seen him cry. My mum remained facing the hot plates but I could see by her slightly shaking body she was also distressed.

'The Court in Delhi assured us you were the only surviving member of your family when we applied for custody. This we were granted, and the right to take you back to Australia under the Guardians and Wards Act set in 1890. We later appealed and won the right to adopt you into our permanent care. You came under the Juvenile Justice, Care and Protection Act, set down in 2015. Children deemed to be orphaned, abandoned, or abused have the right to be offered a better life chance. That's all we ever wanted for you. Aanya, please forgive us, we did not know.'

He was sobbing into his hands now.

I didn't know what to say, overcome with the intense emotion in the room.

Mum turned toward me. Her eyes red from crying. The lines seemed deeper surrounding them, expressing the tension she was feeling. This confronting scene was almost too much for me. I wanted to run, but all we had was each other.

'Aanya, did you know your name means limitless? That's what we wanted to give you, a limitless life. But had we known, we would have searched for Jiera too.'

I sat in stunned silence. Mum and dad had nothing to feel guilty about. They had sacrificed so much for me. Yet clearly, they too were torn apart by this revelation.

'Stop, dad please. It's nobody's fault. I know that. Mum, come and sit. We need to stick together now, and try to work out what is real.'

I grabbed for their hands, determined to appear stronger in that moment than I actually felt.

Under my façade, I was as fragile as glass, having been dropped, about to hit the ground and break into a million pieces. All I could do was wait for the shatter.

We discussed all possibilities of what could come next. As I knew they would, they had been swift to reach out to every contact they had, in both Australia and India, asking for help. Now we just had to wait.

That was going to be near impossible for me. I wanted to jump on the next plane to India.

As the hours unfolded, evidence had come to light, suggesting the mystery letter was more than likely non fraudulent.

I knew it!

But mum was right, we needed to give our contacts a few days. Knowledge was power.

It seemed all so surreal.

I ate mum's pancakes, as instructed, but tasted nothing. I barely remember chewing and swallowing the food. Mum knew I needed to eat to get my strength back, and with each mouthful, I felt better. Dad had collected a number of old photo albums and placed them in front of us. It was like I was viewing another family's life. In a way, I was.

You are too late. You will never find her.

No, no, no!

Never would I believe that.

I found myself wandering aimlessly around the house, an unrelenting restlessness had settled over me like a thick fog. I longed to see Tilly. Where was she, anyway?

I found my parents still in the kitchen late in the day. Mum was searching through old documentation. Dad was intently focused on Google Maps.

'Mum, I should have asked you more about my life before. Is something wrong with me, that I didn't?'

She looked up and smiled, gesturing me to sit beside her.

'Everyone handles things differently. There is nothing wrong with you, my sweet girl.'

Would mum still think that if she knew about the voice in my head?

'Maybe I was protecting myself. In all these years, I've never really asked for the details. I've avoided them, and counselling. I am grateful you never pushed me on this. But I thought I had nothing back in India except trauma. My new life here, with you guys, was all I wanted. But everything is different now. Like it or not, I need to know. If you are up for it, could you tell me what you remember?'

My parents looked at each other, drawing upon the invisible

strength between them. Dad reached over for her hand. I admired the unassailable team they were. I hoped to find that again one day. I knew without doubt Jiera and I must have been the same.

Until you left her to die Aanya.

The voice was always the same. Low, venomous and angry. His foreign accent was heavy, yet somewhere deep inside, I knew I had encountered it before. I shook him off. I couldn't help but think about how alone Jiera must feel. This very minute, she believes I am dead. It made my stomach turn and acid build in my throat.

'What we haven't told you is simply to protect you Aanya, not to betray you in any way. You know that, right?'

'Of course, I do Dad. You are incredible, genuine people. I am so lucky to have you. In no way is this on you guys, okay!'

'Let's get ourselves a fresh cuppa. Are you sure you want to talk about this now, Aanya? You have a lot to deal with emotionally already.'

'Please mum, I need to know everything you do, to trigger mymind into remembering, somehow.

Tilly arrived in a fluster.

'Sorry Aanya, I was at the hospital having a treatment.'

'What! Why didn't you tell me?

I hugged her for the longest time. She always seemed to breathe life back into me in moments that mattered. She just smiled, then burst into tears. I felt like a different person from the last time we had met. Did I seem different to outsiders?

'I think you have enough going on right now Aanya, but I'm here now and I am fine.'

Tilly continued to cry as she read through the letter and looked at the photos. Now we sat huddled closely together, turning the pages of the dusty old albums in silence.

So many photos of my younger parents. Always surrounded by the people and culture of India.

I had many questions, yet didn't know where to begin.

I tried to place myself in this foreign world, but still, I couldn't.

This was so frustrating, trying to will my mind to reveal its truth. Why was I not capable of retrieving my past? I knew the information I needed was there, I just had to get my mind to trust enough to release it.

'This will show you how we lived and some of the things we witnessed, Aanya. It was both a beautiful and heart wrenching time. But we wouldn't trade it for the world. The best four years of our lives, until you came and completed our family. We realised then, every moment we were there, was the lead up to meeting you, our precious daughter.

Mum smiled, but deep sadness remained in her hazel eyes, clearly reflecting her truth.

Tilly sat listening as intently as me.

Dad interrupted her, eager to share their memories. His tone was more animated than this morning and I took comfort in this. Trying to ease some of the tension in the room, I smiled, raising my eyebrows at Tilly, hoping she would catch my drift. We had always shared a joke that my dad was a walking, talking encyclopedia. He relished in sharing knowledge, and I knew this was about to be another of his shining moments.

'The people are so unique because of their unity amid diversity. Many cultures are intertwined, yet live peacefully despite their different languages, routines, foods, beliefs, and even dress codes. It's quite an upcoming and progressive democracy. One thing all the people have in common, is they are big on community, festivals and family.'

'That's so different to how I pictured it, to be honest. But I suppose we only see what the media wants us to at any given moment'

I agreed with Tilly on that. Dad continued enthusiastically, 'Unbelievably India is made up of 1.3 billion people. Now, considering Australia is 2.4 times larger than India and has a population of only 2.4 million, you can imagine their overcrowding and the difficulties they face changing. Indians are heavily influenced by religion, with nearly 80% of them being Hindus. Yet it is a multicultural and pluralistic society where several belief systems, including Christians and Muslims exist side by side. Sadly, as the population keeps burgeoning, so does the poverty rate.

I could all but stare as I tried to comprehend. Dad sighed as he went on.

'One child is born every eight minutes, you know. And statistics show, around 42 of every 1000 children born, die before their first birthday. Of those that don't die, 1/3 of India's children are stunted and wasted.'

Tilly's gasp said it all as she spoke, staring intently at my dad. 'That's horrendous. Why? What do they die of?'

'Malnutrition mainly. But, also from disease resulting from inadequate sanitation, pollution, poor health care facilities. There are many reasons. A huge number of children die from unintentional accidents.'

Mum interrupted him. 'It's like a vortex of degradation, disease, desperation and death.'

'What do you mean by degradation?' Tilly beat me to the question.

'Dalits are treated with contempt, and appallingly disgraced and ostracised, even to this day.'

Mum shook her head as she spoke, I could see it was making her angry.

'Who are the Dalits? I've never heard of them.'

Tilly agreed with me as I piped up. Dad waved his hands around, eager to take over again.

'Well girls, I need to explain India's traditional Caste System firstly. For thousands of years all Hindus in India have been controlled by a hierarchical social stratification framework. At the top of the pyramid are the Brahmins who are the priestly class, then the Kshatriyas, or warrior class. Then follows the Vaishyas, or merchant class people. And at the bottom Shudras, laboring class. Each caste defines and dictates one's occupation, dietary habits, social interaction, income, resources, even who you could marry. The higher up the pyramid you are, the greater your privileges and superiority. You were born into and died in your caste.

I couldn't believe what I was hearing.

'So, Dad, you mean there was no social mobility at all? And where were the Dalits in the system?'

Dad grimaced.

'They are not in it; they are below it and outside this system. The Dalits are regarded as untouchables and considered impure. Dalits are regarded as unclean, as they had to perform many menial jobs for a pittance of pay. Millions of Dalits work as manual scavengers, clean toilets and sewers by hand, or clear away dead animals.'

As dad drew breath, mum interjected.

'Although the caste system was officially abolished in 1950, its mentality loiters and even today directs and dictates social behaviours. The poverty is devastating; it spreads far and wide. Yet the wealth of the rich is quite mind blowing.'

Dad nodded as mum became lost in thought. Tilly and I stared from one to the other. My parents knew so much. I was starting to feel agitated at the injustice.

'This is 2018, surely the world has learnt people are to be treated equally. How can a society class them? That seems far from equality. Does the Indian government still allow this? What about the people? Surely, they protest? So, you wanted to help the people of India? What was your main role? That's a massive thing to do, to move countries and all. Did you have training in Australia first?'

My rapid questions reflected my static state of mind. All the while, my appreciation of the bravery engrained in my parents was certainly deepening.

How could I have turned my back on my culture?

I felt strangely ashamed. But was this my culture? I originated from Nepal, didn't I? Everything I'd taken for granted felt like it was called into a question.

Could I ever be as courageous as my adoptive parents?

'Goodness Aanya, take a breath, slow down a bit. You're going to explode.'

Dad smiled as he patted my hand encouragingly.

'Had either of you heard of the Caste System?'

Both Tilly and I shook our heads. Dad took his cue to continue, puffing his chest out slightly with the thrill of imparting his wisdom. Tilly poked me under the table and we both stifled a laugh despite my agitation.

'Sadly, many children are trafficked from these slum areas, and the common belief is, they don't matter anyway, so nothing is done to rescue them.'

I couldn't believe what I was hearing.

'So does Nepal also have the Caste System dad?'

'Well, it was adopted by Nepal, then abolished in 1963 when Nepal became a secular state. Then in 2008 Nepal became a republic.'

'You are quite incredible, Papa Jeff. A wealth of knowledge.'

Dad was clearly impressed with himself needing no encouragement to continue.

'Although illegal, most of the Dalits are bonded, working to pay off debts or to eke out a living. According to the Human Rights Watch 1997, 15 million children work under slave conditions, hauling rocks, in fields or factories for less than a dollar a day.'

'Why aren't these children at school?'

'Good question Tilly. Since 1880, Australia has made education for 6-14 year olds compulsory; the same was legislated in India as late as 2010. The illiteracy rate is huge, especially in rural areas and the poor class. Over 287 million people are illiterate today. Many who become educated don't necessarily get better job opportunities as the jobs just don't exist for them. Many families can't afford for their children to go to school.

'But surely education is free in India?' Tilly scoffed.

'Yes, but abjectly poor families can't afford to lose even the paltry income their children can earn. It is the lack of enforcement of laws and not the laws that's the problem . You get what I mean girls? Police, village council and government officials still often unofficially support the Caste System.'

Mum leant forward as she spoke, placing her hand on dad's.

'It is a vicious cycle of high population, poverty and illiteracy. With lax re enforcement the cycle cannot easily be broken.'

'Yes, but there is hope. Remember India is still regarded as a third world country, but the silver lining here is that it is developing. More children than ever before are being educated, millions have been lifted out of poverty; and a quota system has been implemented where by a large number of poor Indian citizens are entitled to gain access to higher education and certain jobs.'

I could see dad was trying to be positive. My parents were reflective as we all sat in silence. Mum was the first to speak again.

'Sadly, corruption is still rife. Bribery, debt bondage, child labor, collusion with the police force, even incomplete voting lists exist, however every country has its dark side I'm afraid. Never should the people of India be judged by the evil trade of slavery. But once we learnt about it, both your father and I knew we couldn't simply turn a blind eye to the problem. Child trafficking was foremost in our minds.'

'When you say child trafficking, you mean children sold into the sex trade right? That's so gross. Makes me want to spit on those vile humans.'

Tilly was never shy about putting things out there. I loved this about her.

'Well yes Tilly, the sex trade is a huge part of it, but unfortunately child trafficking is a term that umbrellas a number of smaller trades. Like in Aanya's case, we believe she had been sold into the slave labor trade.'

Mum was struggling relaying this to us. She blinked rapidly as her shoulders hunched even further. Without saying a word Dad put his hand on her back. For as long as I could remember, Mum had referred to India and its culture as 'beautiful people'; they were clearly very important to her. Funny, you go through life hearing news reports, watching images from other countries, but somehow you manage to keep it separate from your life. I'd always known the problem was there, but managed to block it, focusing on my own world.

Until now.

I felt selfish in that moment. Was I self-centred and egotistical? Had I taken my second chance for granted?

All this time, my sister had been living this hell on earth.

Please Jiera, forgive me.

Dad took over again, whilst mum got up and made some more snacks we neither wanted nor needed. I'd actually never seen her this unnerved. She moved swiftly around yet almost like she couldn't settle on a real purpose Tilly remained glued to their every word, as was I. She was much quieter than I had ever known her. Perhaps the reality of another life was hitting Tilly too.

'Child trafficking is a multi-million-dollar industry. I was reading just yesterday, they estimate at present in 2019, over 1 million children are being trafficked and exploited. 70% are trafficked from the Asia Pacific Region. $99 billion is generated through the trade each year, estimated at $11 million every hour.'

Tilly hugged me tighter. Her face whiter than before and her voice quieter.

'Thank God you are here Aanya.'

'But Jiera isn't.'

My words were strangled. I stared down at the wood grain on the table. The crushing burden was causing sharp pains in my chest.

'She will be Aanya. I know she will, and she can join us. It will be like I have two best friends from now on. We can do this. I know we can.' Tilly squeezed my hand and I offered a wobbly smile.

She was always the optimist, despite the small fact she lived with a disease that aimed to kill her.

Dad cleared his throat before continuing, 'No age limit applies, unfortunately. In India it is estimated one child disappears every 8 minutes. Either bought, sold or stolen. With the population sitting in the billions, it is almost impossible to trace the child again. As mum said, child trafficking is not only the sex trade, it is many other forms of exploitation.

'Like what?' I knew bits and pieces fed through the media, but clearly not enough.

'Through horrendous work in child labor jobs, organ stealing and even training children to work as professional beggars.'

'I don't understand, why don't leaders around the world stop this!' Tilly was becoming animated.

'As we said, every country has a dark side Tilly. We chose to go to India believing we could make the most difference there. I only hope we did, at least to some degree. Some of the things we saw….'

My dad could not finish, his voice becoming a husky whisper. Standing abruptly he bumped the table as he turned away fighting to compose himself.

'Call me naive, but why would any parent allow their child to be taken? I get it, I was in an orphanage so maybe I was easy pickings, but I can't imagine a family letting their child go. How does that happen?'

Mum sighed, reaching for my free hand, while Tilly maintained her grip on the other.

'My darling Aanya. Life is so different in a developing country

Unfortunately, the most vulnerable are children from low socio and disadvantaged backgrounds. Parents and caregivers of children in poor communities are frequently betrayed or lured into the scam. In some instances, families are forced to 'sell' or 'send' their children away in the hope they will have a better life. Sometimes families simply cannot afford to feed and keep them. Traffickers promise wages will be sent back to the villages, that their child will be educated and so on. But the reality is, these children are seen as a commodity. Sent to big cities such as Delhi where we lived. Slaves to their masters, in any way they see fit. Most families never see their children again.'

My past was being sketched for me. No wonder my mind sheltered me from recalling it. I hated the man who did this to me. A man I knew little about, yet despite this, a man who made the bile rise in my throat, and my blood boil. Every fiber in my body was enraged. I'd never recalled this level of resentment in my life toward anyone.

But surely, I must have before? I would have loathed him, for forcing me to live as a prisoner.

Until now I had never wished anyone dead.

I wanted revenge so badly.

I would never tell my family, but today a strange new feeling had begun to take hold. Was I willing to kill him to save my sister? My internal monologue shocked me a bit. Yes, my intention was to make him pay. Whatever that looked like.

Maybe now I was ready to hear my story, my past journey.

Maybe not.

It was irrelevant really. My focus had shifted big time. All I cared about was finding Jiera, and rescuing her. And to do that, I needed to face a few harsh realities.

Piecing together the life of a stranger, was going to be tough. But this stranger was me, not a narrative from a fictional tale. My past was real, and my parents held one of the keys that could unlock it. I knew I was born in Nepal. I also knew my biological parents died when I was just two years old. I lived under the care of an orphanage in Nepal until I was sold into slavery and taken over the border into India. Jeff and Nancy had told me this from the start. That's what my official child protection paperwork had said apparently. My life written on an old piece of paper.

As soon as I recovered enough from my injuries, my parents shared everything they knew. Mum and dad had little information on my exact birth location. They didn't know when or how I had been taken from the orphanage. Mum had openly told me, to this day, it is not uncommon for children to be smuggled over the open border which runs between Nepal and India.

I knew my story was not unique.

You were just a number. Part of the trade. Nothing personal.

Wrong, arsehole. It was personal alright.

My thoughts returned to my first memories after waking and returning to my new home. I had sat in silence around our comfortable kitchen table. How strange it had felt. My parents might have well been aliens. Australia was a foreign country. Even my clothes seemed odd on my body. I had to learn almost everything from scratch. I spoke fluent English, so this made my transition easier. Someone had educated me. Had it been Ami?

Although I'd made a conscious choice to trust my adoptive parents from the beginning, I could remember many nights privately questioning everything they told me.

How could I possibly know the truth?

Maybe I had never been a victim of child trafficking in India, but instead I was now captive to these strangers, and they were inventing my past.

And what if I was never an orphan?

So many times, I dreamt of my real parents. What did they look like?

If they were alive, were they looking for me?

And then I had made my personal resolution. It was a powerful moment for me. I knew I could not continue with this sense of being detached from my emotions, from myself.I had a distorted perception of the people and life around me.

So, I made a pact with myself. I was no longer going to look back. What was done was done. I had survived for a reason. I intended to make the most of life going forward.

As the months had moved on, I sensed my adoptive parents were like no humans I had ever known. The missionary agency had been swift in offering me many types of services and counselling to help me in my rehabilitation, embarking on my new life so to speak. I had refused them all. If I couldn't understand my past, how could they?

I am the first to admit now, for many years my personal agreement had been enough. That was how I survived emotionally.

But not now.

Was I stupid to have ignored the niggling feelings deep inside me?

Were my unexplained pain attacks a way for my body to punish me?

Or were they reminding me perhaps, that just beneath my Aussie facade, lived an unknown monster.

If you knew who you really were Aanya, you would see the evil you are.

ॐ

Tilly and I had been holed up in my room for what seemed like hours. Agitation was setting in, and my mood was darkening. I had to get some fresh air, clear my head. Tilly knew as she always did, without me saying a word.

'Do you want me to go home Aanya? I get it that it's private family stuff.'

Tilly reached for my hand as she spoke to me, her eyes wide with concern. She had slept over again. We had searched our computers long into the night for anything that might help.

'No way Tilly, you *are* family, I want you here, if you feel up to it?'

'I'm fine! I want to help.'

She would have told me that, even if it was her last breath.

She lay contently, resting amongst the pillows on my bed. Tabitha was curled up beside her and her laptop rested on her stretched out legs.

'Go Aanya, go run around the block or something. I don't want your mood to cloud my rainbow. Hey if you do go out, can you get me a KitKat and maybe some lollies?"

She never failed to make me smile. I nodded and blew her a kiss as I left.

As soon as I entered the living room, I knew it wouldn't be possible for me to just leave our situation alone. My brain was bursting, I needed information. I needed action. I just needed to find Jiera.

'Mum, can you help me to understand? Tell me please, how did you find me?'

Mum was folding washing, Dad had escaped outside to his shed. To outsiders, we would have looked like a normal family. But we were far from it.

The new day had started with false calm. The household quiet and subdued as we absorbed our new reality. But that was short lived. My new found anger and impatience to be with Jiera returned with vengeance. Patience was not one of my better qualities.

'Maybe ask your father to come in if you want to do this now Aanya.'

She was white as a ghost and sat heavily in the armchair, as I marched past her heading for the shed.

Dad looked jittery. Never had I seen them like this.

Just how bad was it when I was rescued?

'When we found you Aanya, it was simply by chance. Nothing short of a miracle.'

Mum's voice was gaining strength as she spoke. Dad was

nodding, smiling with encouragement for her to continue.

'As you know, we lived and worked in Delhi. It's a bustling, vibrant city, full of many businesses, all types of manufacturing buildings. Everything a city comprises of really. Delhi is extremely crowded, with apartments and dwellings all built on top of each other. Parts of it look so unstable like the buildings are about to fall to the ground. The metro area alone homes around 30,000 people. It is mixed with all sectors of the socio-economic scale. Structurally it has old and new buildings and many precincts. In amongst all this is New Delhi, a small city in itself.

But we were there to specifically help children who had found themselves victims of the child trafficking trade.'

Dad took over. My mind was racing trying to keep up with all the information and somehow connect it with anything stuck in the dark crevasses of my brain.

'We lived in the Eastern part of Delhi. In a large apartment building owned and run by the missionary organisation. They also provided safe housing for children or families in need. This was next door. To this day it is a huge facility, but with very few funds to keep it going. Still, the people there are kind and motivated, truly inspiring. The place made us want to be better humans; you know what I mean?'

Both Tilly and I nodded.

'It is hard imagining you guys living that life, dad. You should be so proud of the work you did.'

He stared absentmindedly at the table. I'd never seen dad pick at his finger nails before.

'Anyway, the day we had found you had been a gruelling one. We were in the back of a taxi, heading home. The raid, that day, on a brothel in GB Road had been tough to witness. Girls as young as 12 were being rescued; they were not in a good way.'

'What exactly is GB Road?' Tilly said. I could tell she was blown away by their story.

Mum took over.

'GB Road is an infamous part of New Delhi known for its brothels and illegal sex trade. It's said that no girl working on the GB strip does so voluntarily. It's hard to even explain. Sadly, to this day, it remains very much an active yet dangerous place.'

I gasped for air. I didn't see it coming, but suddenly I couldn't breathe. I felt dizzy and faint. My chest was constricted. Mum jumped up and sat by my other side.

I didn't have to say a word, she knew.

'No Aanya. I know what you are thinking. That's not where we found you. You were not part of that world, I promised you that when we first met, remember?'

Slumping over on the table I covered my face with my hands, tears of relief spilled. But I was only eased in spirit momentarily, because then I thought of Jiera. Soon that would be her world if we couldn't find her.

That's where she belongs Aanya, she is scum like you.

'Honey, we found you on one of the streets which runs along the Yamuna River in East Delhi. We had decided to take the scenic road home. Just to help us unwind a bit. We had stopped at a lovely spot. The afternoon was warm and for once the city seemed relatively quiet. Just as we were about to sit riverside, we heard you. A moaning cry, much like an injured animal, could be heard coming from the low tree line just ahead. We followed the sound not knowing what to expect, and there you were.'

Mum hesitated, looking down at the table but not releasing my hand. I could tell the memory was difficult to discuss. She was breathing rapidly and her grip was intense. I could only stare at her. Once again dad picked up where she left off.

'Aanya, when we first knelt beside you, you were very close to death. Even with the little strength you had left, you continued to fight us off. You kept whispering the same name. Rahul. Does that name mean anything to you?'

Shaking my head in frustration, I knew straight away it didn't.
I wish it did.

You do know me Aanya. You betrayed me and your sister.

I shook the voice off. *Piss off you bastard*, my own angry thought blocked his tone.

'Anyway, your mum phoned for an ambulance. You were in and out of consciousness, shaking and jittery. The only time you settled was when I told you Rahul was not with us, then you drifted away.'

I tried to visualise myself in this state.

How could they be talking about me?

It was a lot to take in.

'Did you ever find out where I had come from?'

'We tried. Let me tell you baby girl, we worked night and day. The police were actually helpful, which is not always the case, and our missionary team dedicated much of their time also. It was clear you were a victim of child trafficking.'

'What do you mean it was clear? It's not clear to me.'

Tilly blurted out her thoughts, as intrigued as she was upset about my past. I didn't mind her questions; I was about to ask the same myself.'

Mum smiled despondently. Responding softly, stroking my hair, she was trying to reassure me. That was not possible at this point; I had lived a horror story. She glanced at Tilly as she spoke.

'The evidence was overwhelming Tilly. Aanya had bruises on her wrists and ankles. Children who are kept as slaves, are often tied up with a chain or rope. She had whip marks across her back and her legs. Cigarette burns on her arms and neck. Aanya's hair had been dyed and chopped short. She wore clothes typical of a factory worker. She was skin and bones and looked jaundiced. Often rescued victims are like this due to poor diet and lack of sunlight. As you know, she was also number branded with a tattoo. Unfortunately, all these things are not uncommon for victims to have. We had seen it many times over the years. To add to this, the day we found our precious Aanya, she had been beaten severely.'

I felt the heat of their stares, everyone searching my face for any reaction, I felt my body beginning to detach again, the same protective numbness washing over.

It seemed near impossible that was me?

I deliberately kept my breathing slow. But my hands under the table were expressing my inner turmoil. Without me realising, they had become fisted so tightly, they began tingling from lack of circulation.

'Unfortunately, we never discovered exactly where you had come from Aanya. The area in which we found you encompasses a wealthy precinct. Many estates and apartment complexes use hired help, and it is not a secret that many of those were underage, illegal workers.'

Dad was getting weary; I could hear it in his voice. I could also detect a level of anger. This was rare in him.

Did he blame himself for my unresolved past?

'Thank you both so much, I mean that.'

It was all I could muster up. My head was swirling, yet still the dull, separated feeling remained. Almost like I was hovering above this present scene.

'I owe you both so much,' my voice was but a whisper.

※

Later that night, in bed, I traced the scars around my face. Their slight indentation the only evidence of my previous life. Those and the branding on my forearm. I had many scars like these over my body. What had I done to deserve being beaten so severely?

My parents had wept as they recounted my injuries. I felt anger at their reaction. Not at them, but at the bastard who had administered the scars.

Was it just one man?

Were there others who'd harmed me too?

I wanted to kill him. Whoever *he* was.

Rahul.

But not before my sister was safe. I knew these feelings were not healthy, but they were embracing my soul with the force of a steam train. A broken eye socket and jaw. A fractured arm and hip. Internal bleeding and broken ribs from the blows I had received, most likely by a boot or metal object they had said.

Our heavy conversation had left a strange emptiness. I lay silently, buried deep beneath my warm doona, yet still far from sleep. Tabitha purred loudly beside me. Her breathing brought comfort. I tried to imagine hugging my sister, comforting her. Would she let me? All those years we had lost to slavery. Then in the years after that, we became lost to each other. All of it had been out of our control.

But not anymore. Never again.

I was a victim, but determined not to act like one.

Frustratingly I had no idea how or where to start my search for Jiera.

뀿

Over the following days I became totally consumed.

I longed to be back in India, but as impatient and headstrong as I was, had to gather some information first.

I continued researching anything and everything I could. I had to learn fast; time was running out.

I could sense her now. Had I actually all along? Her heartache, her dreams, her fears.

My pain was her pain. I was sure of that now.

The statistics on child trafficking in India and Nepal were heartbreaking. The Internet offered a plethora of information, more than I could cope with. My mum had warned me of this.

I felt so angry at myself that I had not dared open my eyes to this reality before now.

These were not just statistics, but real life. Why was this not studied at school? Or on breaking news? How the hell did the world just accept this happening?

I cringed at the thought of the children, many very young, working 15 hours a day or locked in rooms to produce bracelets or the like. Many only had one meal a day and lived in squalor. Groups of children were locked in dark rooms and given 2kg of flour every 2-3 days to mix with water. This was their only food. These children had no outside exposure, lived with the fear of being beaten, and were taught to be frightened of the police. Then there were children who were trained to be professional beggars, or drugged and their body organs stolen. Thousands of young girls forced to exist as sex workers in brothels and bars.

None of these children knew where their parents were.

How could this be my world?

I was given a second chance, but up until now, had done nothing to help my people back home.

Shame filled me to the core as I squeezed my eyes shut, blocking the images and confronting information on the screen momentarily.

Being as proactive as I could, I had arranged Skype meetings with the authorities in Delhi. They seemed reluctant to help. I was told my best bet was to hire my own private investigator after being quickly informed that there were thousands of open cases just like mine. Firstly, they suggested I should gather evidence Jiera even existed, before an investigation would be considered. Even then, without a decent side payment it would take many months before my file saw the light of day. I felt angry and frustrated, somewhat helpless, but at the end of the day, I had no room for these emotions, refusing to host them for long.

I read and re read the letter Ami had sent, maybe a thousand times. I could recite it from memory.

Who was this mystery woman?

I knew she held many of the answers I needed.

She was clearly well educated, given her standard of English. I sensed it was she who had taught me to read and write so well.

Speaking with the missionary organisation my parents had worked for, was helpful and gave me a trickle of hope. I was madly scribbling down as much information as I could when Tilly arrived.

'Hey Aanya, how did you go. Sorry I'm late, I really wanted to listen in to your phone calls, but class was running overtime today. Then the practical at the doctor's clinic took forever. We were practising using IV drips. Everyone is missing you. I really think you should consider coming back Aanya…'

Tilly stopped mid-sentence. I could tell by the look on her face, she knew I was a million miles away. Truthfully, I had barely registered a word.

'Sorry Aanya, there I go again, babbling on as I do. Tell me everything. How are you holding up? Any new leads?'

It had been a few days since we had caught up. Seven days since I had received *the* letter. I had not left the house. Tilly was looking me over with a scrunched-up expression.

'What?'

'Aanya, you know I love you girl, right? So, I can say this. Have you had a shower in the last few days? And when was the last time you brushed your hair?'

Tilly was smiling, but I could see the look of concern. True. I had been a little preoccupied. The past days had seemingly blurred together. I looked down at my old tracksuit top and PJ bottoms. My thick woollen socks acted like leg warmers. I pulled my red beanie further down over my hair. Was that a food stain on my jacket?

Perhaps she had a point.

Tilly hugged me anyway, and I welcomed the comfort of my best friend.

'Thanks for coming over. I know I'm a little self-obsessed lately. I can't help it. But hey, I've just had an interesting conversation with the missionary's office lady in India. She is a friend of my folks. Her name is Bina. Tilly, she was there the day Ami came in! Bina said she noticed Ami getting off the bus out front of the building straight away because she looked scared and anxious, constantly looking over her shoulder. She said the strangest thing was, despite this, she hesitated for over ten minutes before finally climbing the stairs into the foyer.'

'Aanya, that's huge news!'

Tilly's animated tone only fuelled my excitement.

'The bus had come from an outer eastern suburb called Shahdar. That's got to be a bloody good lead, right? I was about to check out Google Earth and see it for myself.'

Tilly smiled and nodded vigorously. Her encouragement meant the world.

'What was Ami like? Did Bina have any contact details for her?'

'No, she wouldn't even leave her name. Bina didn't push it with the lady, but she had her suspicions it was Ami. Bina said she was sure she had seen her with a friend that used to work with the missionary centre, many moons ago. But Bina had kept this to herself, not wanting to scare Ami away. Bina said Ami was an older Indian woman, dressed in house maids' attire. Oddly she carried a large yellow bag. She was well groomed and spoke fluent English. Ami became agitated and insistent Bina help her, showing her photos of me, and clothes I had owned to plead her case. Bina said she was very adamant my sister needed me and was in grave danger. Because the agency had my past file, they gave her my address in Australia. Ami pleaded with her that they must never disclose her coming to inquire, for she would be severely punished'

Tilly's wild eyes were enormous, she was clearly startled and bewildered. I didn't blame her one bit. It still felt like I was going to wake at any moment from a nightmare.

'How would Ami have known to look for your information there do you think?'

'I asked the same question of Bina. She said the hired help talk. It wouldn't have been difficult to discover I was alive and relocated.'

'But that means the man, Rahul, he could also know, right?'

'He doesn't scare me anymore Tilly. He should be more worried that I am coming for him.'

I could tell by her look, Tilly was shocked not only by my words, but with the venomous tone which I had spat them out. I didn't care. I meant it. I could taste the salt of my tears before I even realised they were there. Angrily I ripped my beanie off. Feeling flushed, my entire body seemed to be tingling and hot. I sat tense and wired in front of my computer, motionless to the outsider, raging internally.

This was so much bigger than me.

Tilly sat silently in her wheelchair, her hand gripping mine.

Then the strangest feeling started to creep through my body.

And in that moment, for the first time, parts of my hidden self began creeping out from the shadows.

I began to remember.

Yellow. Ami's bag was yellow. That's why I picked yellow for the front door of our house. I remember Ami had often hidden food or medicine in her bag for us. Sometimes she even had a washer to clean our faces, or a book for us to read. I smiled despite my confusion.

It was a start. A calm came then, and with it, determination.

꙼

Dr Belshar sat across from me in her office. It felt like groundhog day and I didn't want to be here. Overheating I stood in an attempt to relieve my feeling of claustrophobia.

I was exhausted.

During the last few days my mind had not been my own. At least not in the nights anyway.

'Can you tell me what you saw Aanya?'

I looked over at Dr Belshar. Again, her lipstick seemed far too pink and glossy, her orange jumper too bright. But her smile was kind, and I needed that reassurance today.

I'm coming for you, you little bitch.

No. I was not going to listen, ever. I was better than him. I focused on Ruby's hands. I still couldn't bring myself to tell her or anyone about the voice that was becoming more frequent in my head.

'At first, I woke with a fright, feeling like there was some sort of presence in my room. I felt uneasy. There was a smell I could not place. Then the second time I woke that night, it was like somehow, I knew the presence was closer still. I couldn't see anything, more like sensed it. And the smell was like tobacco, and alcohol.'

'Are you able to tell me about your reaction? Do you remember what happened then? Your mum said when she woke you, you are hiding in the corner of your room and lashed out at her physically when she tried to get near you.'

I looked across at mum. She was sitting in the armchair under the single window. The sun made her look almost angelic as she smiled, but I could see the weariness and worry on her face.

I would never hurt my mum deliberately. I hope she knew that.

'Last night, I was there. Back in India. I was in a dark, cold room. We had only one blanket, and it was so filthy. There were scraps of bread on the floor, but just out of reach. I wanted to protect her. She was not well. Her chesty cough was so bad. I could hear her wheezing. Somehow, I knew he was coming.'

'Who did you need to protect Aanya?'

'Jiera. I was with Jiera. We were so much younger. She had a fever, she needed food and water. So did I. I could feel the emptiness in my stomach, taste the parchness. But we were chained to the wall. I couldn't reach her. Then he came, I could not stop him.'

'Who came Aanya?'

'Rahul. He looked barely human. A big man, overweight.

Disgustingly drunk, stumbling and rambling. He stank, and was sweating profusely. He had a scar on his left cheek. Greasy black hair and black eyes... They were filled with hate, made him look like the devil himself. I peed myself in fear.'

I felt the detachment wash over me again. Making the recount easier to tell, like I was a robot. Was this how my mind had protected me all these years?

'Are you able to keep going Aanya? What happened next?'

'He spat on Jiera and kicked her in the stomach. Her cry was soft, kind of a gurgling sound. Rahul said she was no good to him if she was sick. His voice was deep, with a thick accent. Not foreign to me I realised. He said in the morning if she was still unable to work, he would get rid of her in the river. I remember now, the fast-flowing estuary that ran along the back of the property. Sometimes we carried buckets of water from it. The journey always seemed so long. Then mum woke me.'

My mum was crying silently, her head was down, so she could not look at me. Her arms were protectively wrapped around her body, almost cocooning herself in her thick brown cardigan. Dr Belshar wrote notes in my file. She too seemed rattled. But my numbness remained, like I was simply a reporter relaying a crime scene. Could they tell?

Should I worry that I feel so dead inside?

Was I a monster? At the end of the day, I really didn't know if I had done something unspeakable.

'That was really brave, sharing that with us. Amazing job Aanya. I believe your mind is releasing some shadowed memories. This will be a really challenging time for you, no question, but I believe you are strong enough now, and so does your body it seems. I want you to try to keep relaxed and each time you remember something, I want you to journal it. They are memories, they can't hurt you now. The pieces will come together I promise.'

Relaxed! Easy for her to say!

They were not memories for Jiera. He was still hurting her. I could feel it.

۶

The following day Tilly arrived, flushed from the cold air outside. It was Saturday. Mid-winter in Melbourne. The perfect day to stay indoors. The rain was steady on our tin roof, a soothing sound which had always brought me calm. Not today. As it had been for the past week, I sat fixated in front of my lap top. Everything and anything I found, I scribbled in my notebook.

At least today I had showered.

I continued researching the provinces and districts of India, feeling slightly positive I had some good leads as to the area I had come from.

'I need to talk to you about something Aanya.'

'Sure Tilly, fire away.'

I was only half listening, my finger following the line of the Yamuna River in East Delhi across Google maps.

'Aanya. Look at me.'

Her sharper than normal tone, jolted my focus immediately, and I turned to face her. She looked as beautiful as ever, yet I could tell straight away, something was troubling her. Today Tilly's hair was in a messy bun. She wore huge silver earrings. I knew she loved the green scarf around her neck. She had knitted it herself in one of her long stays in hospital. Her determination to achieve always made me smile.

She lived and breathed triumph through tragedy.

'Sorry, I am all yours. I am listening. Are you okay?'

'Aanya, I am not proud of what I did, but I think I may have just overheard something that well now I can't just forget. I think it can help us find Jiera.'

'What! Spill, tell me Tilly!'

'Well as I came inside, your parents were in the kitchen

chatting. I'd said my hello and was heading to your room. But in the hallway my shoelace got caught in the wheel of my chair. I hate when that happens, it takes ages to get it free. And well, I didn't mean to eavesdrop, but I sort of couldn't help it. Obviously, they didn't know I was still close.'

'Tilly, get to the point. I don't care about eavesdropping for God's sake. Tell me, what did you hear?'

I felt a mixture of intrigue and annoyance at having to wait. My tone was harsher than intended.

'Well, they were kind of arguing. Or debating I think, about whether or not to contact a guy called LJ. Do you know him?'

'No, I don't think so, should I?'

'Your mum was trying to convince your dad to go and see him. Tell him about the Jiera situation. Apparently, he lives just on the other side of Melbourne. She said he was a detective who worked in India for a long time. Rescuing kids, just like you Aanya! Obviously, they know him personally.'

Tilly had my full attention now. My stomach did a flip and an electric current seemed to run through me.

I knew it in my gut.

I knew he could help.

I stood, a little light headed. My intention was clear. To beg or even demand my parents to take me to him.

'Wait, Aanya, sit back down for a minute. I'm not done, there's more.'

I wasn't sure I needed to hear more. I needed action.

'Your dad said he was unstable Aanya. He argued the point with your mum, saying he was not who he used to be. Your dad said LJ had a horrible breakdown, just after his last rescue went really wrong. Now he just hides away, and drinks way too much. Apparently, he's on a path of self-destruction. LJ doesn't like to see people anymore. Sounded to me like he has fully lost his shit and is pissed off with the world. Do you really think you should get involved with a guy like that Aanya?'

I sat heavily, trying to take it all in. I was willing to take the risk. LJ. What was that short for? This guy was the key. I could just feel it.

Surely if he knew my situation, he would help. Maybe he just needed a fresh start. A reason to move on from whatever had happened to him. Without question LJ would know India well, both the people and the geography. I had to give it a shot.

My brain was processing seemingly a million things at once.

I could offer him money. Even the little bit I had. I would promise to pay him back, whatever it took I would do it.

'Thanks Tilly. That's incredible, you did the right thing telling me. I'm going to find him, pay him a visit. Plead my case.'

'But Aanya, your dad was a firm no. He said they would never make contact with him again. He reminded your mum that was the last request LJ had of them. To be left alone. It sounded like your dad had convinced your mum he was right. You don't know enough about him, including what he is capable of Aanya. Maybe he is dangerous?'

'More dangerous than the traffickers who have Jiera right this second Tilly? More dangerous than sitting around doing nothing? Tilly, you know me better than anyone. Surely you know I have to do this. I'm going to track LJ down whether you like it or not.'

The deep anger bubbling just beneath my surface was growing. I was noticing it more and more. Never had I recalled feeling like this before. The way Tilly was looking at me, I knew she saw it too.

She nodded and gave me a weak smile.

⚜

The physical agony violating my body returned in the dead of night. The pain in my stomach was intense, and the dull ache in the back of my head was acute.

Had something happened to Jiera?

This time it was worse, the pain coincided with another repressed memory.

A shadow in my mind.

Abruptly woken, instantly I felt breathless. An unexplained heaviness crushed my chest.

The images in my mind were like watching an old film, yet I seemed to hover above the scene. So real, I almost wondered if someone else were present in this moment, could they see them too. I sat frozen in my bed; a cold shiver travelling through my veins like I had been injected with poison. I knew I was awake, yet somehow my room seemed cloudy and distant beyond this vision.

Out of nowhere, a dark figure appeared and stood over the tiny frame of a girl who instantly I knew was me.

I was young. So vulnerable.

Somewhere in India, the room where I was captive was darkened; the air was so repugnant, I could actually smell it. I recognised these mixed odours. I knew without question I had spent much time here.

I could smell his stench, see the sweat stains on his shirt.

The picture was clear and distinct in my mind's eye.

His big, dirty boot held me down.

Then I felt a burning sensation across my face.

Bending down the Indian man stubbed out his cigarette on my cheek.

It was Rahul.

Despite my mind forgetting for so long, now I knew, I would recognise him anywhere.

'Stop struggling Aanya. Where have you hidden Jiera? If you little bitches will not work, I can easily dispose of you both. Do you think anyone would know? Or even care? You see Aanya, some people matter and some don't.'

His laugh was disgusting, evil. Again, I recognised his aggressive tone like it had been ingrained within.

He spat on my face and I felt the repulsion of alcohol and cigarettes mixed with his saliva.

Jiera came at him from behind, attempting to bite his arm.

'Get off her Rahul.' Jiera's voice was strong despite her small stature. She wore only a singlet and shorts, both ripped and dirty. Her skin was waxen and bruised. She had burns on her body, similar to mine.

What came next, will haunt me forever. I will never be the same.

What if my subconscious was wrong?

I wanted out.

Wanted it to stop.

'NO NO, leave her' I could hear my own screams. It didn't matter if I closed my eyes or stared into my darkened bedroom. The memory continued to unfold, dominating my swirling head.

The man grabbed my sister. He began pulling a decayed tooth out savagely with pliers. Throwing it at me, the blood trailing behind through the air. Jiera screamed and thrashed.

Stop. Please stop. I couldn't take anymore.

The pain in my own body now was excruciating. I grabbed at my face, clenching my own jaw, desperate for the infliction to stop.

I swung my legs over the side of my bed, gasping for air, sweat poured from my body and I was shaking profusely. I felt so alone. It was 3am.

How could anyone ever understand?

Despite my rational brain knowing I was safe, subconsciously I felt far from it.

The shadows in my mind had retreated, for now. But for how long?

I knew I couldn't, but I wanted to lock them up forever.

Now I understood. I was sure.

Not that it made any sense.

Somehow, I was feeling Jiera's pain.

I wasn't crazy after all.

I'd never held secrets from my parents before. Trust was very important to me, as it was to them. But for the first time today, I knew my new reality would force necessary change. I hadn't asked for it, but nothing was going to stop me doing what I knew I must. A heavy fog continued to weigh me down. My surrounds, my home, which had been of great comfort in the last 5 years, now left me unsettled.

Where did I belong?

It was becoming evident I was more alone than I hoped in my quest to find Jiera. In the way I wanted to go about it anyway.

I was left with little choice now but to defy my parents' wishes.

Although I felt sick at the thought, the despair of doing nothing superseded the nausea.

One day they would understand.

It was nine days since I had received the letter.

Such a small space in time, yet emotionally, the toughest I could remember. Jiera was now the centre of my world, so 9 days apart was far too long. While she remained a prisoner, I had failed her. In my mind it was as simple as that.

I'd been reading up on the phenomenal connections shared between siblings, particularly identical twins. It all made sense. Even down to the pains I'd been having. Could it be I was actually experiencing Jiera's torment? Twins shared a special bond for life, there was much research to support the inherent understanding of a co-twins emotional state as well as abilities to feel our twin's physical sensations. Then there were all the studies into twin telepathy, a staggering 40% of twins even have their own shared language, beginning interactions in the womb at just 14 weeks. We had been created from a single egg, split in two. Our DNA was 99% the same. We even had almost identical brain wave patterns. It blew my mind that there was someone else, just like me.

There were two facts dominating my mind and becoming all consuming. I had left my twin in the hands of a monster. I had run away... Why? Then I had managed to forget Jiera even existed and create a new life for myself.

I was the real monster.

I willed my mind to search for the events that led me to abandon Jiera. All I could sense was a murky blackness, so much so, it made the hairs on my arms stand up and a chill run deeply through my core.

What had I done?

Unable to face eating much for lunch, I retreated directly from my car, to my bedroom. Tabby yawned and stretched in her way of greeting. Her beautiful soft fur always calmed me. Her purr was so soothing. Of course, she was sleeping on my computer keyboard. Shaking my head, I couldn't help but smile.

As I stood in the middle of the room, I noticed the stillness. Our house was eerily quiet. My parents had headed out early to work. I should have been heading into Uni, but today, I knew once again that wasn't going to happen. How could they just carry on like nothing had changed? It pissed me off. I knew I was being harsh, thinking in such a way. Still, it irked me.

I recalled the heated debate last night between my dad and me. Mum had backed him, which had angered me further. Squeezing my eyes together now, rubbing my temples, I tried to dissolve the headache forming. We had disagreed on what should happen next, and somehow I had hoped mum might be on my side. I had expressed my will to return to India, and as soon as possible. Jeff and Nancy had all but forbidden me to do so. My rational brain understood the dangers of such a mission, I had very little understanding. I possessed limited knowledge about the country, thanks to my stupid memory and had very few contacts there to help me. It was nothing like Australia they had said. Obviously, I knew that. Honestly, I didn't care.

I had survived there once before, after all.

Sitting heavily at my desk chair now, I sighed, trying to release some tension. I was restless. Angry, at my folks. But I knew it was more than that, I was so pissed off at myself.

If only I could remember more. Why couldn't I just click my fingers, and tell my brain I was ready. Then bam, the flood gates would open and my memories return. The spasmodic way the information was resurfacing, was tough. There was no pattern to the memories, no control. Frustrated, I kicked at the wall behind my desk, my jaw was clenched so tight, my teeth were beginning to ache. This anger was so unlike me. Tabby meowed and retreated quickly under my bed. If I just could control the way the shadows were returning, then I would be able to lead the authorities straight to Jiera. Unless she had already been moved of course. What if Ami had been discovered contacting me?

Time was running out.

❧

My parents believed the best course of action was to remain in Melbourne, at least until a firm lead had been established. I knew deep down they were doing all they could. Mum and dad continued to liaise with their contacts both in Australia and India daily. Still the Indian police were taking little action. I understood why, at this point it was like finding a needle in a haystack. And truth be told, there were thousands of other children in the same predicament.

Today, my earlier appointment with Dr Belshar, had taken its toll. I moved to curl up on my bed, barely registering I was still yet to take off my coat and gloves. I felt mentally and physically exhausted. Then ashamed, I reminded myself, surely it was nothing compared to what Jiera was feeling today.

This was no time for a pity party.

Tabitha returned to my side, needling into the arm of my coat.

I closed my eyes and let her purring calm me.

Last night my dream, or 'suppressed memory' so Dr Belshar called it, was brutal, perhaps the worst one thus far. It remained crystal clear in my mind. Again, I had watched, like I was hovering above in the clouds. My subconscious was presenting this to me in the third eye, so I was told.

The vivid images saw me walking along, holding the hand of my sister. It seemed as though I was willing her to move faster. I almost dragged her along the dirt path. We carried huge knapsacks. What they contained was unknown to us. Jiera fell, she was crying. I could see myself anxiously trying to convince her to move more quickly, despite struggling with the heavy weight of the bag.

We looked like we were about seven. But it was hard to tell.

We wore no shoes. I could see sweat glistening on our pale, scabrous skin. Like the photo and previous memories, we were filthy. Our clothes torn and old; too big for our tiny frames. My hair was longer than Jiera's. Hers was almost shaved to the bone, uneven and patchy.

Despite the bustle of the city beyond, the track we travelled on was barren and partly hidden, winding in between low-level housing and a valley with a steep descent of dense shrubs. Household rubbish lay at its edges. Discarded barbed wire and broken car parts made it difficult to pass. Rats scurried away as we disrupted their foraging.

Laying completely still now on my bed, I willed each and every detail to present as I journaled the memory. It had been mum's idea to do this. If I could just recognise something, it may lead me back to my sister again. Dr Belshar had assured me the details would eventually come. I just had to be patient and keep relaxed. Was she for real? I almost smirked with dissent as she reminded me again, not to be afraid of what I was seeing. It was in the past. The memories cannot hurt me anymore.

But what about Jiera? I had almost spat at Dr Belshar, once

again my tone harsh. My frustration was unable to be hidden a minute longer.

Could I really trust this woman?

Even Ruby couldn't deny, despite them being just memories for me, we had to assume it was still Jiera's very present reality.

My dream last night had been set late in the day. I could see the sun starting to lower in the smoke-filled sky; its red glow disappearing behind the tall structures beyond. There were so many buildings. I watched myself and Jiera as we were stopped by a man in an old white truck. The logo on the side panel, I couldn't quite make out, but could see the gold and black lettering. At first, I had thought it Rahul, but as I focused harder, I could see the Indian man was someone new.

He was swift and rough as he took the large bags from us, and threw them into the back of his vehicle. I must have mouthed something to the man. He stilled, then berated me before looking at his watch. Jiera glared back at him, I had stumbled back, cowering behind her now. He slapped me forcefully across the face, and I fell hard onto rough dirt. Jiera reacted protectively, and began to kick at the man. Pushing her away, he picked me up roughly with just one hand, kicking me into the bushes lining the track. I tumbled hard, down into the thick bracken below.

As much as I didn't want to see any more of this memory. I couldn't escape; my subconscious had other ideas. The man left the scene quickly, flicking his cigarette and shouting profanities at Jiera before he departed.

How could this man show such disrespect for human life? Children no less?

He had hurt two little girls, then simply left them to fend for themselves. Obviously, someone had sent us to make the delivery. I wondered how often we had been given such a task?

My guess, it had been a demand of Rahul.

Bastard.

I so wanted to kill him.

I watched as Jiera frantically called to me. I was non responsive. My nose was bleeding profusely from the impact of the earlier blow. I had fallen into thick prickles and was covered in blood from the plethora of thorns I was now entangled amongst. It looked as though I had hit my head. Jiera couldn't reach me, as the embankment was far too steep. It was the strangest most unnerving feeling I had ever had. Watching my own person injured, perhaps close to death.

Jiera fell to her knees, dust floated in the air as she began banging her fists into the ground. She started chewing on her lower lip and she began to tremble. At first, I thought Jiera was scared, but soon I could see she was plain angry, at breaking point.

From behind I watched as a shadow emerged from my peripheral vision. It was an Indian woman. She was calling and gesturing for Jiera to stand up. Jiera frantically ran to her screaming

'Ami Ami, help us,' pointing to where I lay.

The woman, clothed in a pale blue servant's dress began berating Jiera, yet hugging her at the same time. Then without hesitation, despite cutting her own legs, she swiftly descended and began to lift me from the bushes.

Somehow, I could feel she was kind, and had cared for us. I wondered if that was how we had survived our prison.

Carrying me out, she called to Jiera to hurry behind her. I watched as the three figures scurried back the way we had come. Disappearing from my mind, it was almost like they walked into a thick fog.

Where were we returning to?

I had willed my mind to focus. I wanted to follow them.

It's impossible to articulate how strange it is to watch yourself in an event of which you have no memory, yet at the same time, is not entirely unfamiliar. You know it's part of you, despite it being foreign.

How could I ever explain that to mum and dad, or Tilly?

That same numbness washed over me. It rose from my toes, and made even my eyelids feel heavy. I was so tired, and laying on my bed I felt myself begin to recoil again.

I was beginning to see how good I was at detachment.

Was that normal?

⁂

So here I was. The old, grey building in front of me, was not dissimilar to those surrounding it. I'd never been to this side of town before. Perhaps it wasn't the safest of places, but I cared little. The city moved at a fast pace, yet I felt almost oblivious to its noise and chaos.

The icy morning did its best to dull my senses, but I barely registered the chill. I willed myself not to doubt in this moment, I was right coming here. I pulled my beanie further down my forehead. The swirling wind carried sleet which stung my eyes. The whole scene seemed almost surreal, until the familiar beep of my phone vaulted me back into the moment.

I needed to focus. I knew who the message would be from. Tilly was the only one I had told. Not that she had agreed with my decision to come here. But I knew unless I found myself in trouble, she would never reveal my whereabouts.

It hadn't been hard to find the mysterious Ex Detective Leo James Warren. You can find almost anything or anyone online if you try hard enough.

I returned Tilly's text, my frozen fingers making the task harder than it should have been. I assured my best friend I was alright, but that I had not seen him yet. I promised I would keep her in the loop. Today I wished more than anything she could be by my side. Tilly's health had taken a downturn again this week. It often did that, and she had no choice but to rest. A trip across town in the freezing conditions was simply out of the question for her. Of course, she had begged me to pick her up for the journey.

Was my situation adding to her ailing health? The prospect caused a flicker of guilt in my stomach.

I looked around, gathering my bearings. Perhaps I should have asked the Uber driver to wait. Then my fingers found the sharp edges of the lifeline Ami had sent. I had tucked it protectively into the pocket of my duffel coat. I hadn't trusted the letter's safety to the backpack I carried, in case we had got separated.

Any doubt vanished as quickly as it came. Just the touch of the envelope reminded me of the importance of its message. Nothing else mattered. Without wasting another moment, I pressed the copper buzzer labelled '205'. LJ's apartment was one of many, judging by the number of buttons beside the huge gated doors. They opened directly onto the dirty street, straight into the mayhem of movement and sound beyond.

There was no answer, so I pressed the buzzer a couple more times. I had been waiting outside the building now for at least half an hour. Obviously, he wasn't home. Then again, my dad had said he was a loner these days, and wanted as little as possible to do with the outside world.

Maybe he was in there. If so, my constant intrusion surely would irk him eventually. Any reaction was better than none.

Dad had told me the guilt LJ was now consumed with was not justified by a long shot. He was a hero in the eyes of many. But LJ was never able to forgive himself. Dad didn't elaborate, but indicated the last job he ever did in India went horribly wrong. So instead, now he washed his feelings down with copious amounts of booze, shutting the world out. Pretty cliché, really. I'd seen more than one movie along those lines. I felt sad for him.

As I shivered in the cold, jogging on the spot so I could feel my toes, I prayed he would listen to me, should I finally get his attention. I wasn't going to give up easily. I'd just returned from getting a coffee and bagel down the street, when I saw my chance. The buzzer released the steel gate locking the entrance.

Someone was leaving the building. Determined to get inside, I smiled at the elderly lady as she exited, sliding into the building, before I was locked out once again. I scrunched my nose as the potent smell of mould and urine hit me. The lighting surrounding the small entrance was dull, washing the world in a sepia tone. Graffiti covered the walls. Directly opposite the entrance door was a thin staircase. Wasting no time, I took a deep breath and began to climb.

It was now or never.

Did I have a plan? Not really.

Except to say, my plan was not to fail.

On the third level, I found the door to LJ's apartment, number 205. It looked as dreary as the rest of the doors lining the dull hallway. The only distinction was a sign hanging from his door handle saying 'DO NOT DISTURB'. The hallway between the doors was narrow. Plaster peeled from the walls and black stains from water damage ran down them. No wonder it reeked. Taking another shallow breath and willing myself to stand straight and portray confidence, I knocked. Quietly at first. I could hear nothing but my own heartbeat thumping.

There was no movement I could detect. Somewhere down the hall I registered a baby crying and a TV blaring. I pressed my ear into the door as I knocked again. This time my knuckles used greater force.

'What the hell?! Stop with the bloody knocking. Go away. Get.'

The venom in the gruff words penetrating from behind the door shocked me. I reeled back, almost hitting the wall opposite.

I felt a little stunned. I had not heard movement until now. Had he been just behind the door all along?

It was now or never.

'Hi, Sir. My name is Aanya. LJ? Is that you. Please, can I just talk to you for a minute.'

'Girl. I've got nothing to say to you. Get out of here before I call the police. Do you hear me? Scat. You'll be sorry if ya don't.'

Was he trying to threaten me? My anger began to pulse through my veins.

I could have retreated. Maybe I should have. But there was no way I was going to.

Obviously, he was really angry. But he couldn't hurt me. This building was filled with people.

And I had everything to lose by walking away.

'Please sir. I know you are Detective Leo James Warren. I really need to talk to you. It is urgent. I will not take much of your time but you've just got to listen to what I have to say.'

The words had barely left my mouth when I felt the building almost shake, as the door, only inches away from my face was wrenched open. He used such force I thought it might come away from its hinges. Within seconds, I was pushed back against the hallway wall.

He was not like I had imagined. He seemed older. He was tall and thick set. His skin was darker and he looked Middle Eastern. His eyes were wild and black, his dark hair pulled back into a band at the back of his head exposing a tattoo crawling up the left side of his neck.

I dared not speak.

Pinning me up against the rough surface of the wall, he eyeballed me. His bloodshot eyes were angry. His strong hands had a slight shake despite their force, and he smelt like he'd had a heavy night on the turps.

Yet I refused to look away. I locked into his gaze, trying to portray a bravado contrary to the fear I was feeling. For a split second I thought I saw a flicker of doubt in his eyes, or maybe it was confusion.

'That's where you are wrong see missy. I don't have to listen to anything you have to say. Was that you all morning, ringing the doorbell?' His hands gripped my arms, shaking me slightly as if to get me to respond. I held my ground. 'I want nothing to do with whatever the hell it is you want. You got that?' His words were slurred, probably from his recent intoxication, 'Do ya think you are the first Uni student wanting to interview me? Rack off the lot of ya. I have nothing to say. Do ya bloody research project on someone else.'

'Let go of me LJ. You're assaulting me.' I yelled back and used every bit of energy I had to push him out of my space. He barely moved. 'I'm not here to interview you. I need your help. I understand what I am asking sounds crazy, but I need you to come to India with me. There's a child trafficking situation. I know about you and the incredible things you have done over there.'

'You know nothing about me, dumb bitch.'

He dropped his hands from my shoulders yet remained close, continuing to tower over my frame. He was trembling, and seemed slightly disorientated. I slowly breathed out. Holding his stare, I waited for his next move. I couldn't tell whether I had bought myself a little more time, or whether I would soon be running for my life, out of there. My fingers examined the envelope in my pocket again.

I am coming for you Jiera.

Could she feel me, the way I could feel her?

The anger in his eyes remained, yet I detected a hint of curiosity. Then he laughed.

It was not exactly friendly, more like the evil sound a villain makes in a movie before he or she unleashes a punishment. His chesty bellow was quickly proceeded with a coughing fit, leaving him bent over supporting himself, hands on knees.

'Are you okay? Can I get you some water?'

This man was clearly *not* okay, on many levels.

LJ straightened up. Regaining his composure, he refocused his stare directly at me. Moving closer still.

'There is nothing I want from the types of you girl. I am going to tell ya one more time. Get out of here, and do it now ya little bitch.'

Somehow, I was not swayed.

'Please, I need to talk to you. You have to listen to me, just for a second, then if you still want me to go, fair enough.'

Despite feeling threatened, I also felt a determination I had never experienced. I wasn't going to give up easily. I lifted my chin, waiting for his response.

'Last chance. I'm not going to help with ya little project saving the world or whatever the hell ya doing. Bloody Uni types, think they can get some insight into India, or the trafficking game, write a bullshit assignment. Bloody little upstarts, think you know everything. All you want is to feel a little better about the bloody naive privileged life you lead. Done your bit for the 3rd world bla bla. You can tick that box and move on with your yuppie little existence. Rack off. You will never understand what life is like for some over there. Now go.'

He shoved me and turned to go back inside his apartment.

My skin prickled with the heat of my anger returning with vengeance. How dare he judge me.

I began to yell at his turned back, 'So, you think you know everything hey! You are a naive prick!' yet he continued to walk away, but I was undeterred. 'I am a victim myself. So that makes me a little closer to the situation than you. I was born in Nepal and trafficked into India. My adoptive parents rescued me. My sister is still in slavery. She needs us, it's her last chance. I was warned not to come to you, but I did it anyway. Maybe you don't believe in yourself anymore, but stupidly I do. You are not the only victim LJ!'

He stilled momentarily; I saw the veins in his neck tighten. His face turned a deep red. Then without turning back, he slammed the door in my face. Bits of plaster fell around me in the darkened hall. I stood stunned, in disbelief.

'There is no "us" girl. I can't help you anymore. Find someone else. Now get lost. I mean it.'

Bastard.

I stomped down the stairs, wired with antagonism. My blood was boiling to a point I had not recalled feeling in my life before.

This was not over. Not by a long shot.

❧

That night I slept very little. LJ swirled around my head. What made it worse, was the pain of knowing I couldn't tell my mum or dad. With that would come the admittance of betraying them. I had even fobbed Tilly off, promising to visit her the following day and tell her everything. I just needed some time. Time to try to figure out my next move. I was in the midst of a storm.

As I lay on my bed drained and unsettled, I searched the picture of my framed eagle for insight. This image had been the first thing I had noticed when I came home to my new bedroom from the hospital five years ago now. It was the words underneath the image of the soaring beast that caught my attention.

'But those who trust in the Lord will find new strength. They will soar high on wings like eagles. They will run and not grow weary. They will walk and not faint.'

The words were from the Bible. Although I am not overly religious, they were enough to leave me wanting to find out more about these amazing creatures. Its metaphor somehow resonated deeply.

When had my obsession with eagles actually begun? Was it before I lost my memory? I felt connected with these mysterious and majestic creatures.

Eagles were so brave. The only feathered creature not to shy away from a storm. Fearlessly an eagle will fly directly into the eye of fierce winds, using its power to help it glide, instead of fighting the force. Somehow, this animal understands a storm will pass, and on the other side, is peace and security.

Tonight, I needed to believe I, too, could possess such strength.

Did I have the courage?

It wasn't until the early hours of the morning that I felt the respite and clarification I needed wash over me. I knew what I had to do next.

Early the next morning, I left my house as silently as I could. My parents were still asleep. It was easier for me this way. Once more, I returned to LJ's apartment.

Damn him. I was not done.

This was plan B.

Today, I was grateful to be filled with a new confidence. My anger had not entirely dispersed but was superseded with determination.

This time, in the pocket of my duffle jacket, I was armed with another detailed letter. One I had spent much of the night working on. It explained my circumstance, including a photocopy of the photos and correspondence I had received from Ami. I figured it was my best shot to get LJ to listen.

Surely once he knew, LJ would help me. Despite his exasperation, I felt without question he was a good person. He just needed to remember who he was, before the darkness within had overtaken. Anyone who could give up their time as a mission worker was undoubtedly a saint. He was clearly dealing with some dark shadows in his own mind in recent years.

Question was, could he get past them?

It made me wonder, was it better for a human to be able to remember a traumatic event, or live life not knowing what had really transpired? My mum always says, every behaviour, especially the bad, has a reason behind it.

I could see LJ was trying to protect himself.

Would this once great man be able to let another person close to him ever again?

Waiting to get access to his building felt like an eternity. Ascending the stairs quickly, I slipped the letter silently under his door. Hastily I retreated, not even daring to breathe, I was not ready for another confrontation today. Yet at the same time desperately I hoped LJ would make contact with me after reading my story.

The Uber ride home was turbulent, mostly in my mind. I was going to India alone if I had to. The decision was made. Not that I had disclosed that to a single soul.

But truth be told, as frustrating as it was, I needed this complete stranger, LJ's help. I didn't want to have to trust him. It didn't make sense to do so. But then again, neither did it seem rational to board my booked flight to India in less than 24 hours. But I was going to do just that. Like the eagle, I needed to fly with the storm to find peace on the other side.

My peace was Jiera.

⁂

'Hey Tilly, how are you feeling?'

I'd headed straight for Tilly's house after gladly leaving LJ's suburb behind. Not that I had told her I was seeing him first. As always, her smile made my heart melt. Her light never dimmed, even when she was in agony. I could tell today she was. I hugged her like my soul depended on it. In a way it did. Ironic how I needed her strength. I felt a little selfish.

She looked at me in her knowing way, a slight smirk now resting on her lips.

'Hey Aanya. Come sit.' She patted the bed beside her. 'Tell me everything,' she said, before arching a brow as her eyes roved over my face. 'Have you even slept in the last few days? No offence but you look shithouse!'

I felt a rush of tears as I flopped onto her bright quilt. Not because she had offended me, but because the oppressiveness of all the rapid change made me feel like I was drowning. Nothing would be the same ever again. My situation brought with it a heavy burden. The plans I had were going to prove a lot tougher in reality. Yet I had little choice.

My friend's eyes filled with compassion, before my own registered her outfit. Without warning, laughter burst from my lips, superseding my tears.

'What are you wearing?'

Tilly proudly raised her arms, almost as a celebrity would greeting fans. She battered her eyes and pouted dramatically in jest.

'What this old thing? It's my new leisure wear. You like?'

This girl cracked me up. The new tracksuit certainly was flamboyant, patterned by rainbow tie dye, as were the orange socks and lime headband. I smiled through my tears. Despite this, nothing compared to the brightness her spirit projected.

'I will tell you everything, but you first Tilly. What did the hospital say? What is going on?'

'It is good news Aanya. I was really relieved. I didn't say it aloud, but I was worried my MS had progressed. That would have really jacked me off majorly, you know!'

I grinned at her with genuine love and affection. I did know.

'Turns out, it's just what's called remitting MS. Just a relapse in symptoms, a harsh onset of a bunch of them. But it will settle down the doctors think. I just need to push through, wait for my new meds to kick in. My memory has been fuzzy, and I'm a bit lost for words at times. That's not easy with uni. I feel like I can't keep up sometimes. And I'm just so tired, but I know it will pass. The one thing I want is to come to India with you, Aanya. So, I'm getting my shit together for that.'

It saddened me so much to think about my beautiful friend suffering. I would give anything to see her cured, or even in remission for a while. In this moment, existing as we had so many times before, we didn't need words. Some things were best left unspoken. Then maybe, just maybe, they wouldn't come to pass. We both knew Tilly would never make it to India with me, no matter how much we wished for it.

'Enough about me, I'm bored. So, spill! Tell me, what happed at LJ's this morning?'

I stared at her in disbelief. How did she know?

As if reading my mind, Tilly laughed, throwing her head back.

'Aanya, I can read you like a book, remember. I know the moves you are going to make even before you do.'

Yes, that she did.

I spared no details. Tilly, sat captivated by my adventure as I shared every move I had made over the last few days. Reliving the moments aloud for the first time, I saw something in myself I had perhaps overlooked. What I had done was audacious, but I felt a little proud. I would need every bit of bravery and courage I could muster in the days to come.

But I wasn't brave enough at that moment to tell Tilly what was coming. No one could know I was going to India, tomorrow.

Aanya

India, 2018

A jolt pulled me from my already maladjusted sleep. A sharp pain shot through my neck, and I instantly registered the dull ache behind my eyes, now beginning to pound through my head. I had been dreaming about Tilly. She was so angry at me, and it was making her sick. I kept calling to her, but she wouldn't turn and face me. When I grabbed her and forced her to look at me, her face was missing, just a shadow.

Disorientated, I willed myself to comprehend where I was. The cramped, claustrophobic space I was constrained by, brought my reality flooding back with force. I was sweating, and a hot flush of unwanted nausea turned my stomach. The smell, the noise, the turbulence. Had I done the right thing? Too late now...I couldn't turn back even if I wanted to. From my tiny window, I could see the city lights below, sparkling through the blackness of night. They were getting closer. I'd been lucky to have a window seat. The plane was packed, all of us squished into tiny seats. Two business men sat cramped beside me. They seemed nice enough, but the whole closeness thing made me uncomfortable.

It seemed like I was the only foreigner in economy, and almost the only woman. I'd felt prying eyes many times during the night. In a vulnerable moment, I almost wondered if my fellow travellers knew why I had returned. I kept my headphones on the entire trip, small talk was not on my agenda. Many of the other passengers around me seemed familiar with one another, their voices unrelenting.

What would I possibly say anyway, should someone ask why I was travelling to India?

I had little comprehension of time or how long had I slept. My stinging eyes suggested not long enough. I tried to calm the storm of untamed hair surrounding my face. My mouth was dry, and I could still taste the vile food that had been served to me at some stage during the night. The cabin felt too hot now, and I longed to be far away from the stale air. The mixed smell in the small chaotic space was too much. Coffee, body odor, tobacco, and food aromas reminding me of my high school cafeteria. Someone close was wearing far too much cheap cologne. Maybe that was the source of my headache.

The plane was bumping and swaying, obviously we had begun our descent to land. Daring to look out the window I could see the brightly lit tarmac. Soon the wheels of this flying beast would kiss the same soil I had been so desperate to escape. The dull throb of pressure was building in my ears. I desperately searched for the chewing gum in my bag, knocking the cup of water sitting on my food tray in my groggy attempt. As eager as I was to get the hell off this flight, I was terrified of what lay ahead for me.

You should not have come back here Aanya. I will make you pay.

No question, my family would be pissed off and disappointed in me. My decision will have hurt them, Tilly too. I felt ashamed after everything they had done for me. But what choice did I have? Honestly, in my opinion, none.

Somehow, I had to block the voice, his voice. These guilty thoughts too. I couldn't afford to engage in the negative energy swelling inside my head. I was here now, and determined to find Jiera. Just over 12 very long hours ago, I had set off from Melbourne. I'd never felt so alone or out of my depth. But that was never going to stop me, nothing would. The sudden determination made me smile.

Screw you Rahul, I am coming for you.

ᚹ

It had to be the early hours of the morning in New Delhi. My watch read 9.19am, which meant here, it was only 4.49am. My family would know by now that I had gone. I'd left a brief note promising I'd contact them on my arrival. That I dreaded. I forced some gulps of water, stretching to relieve my tension as best I could. I needed more than water truth be told, but it was better than nothing.

Searching the depths of my mind, I willed any memory of my last plane trip. Nothing. How do injured passengers get transported anyway? Last time I flew I was escaping my childhood of torture and captivity.

And now, I was back.

Was I really ready to face this world again?

Dear Mum and Dad,

I hope one day you will understand and forgive me.

Part of me hates myself for hurting you, but the other part of me, I hate even more for betraying Jiera. I left her when she needed me the most. I have to understand why.

I know you have sacrificed so much for me. Travelling to India will seem selfish and is obviously against your wishes. Had there been another way, I would have taken it.

I have arrived safely in New Delhi with the intention of bringing Jiera home. I have an open ticket and intend to stay for as long as it takes. I have deferred my nursing studies for now. I also must confess, before I left, I went to see L.J. Let's just say, he was very reluctant to help.

I have a plan, don't worry. I will soon be leaving the airport, to travel to the Missionary Centre in East Delhi where you lived and worked. My intention is to let them know my plans to find

Jiera, and ask them for a safe place to stay. I have not told them I am coming, as I feared they would contact you. I am obviously hoping they will help me actively search and investigate going forward.

Please give Tilly my love.

I have transferred my phone to international roaming, and hope to talk with you guys often. I've organised enough rupee from my savings before I left. I promise I will be careful. I am hoping my repressed memories will continue to return as I travel through areas I have been as a child. Ruby said, most likely they would return with environmental triggers.

Mum, Dad, please know I'm not afraid. Just determined. I have survived here before, and I will do it again.

I love you both so much. Please try to understand. I hope you will forgive me.

Yours,

Aanya.

Email sent.

My fingers were shaking, and the rich heavy coffee I'd downed earlier in the terminal, threatened its return, I could taste the bile in my throat. I watched as the icon left the bright screen, headed into the abyss. I let a slow breath out, closing my iPad. Sending an email felt a little cold, but it was the best I could do right now. I couldn't hear their voices on the phone, not yet. I had to detach from some of the emotion. I'd come this far. I couldn't risk them talking me out of my mission.

I was procrastinating, tiredness and sentiment swirled in my head. I was thinking slower and I found it hard to concentrate. Nothing annoyed me more.

It was exactly what I didn't need.

The red sliding doors across the busy terminal loomed. Having sat for longer than I'd intended, I watched the doors, almost like they were my enemy. Each time they opened and closed I could see the bustle of another world, hear the traffic and congestion.

I'd YouTubed many Indian survival guides before I left, and in my restless early hours of the flight. Although India was a country of much history and beauty, there were also many nasty surprises that awaited the naive tourist. Just beyond those red doors was potentially one of them. I felt a little more at ease knowing I had pre booked an Uber and written details of the Missionary Centre's address for the driver. I stuffed my iPad deep inside my bag, securing all my belongings as best I could.

Scanning my surroundings, the airport seemed anything but ornery. It was pristine and modern, decorated with spectacular wall art. The air was cold, almost like the air conditioner was set too high. The mix of food, perfumes and people overwhelmed my senses. People seemed loud, and rushed by in a constant stream before my eyes. I had noticed instantly when stepping off the plane, security was high. I'd read that the Indira Gandhi International airport was one of the busiest and well-run airports in the world. It certainly was a culture shock.

Named after the very well-respected former PM of India, I could see the airport was almost shrine-like. Clearly, she had been a very successful and powerful woman leader in her time, inciting many political changes both in India and around the world. Unfortunately, she was assassinated by her own bodyguards in 1884. History was so brutal in many ways.

That I knew first hand.

Do you really want to know about your past? When you find out, you will run. Just like last time.

It had taken me over an hour to summon the courage to pass through the red doors, exiting the safety of the terminal. But no amount of fortitude could have prepared me. Dr Belshar had warned me about triggers such as smell and sound, potentially evoking memories. I had only been half listening at the time.

It was the smell that assaulted me first. The air was heavy, like I could almost taste its poison. A mixture of smoke, pollution and garbage. As soon as the stench hit me the memory presented, it was all consuming. Again, it brought with it a kind of tunnel vision and inability to refocus on the chaos India presented around me. I staggered to the nearest wall, hoping to avoid attention from anyone and everyone.

I was locked in the back of a moving vehicle. Darkness engulfed us. What little air remained, was stale and thick. I could barely retrieve a breath, my chest felt like it was being crushed. I desperately tried calling out to my sister, but no sound would come. It was then I realised, my mouth was taped. I could feel Jiera's tiny frame pressed up against mine. She was shaking profusely; her body clammy and cold. Thick ropes tightly bound us together at the waist and feet. They hurt, cutting into my flesh. The road we travelled was bumpy and seemingly endless. The driver was reckless, taking the bends with speed. Each swerve caused us to hit our heads on the sharp metal edge of the boot. I could taste the blood now, which had begun trickling down my cheek. Muffled music, and the laughter of the men travelling up in front, reached us spasmodically. Their stench was relentless, a mixture of tobacco, alcohol and filth.

Or was it the smell of death? How close were we in that moment?

I nearly dry retched as I clung to the wall of the outside terminal, desperate for my racing mind to ease. I felt hate, anger, fear and weakness. I was so alone here.

Bracing myself against the filthy wall, fighting for composure, I saw more in my mind's eye.

The memory of the smells. The mixture of cooking fires from the slums, the waste of industrial sprawl, diesel fuel, and exhaust fumes from too many cars. Then there was the desert dust from Rajasthan.

How did I know this?

It all came whooshing back, overwhelming my already unbalanced senses.

I crouched down, using my bags to ground me, begging silently for my mind to return to the present. Was I going to pass out? Overcome with the oppressive heat, I began stripping off my heavy jumper. Somehow I managed, despite my shaking hands, to tie it awkwardly around my waist.

Breathe Aanya, breathe.

As quickly as my memory came, it vanished.

I warned you, Aanya. Stupid girl.

No. No way am I listening to you.

Despite my body reacting like this, I had to believe, I did believe, I was stronger than any memory that was returning to me... I had survived them when they were real.

'You want taxi miss? Please come with me. I have taxi.'

I was jolted back into reality.

A man was pulling at my bags.

'No thanks, no, please leave me here.' My voice sounded weak and unconvincing.

'You come miss. I look after you, give you very cheap price and nice drink of water. You feel better with me.'

He attempted to pick up my bag again. I had been warned of the scammers residing outside the famous red doors. Be firm, but polite, was the advice I had read. I pulled my bag back assertively into my chest, causing me to fall all the way to the ground now.

'No thank you. Please leave me alone.' Yep, if nothing else, I was a fast learner. My abrasive tone changed the look on the man's face immediately. I stared him in the eye without relenting. He turned without another word, spitting on the ground beside me as he retreated. I had no doubt he would shortly be buttering up his next victim. I took courage in my actions. It was a start.

Detective LJ

Australia, 2018

LJ squinted at the invasive morning light, burying himself further under the covers. He could smell his own filth. The potent combination of urine, vomit, empty spirit bottles and cigarettes swirled around him, making him loathe his existence only further.

His mouth was dry and crusty. The last thing he needed was the daylight; that would mean he was still alive. He had hoped never to see the darkness end. Bloody typical he thought, he couldn't even end things right. He wondered what the constant banging next door was? Why was the street outside so loud? LJ was sweating profusely, and his heart beating so rapidly, he clutched at his chest. The effort of banging on his heart with his hands, caused him to become dizzy and light headed.

Truth be told he had drunk enough last night for 10 people.

His aim? To wash himself away. Away from his past, away from his present, away from this world.

Surely hell couldn't torment him more than his mind did already. LJ had cared very little of the outcome of last night's binge. He felt that perhaps it was best for everyone he never woke up again.

He had made it through another night. LJ was accustomed to being hung over. It was almost like a comfort to him these days. At least he knew what to expect. But not today, this was different.

As he fought to regain any memory of the last 24hours, even the slight movement of rolling over brought with it a wave of unstoppable nausea. Without warning LJ vomited down the side of his bed. Judging by the malodor surrounding him, obviously this was not the first time.

The dry retching subsided, leaving him shaky; he could do little more than lie where he was. LJ craved a cigarette. His body felt weird, like it belonged to someone else, hovering above a crime scene.

Whose blood was on the floor beside the bed?

Had he taken something other than the booze?

He wished again he were dead.

The panic attack, triggering last night's binge, had been the worst he'd experienced in over a year. PTSD the doctors had diagnosed him with all that time ago. Only LJ really knew what was going on inside his head. He wished he didn't, wished he could have his own memory wiped.

That stupid girl, Aanya, she didn't know how lucky she is. His trouble was that he couldn't forget. Remembering was a curse. LJ had fought hard, but now felt he was unable to just get on with life. Life after *the* incident.

He saw them, wherever he went, whatever he was doing.

They were always there in his mind.

Their wide eyes, pleading with him.

Their fear, bodies trembling.

Their arms, outstretched toward him, willing him closer.

Their voices, whispering, begging him.

Then the blackness.

⁂

LJ attempted to roll out of bed again. He needed water, or maybe even more booze. Landing heavily on all fours, he reluctantly crawled toward the kitchen, unsure how his body would react. All around him, evidence of the carnage from last night's personal war. At some point he had obviously been in a rage. His TV and wall cabinet were broken into pieces, and the single window, facing the street below, smashed. No wonder the traffic seemed noisy.

Then he saw it.

He willed his eyes to turn away, but it was too late. The memory of the letters confronting contents came flashing back, causing him to curl into a ball amongst the rubble.

Why had she done this to him?

Then the blackness returned and he welcomed the respite it brought.

※

LJ woke again, startled, still on the floor. But this time to constant banging. Someone was knocking on his front door. It penetrated through his head. He stumbled up slowly, the spinning sensation and pain throughout remaining. He stepped on the letter as he crossed the room.

The cause of his latest meltdown.

'What?'

LJ's tone was harsh.

'LJ it's Cory, your landlord. Just checking mate, is everything alright? I've had some complaints from your neighbours.'

LJ rested his head against the closed door. He had no intention of opening it, that was for sure.

'Yep. All good here. Thanks for checking. Now rack off will ya.'

'LJ, you know I just want to help you right? But I can't keep covering for you okay. I need you to get yourself together mate. Get some help if you need it. I don't want to have to evict you mate.'

Mate? What a joke, LJ thought. Cory was not his mate. Taking a deep breath, LJ knew he had little choice but to be passive. Last thing he needed was this wanker on his case too.

'Sorry Cory. Yep, a rough night, but I've got it all sorted now. Was just heading out to the doctor, actually. Thanks for stopping by. Won't happen again, mate.'

LJ slid heavily down to the floor, back against the wooden door. Rubbing his eyes, his focus landed again on the letter.

Why did she have to pick him?

Aanya had been straight to the point. She wanted his help. She wanted him to travel to India and help her find Jiera. Aanya had been clever enough to include the photos of the young victims, her sister and herself. Also, the letter from the house maid. Ami, yes LJ had known her alright. Aanya had written her flight details, even where she would be staying. LJ knew the missionary in East Delhi well.

Who the hell does she think she is?

It made him furious.

If she knew him at all, she would never have asked.

What the heck did she expect him to do now? Just drop everything, and follow her?

Did she not understand?

He wouldn't risk messing up again.

He couldn't do that anymore. He had failed them, all those years ago. Failed the young, innocent girls he had been sent there to protect. LJ had vowed never to set foot in India again. Never to work as a detective again.

The world was safer without him.

But even as he ranted to himself, attempting to rationalise all the reasons why he couldn't, his mind wavered. LJ reached for his lighter, intending to burn her letter and forget about Aanya forever. But again, something stopped him. The niggling feeling inside him returned.

The same irritating awareness which had caused his meltdown last night.

Was it his conscience?

That little bitch had gotten under his skin. Aanya believed he was the one who could help. This revelation was beyond LJ's comprehension right now. Even after the way he had treated her, she had pursued him. If he was to be truthful with himself, and push fear aside for a brief moment, there was something else. Something about Aanya, he just couldn't let go.

No one had believed in him for a long time now, least of all himself. Did he dare even think he could be more than a washed-up failure, a worthless piece of shit?

Resting his head against the door, LJ began to cry. He had not let himself feel anything but anger and hate for so long now. The sun danced on the wall around him, almost magical in its speckled glow. LJ could all but stare through his bloodshot stinging eyes. The consuming weariness from fighting his demons weighed him down, yet somewhere underneath this he felt a shift. He felt like a tiny bit of the sun had penetrated his soul, stirring it. The wall he had built so carefully to protect himself from further hurt, to keep the world at bay, began to form a crack.

LJ knew he wanted more from life again.

Was it too late?

Aanya

India, 2018

The Uber came to a screeching halt, the driver gesturing this was my destination. He seemed in a hurry for me to get out. I peered out of the car's window. So, this was it. It was nothing like I had expected.

The missionary centre towered over the other buildings in the crowded street. My body felt like lead. Already struggling with the sensory overload India presented, this car trip itself had been a stressful experience to say the least.

Vanquished, I remained inside the Uber, staring at the grand concrete stairs gracing the entrance of the decrepit salmon coloured building. I barely registered my driver's animated tone. He clearly wanted me to move on. But the last couple of hours had been massive, and I held my hand up to him indicating I just needed a moment. Honking horns, swerving cars, noise and congestion. It sure was a crazy city. It appeared there were no road rules for the cars, buses, motorbikes, tuk tuks and trucks travelling down the highways. My driver, however, clearly did not share the same view. He seemed relaxed, humming to a local radio station, sucking on cigarettes like each one was his last. I had sat gripping the ripped leather of the back seat with one hand, and door handle with the other, wishing a seat belt had been on offer. Maybe I should have attempted conversation, but had remained silent for the journey.

The infrastructure was staggering. Never had I witnessed

anything quite like it. Buildings, new and old, crammed upon one another. Shop fronts literally spilling out onto streets. And people, there were so many people. Animals appeared to roam freely; rubbish was strewn everywhere. Even from the back seat of my Uber I could sense a chaos through the closed windows. Vibrant splashes of colour seemed unmatched to its environment. Produce, commercial goods and artefacts spilled haphazardly. The mish mash of buildings without question, looked structurally unsound. Yet as we moved along, I was surprised at the lush gardens, grand temples and tourist attractions which randomly popped up amongst it all.

So here I was. This was it.

Although it had been many years, my gut told me I was no stranger to these parts.

Somehow, I felt as though I was viewing Delhi through wise eyes. Yet until today, I had not known those memories existed. Although there was nothing specific I could yet pinpoint, it was more like a knowing. It gave me a new confidence. I could do this.

Outside, the air remained densely hot. The morning was smoggy. Squinting at the sky I could see the sun trying to push through the thick air. The missionary building, which had been home to my parents so long ago, was larger than I had expected. Its paint was now faded and peeling, some of the windows cracked. Certainly, its tall box like façade overpowered the surrounding low-level buildings. I counted four levels and wondered if most was accommodation above. Lawn encompassed both sides of the stairs, and a few people sat on its gentle slope which flowed toward the narrow street.

I imagined Ami, stepping off the bus that day at the shelter to my left. She must have been filled with fear herself as she had headed up these very steps. But she had done it anyway, taken the risk. Ami was obviously a brave woman, and I intended to thank her when I could. I longed to meet her. I knew she would help solve so many pieces of my puzzle. Would she be willing to meet me?

Too late you stupid girl. Jiera is somewhere you will never find her.

No.

It was my turn to be brave. I picked up my bags with shaking hands. My body struggled with the heat, exhaustion and uncertainty. I could feel the beads of sweat dripping down my neck. I felt clammy and light headed. But my determination reigned and I began the journey toward the unknown.

I willed a false bravado as I gingerly took one step after another. The people around stared, like I didn't belong. They were wrong. I knew I did, and forced myself to smile and nod.

My mission was foremost in my mind and I silently recalled the aims.

1. Find Jiera.
2. Find the man who had done this to us. I hated him to the depths of my core.
3. Make him pay, no matter the cost to me.

Rahul was going to wish he had never met me.

ॐ

'You must be Aanya. We have been expecting you dear one, with great excitement I might add.'

The voice was loud and animated. The outside glare behind me blurred the figure standing just inside the entrance. I froze, waiting for my eyes to adjust.

Confusion reigned. This was far from the greeting I had rehearsed in my mind. I blinked, dropping my bags to the floor, not daring to take another step forward just yet. I met the eyes of a woman, the receptionist perhaps? She beamed at me, her warm smile relaxing me somewhat. The elderly Indian woman was striking. Her shimmering dress was a vivid purple. A traditional sari, with a choli top. Her arms, neck and ears were adorned with rose gold jewellery. Her long dark hair, sprinkled with grey, was plaited down her back.

I stood motionless, trying to make sense of this moment. As if feeling my reluctance, she strode out from behind the desk greeting me warmly. She was short, but rather voluptuous. Her bare feet revealed toes coloured in bright orange, her anklets jingled as she walked. I was taken aback by her sudden embrace, not knowing quite how to receive affection from this apparent stranger. But she felt comforting, and needing that right now, I let my body relax against hers. When she released me from her hug, tears were spilling from her heavily made-up eyes.

'My Beautiful Aanya. You are a miracle. A blessing. Never, ever, did I think I would live to see such a tremendous day.'

She held my hands, inspecting them carefully, before kissing each gently. Then she reached for my face, cupping my head, outlining my scar which still lightly remained.

Had I known this woman before?

'Forgive me dear child. This all must be such a day for you, such a big, huge day. Come and sit, come on, you need my tea, yes that will fix you right up. And you must be famished...'

She spoke quickly but with much vivacity. I felt like I was in a trance. She remained holding my hand, pulling me away from the door. I stood my ground, suddenly reluctant to take another step. I was confused, and felt suddenly protective of myself. The last 24 hours had left little emotional reserve.

'It is okay, I am Bina, we spoke on the phone remember? I did not feel it the right time to tell you the whole story my child. But my dear Anya, I knew you before. Before you returned with your family to Australia.'

All the nervous energy drained from my body, replaced by a welcome calmness.

She knew me before.

Bina would help me. A tingling sensation raced through my body, as silent tears escaped. I resisted no longer, letting her lead me further into the building. Exhausted, I could all but drag my bags behind me.

I remembered now too, distantly, but the memory was there. Her smell, her embrace, her love. Yes, I had known her.

Over spicy tea and sugared biscuits, my energy began to return. I was more than curious.

'Aanya, we have much to discuss. But for now, I am going to show you to your sleeping quarters. I assume you need a place to stay? You must rest a little first before you do anything more.'

I didn't want to rest. I wanted to hit the streets and begin my search.

The room we sat in was huge. A big communal area with large kitchen, couches, books and games. People, families, children, single figures, came and went as we sat. Bina smiled at them, as she had me.

'Bina, how did you know I was coming?'

'Great news travels fast my young friend.'

She laughed heartily before continuing.

'You emailed your parents this morning, correct? Well, they contacted me straight away. They are like family to me, wonderful people. You do realise, we all want to help you, right, Aanya? You are not alone in all this my child.'

But I was alone. How could anyone understand the sickening, all-consuming urgency I felt inside?

'I don't know where to start Bina. This place is so huge, and busy and crazily different to what I know. I don't remember much, but I'm trying to force the memories to return. I can't waste any more time, I need to go to the police, today. Surely if I am here now, they will take this investigation more seriously'

I could feel myself rambling, my voice was high pitched, desperate thoughts, fears, questions all spilling out uncontrollably. I was crying again, but had not noticed until Bina handed me a tissue.

'Aanya. All this will come, I promise. But not before you rest a little. If you are not clear headed, the battle will be far greater. Come, I will show you to your old room.'

My old room?

Bina stood, instructing me to do the same. She headed for a staircase toward the back of the lounge area. Stopping mid stride, she faced me, placing both hands on my shoulders. Again, I tried not to flinch.

'Last you were here, I nursed you until you were able to fly home to Australia. Three weeks you stayed with us. Much of the time, it was just you and me Aanya. Your parents were in and out of court, desperately trying to attain the documents needed to get you out of India and take care of you. Every day, we, this community, prayed you would live to see another sunrise. We prayed even harder that *he* would not find you. The man who tried to kill you. Most of your stay, you were unconscious. Occasionally you stirred, mumbling and confused, before fading away again. But there were times, times I saw the real you, and you saw me. I knew you were a strong spirit, even then. So, you see my Aanya, to have you back again, so healthy and full of life. Well, it's nothing short of a miracle.'

With that Bina sighed, before turning back and walking up the stairs. I could see in her eyes I had meant so much to her, yet I'd just left and gone to Australia without knowing.

I climbed silently behind her. Rattled, I tried to process all she was saying. Bina again stopped abruptly, startling me. She was puffing heavily. Grasping my hands, this time she appeared more urgent.

'Please forgive me Aanya. I did not know. None of us knew you had a sister.'

Her eyes seemed clouded, overwhelmed with her grief and shame.

'Bina, how could you have known? It is not your fault'.

Squeezing her hands back, I implored her to look me in the eye.

'I am so grateful I had you to care for me. And all this time, I never knew. I owe my life to you Bina, and I have never even thanked you. It is me who needs forgiveness. I am here now, and this time we are going to find Jiera, okay? I believe we are back together for a reason.'

Bina nodded.

But her eyes said it all. They were filled with doubt.

ॐ

I woke in the early hours of the morning. Again, totally disorientated and soaked through with sweat. Mum was not wrong in saying the heat took some getting used to. My body clock was up shit creek. The room was darkened but not pitch black. As I sat up, swinging my legs over the bed, the coolness of the rough floorboards was a welcome relief. My eyes rested on the only framed picture on the surrounding walls. When I had first entered my room last night, I could all but stare. Goose bumps had travelled over my skin. The giant creature was majestic and bold. It flew gallantly through the surrounding storm. The eagle's eyes looked determined, not wavered by what he was flying into. He seemed to know he would prevail, radiating strength and courage.

It was the same picture as I had back home.

So, this was where my love for eagles had begun. Those weeks I had spent here, barely alive, hiding from my own predator.

Had Bina spoken about eagles to me?

Did I dare associate myself with these glorious birds?

I felt a pinch of guilt, as I still hadn't called my parents or Tilly. Not the greatest of starts. But I just needed some head space. They knew I was here, and safe.

You are nothing like an eagle, Aanya. You are weak, soon you will see.

I lay back on the small bed. The night wasn't still, like I had become accustomed to at home. White noise, muffled and constant, sounded both in and outside the building. I felt so alone. Exhausted, but wired. Determined, yet overwhelmed at the task ahead.

How the hell was I supposed to know where to start?

Out of nowhere came a piercing pain in my stomach. I cried out, unconsciously pulling my body into a protective ball. Then an invisible blow to my kidneys rocked me to the core.

'Stop it, stop hurting her.' I whispered.

I knew Jiera was being beaten. Trying to deepen my shallow breathing, I attempted to calm the tension and excruciating pain surging through my body. Then, sudden pain overtaking the back of my head dominated all other agony I faced in that moment. Murkiness engulfed me, stilling my screams.

Another shadow in my mind was heading into the light, I could feel its intensity.

Ami was shaking me. Pinching my neck, trying to get me to come around. Had I fainted? Jiera was beside her, stroking my face. I could see the three of us were in some sort of factory. An illegal sweatshop perhaps? I watched, again hovering above the scene like I didn't belong.

The room was filthy, packed with other children similar to us. The space was tight, children sat on the floor working, folding and boxing clothes, jewelry and baskets. Some of the workers were so tiny. All appeared to have the same dull expression on their faces, almost like robots, void of emotion. No child should ever look like this. Without question I was witnessing child labor. Question was, where?

Ami reached inside her yellow bag. She pulled out a juice box, instructing me to drink. Jiera willed me to sit up, hitting me on the back of the head gently, insisting I do so. Jiera and I were young. Maybe 12? I was so thin, my skin ashen. Again, pulling something from inside her bag, Ami gave us bread and some sort of broth. She spooned it into my mouth urgently, continuing to look behind us at the bolted door.

Who was she scared of?

How long had it been since we had eaten?

Had heat and starvation caused me to faint?

All around us, other children looked on, famished themselves no doubt. Ami instructed them to keep working. Without warning, I could hear the locks being turned and the heavy door being pushed open. Instantly Ami fled from my view. I watched as Jiera grabbed for my hand. Two men entered the room. Every child desperately tried to look busy, keeping their eyes to the ground.

Why didn't I?

As I hovered above the unfolding scene, I willed my childlike self to look away from them. Yet I did not, instead standing as the men approached.

'*Let us out of here. We have worked for 14 hours straight. We need rest. I will work no more.*'

As frail as I was, slightly wobbly on my feet as I struggled to stand, not once did I drop my stare. The men laughed as they approached. Spitting at us before picking up my tiny frame by the hair.

'*You stupid little bitch. Rahul should have killed you by now. You are nothing but trouble. When will you learn Aanya. You will stop only when we tell you to.*'

I watched helplessly as the tiny little girl, the version of me I had no recollection of, was thrown across the room, hitting a metal boiler in the corner.

I didn't move.

Blackness spilled over the scene like a rupturing tar pit. It moved so quickly I was sucked under and buried with my shadows.

'Aanya, Aanya, stop. You are safe. It is me, Bina.'

I could feel my body thrashing around, but remained unable to return to the present. My mind was caught between the memories and trauma of the past, and the present day.

'Aanya, still your mind. Smell, smell this and lay still.'

What was happening? A heavy weight pushed me down, instantaneously an aroma calmed both my body and mind.

'That's better Aanya, now just breathe child. Breathe.'

Within a few minutes, I felt more grounded. Bina released the pressure from her hands on my shoulders. I sat up in the small bedroom, the window drew my attention as I noticed the sun beginning to fight through the smog filled air of the new day.

Bina, smiling and humming, continued to wave the incense stick above my head.

'This used to calm you every time Aanya. Do you remember the smell?'

I did, it was an aroma I would know anywhere. I loved the peace it brought. I constantly had sandalwood oil burning at home. Till now, I didn't realise how important my connection with it was.

Why wouldn't have mum shared that with me? I didn't want to know.

'Where were you, Aanya? Where did your dreams take you this time?'

How could I ever truly explain myself? My body was still aching, and the headache remained all consuming.

'Jiera is in trouble Bina. I have to do something to help her, and it has to be today.'

'You feel her connection, right?'

I nodded.

'I'm angry at myself. Why didn't I feel her before? How could I not know Bina? How could I have left her there, all that time?'

'Stop Aanya. You must not give those negative thoughts life, by speaking them out loud. Your mind protected you for a reason. You need to trust in your body, your aura is very strong. What's important is that you are here now. I can feel it in my spirit Aanya, you still have time, you will find her.'

'Not sitting around here I won't. I just honestly don't know where to start. This place is crazy, I'm so out of my depth. I feel stupid thinking I could come here and deal with this myself.'

I crossed the room, opening the little window, longing for a burst of fresh air that wasn't to come. Despite the early hours, the stifling heat was prevalent. And the smell, that was going to take some time to adjust to. Bina was smiling at me quietly, as I turned to face her. Her hair was flowing freely down her back, wavy and unkept. She had on a long white nightgown. The speckles of light dancing around the room almost made her look angelic. Her wise demeanor was so calming and spiritual.

'Sorry I woke you Bina. The dream I was having was brutal, another memory it seems. I've been having lots of them lately. They come both day and night now.

'It is okay, child. I am here to help you. You certainly were distressed when I entered. Regaining your memory is going to be exhausting mentally Aanya. Are you meditating at all? You have a lot to deal with, remember that alright, and try to be kind to yourself.'

Meditating? I didn't have the time or the patience for that.

'What do I do now? What should my next move be do you think?'

'The spirits told me something last night, child, and we must never doubt their power.'

I had little clue where this was going, but I was intrigued nonetheless.

'There is something you must believe, and draw upon. Twin telepathy is a real phenomenon. Your heart and mind are connected to Jiera. In my meditation, I saw the image of your bodies joined as one. I believe the spirits wanted you to know Aanya, that if *you* can feel Jiera, then *she* can feel you too.'

I had no idea what 'spirits' Bina was talking about, but the point she was making was profound. I'd never thought about it in the reverse.

Jiera could feel me too.

'So, if twins can have similar thoughts, feelings and even dreams, your first move is to reassure her Aanya. Talk to her. Let Jiera know, she must not give up, soon you will be with her again.'

Overwhelmed I stared at the floor. Picking at my already short and brittle nails, I chewed on my already damaged bottom lip.

Did I dare to believe this could be real?

Better hurry up bitch, or I will get to Jiera first.

The day was filled with disappointments. Perhaps it was me, I was expecting too much. Every minute that passed, was another lost. As the night began to present, I was more unsettled and impatient than ever. The buzz of traffic congestion remained present. How many times did drivers need to honk their bloody horns?

Surprisingly, in the midst of the noise, I could hear birds. Different to the familiar Australian evening sounds, these were chirping and screeching in the few tall trees surrounding the missionary. Down below me in the common room area, Indian music blasted. The room was buzzing with people I had passed earlier. Maybe I should be making the effort to get to know some locals, but I just had zero desire to socialise right now. I'd prayed myself invisible as I headed up the stairs as quickly as I could.

The police had been no help. At first, when I filed a new report, I fought back tears of desperation, but they were soon replaced with anger. My resentment built as little hope was given. The police station itself had been overcrowded and frantic. India was polar opposite to Australia. Everywhere I had been so far, there seemed to be so many people in such little spaces. I tried to plead my case to an officer who barely seemed to be listening. He was distracted by his phone, and the red welt forming on his neck, which he was scratching at. He constantly blew cigarette smoke into our already polluted cubical space. At least his English was good.

Bina took time away from the reception at the missionary and was gracious in helping me navigate Eastern Delhi. Our aim was to expose me, and hopefully my memory, to some local hotspots. My senses were on constant overload as our driver, Madhav, took us from one location to the next. He was a personal friend of Bina, and apparently worked for the missionary. Bina reminded me again to be wary of drivers I didn't know. Madhav would be happy to drive me anywhere I wanted he had said, insisting I keep his details in my phone.

To an onlooker, we were simply sightseers, not that anyone seemed to notice me. India thrived on a frantic pace. My frustration heightened as the tedious day turned into late afternoon, then evening. Not once it seemed, did I recognise or feel a familiarity for any of these local areas.

I didn't belong here. It was true, whoever I'd once been didn't matter; I was a foreigner now. And yet, since discovering Jiera existed, I felt disconnected from Australia too.

Did I belong anywhere?

Maybe I needed to restart my journey in Nepal.

But if the Nepalese were *my* people, why did they not fight for us after our parents died?

My parents had been surprisingly calm and supportive over the phone earlier in the day. I had dreaded making the call. They had said, although they were a little frantic I was here alone, they were not entirely surprised. They knew I had a stubborn, headstrong will. Mum and dad said they understood why I came to India, and would continue to do their best to investigate from Australia. But I knew what was coming next. They wanted to come, to support me over here. It made so much sense. Maybe, if I had no luck in the short-term, it would be an offer I would need to take them up on.

But not now.

I couldn't explain it, but this was something I needed to do alone.

Make my wrong right.

I'd escaped my torment, leaving my only family behind, to suffer. Now it was up to me to find Jiera. This was on me.

I was still yet to talk to Tilly. I had a feeling our conversation was not going to be as smooth. Attempting to dial her number for a third time, I screwed up my face as once again it went straight to message bank.

Was she ghosting me?

Maybe I could text her instead. She couldn't stay mad at me forever.

I flopped onto my bed. Since my arrival, I'd felt constantly clammy and beading with sweat. Today my skin had seemed further irritated by the heat. Yet right now, I could not even muster the energy to get up and shower. The ceiling fan, turning slowly above my head would have to suffice. Once again, I looked over at the Eagle picture, hanging on the thin plastered wall, then my eyes fell onto the bedside table and the photos of Jiera and me. Picking them up, I pressed the precious images into my chest.

'Jiera,' I whispered into the stillness, 'I am here. Please don't give up sister. I will find you and take you home, I promise.'

This heaviness, my scattered mind and deep sadness I think, made me subdued and somewhat cloudy in my thoughts. It was really starting to piss me off. I was better than this. I'd have to fight my way through this numbing emotion, if I was to get anywhere. Time to shake off this frustrating fog.

It'll be nice to see you again, Aanya. Two for the price of one on GB Road, sounds good to me.

I sat bolt upright, exploding with sudden energy fuelled by the onset of rage.

Screw you, Rahul. You are wrong.

I shouldn't have done it.

Deep down I knew it was foolish, and more than that, it was bloody dangerous.

But my rational side took little notice of my building fury. Unable to stop myself, I was on autopilot.

Overcome with grievance and adrenaline, my irrational, headstrong nature took charge.

I needed to see for myself.

Grabbing my backpack, I quietly closed my bedroom door behind me, already dialing Madhav's number as I descended the stairs two at a time.

ॐ

Perhaps it was the dark, eerie streetlights, or the potent air which seemed to embellish this seedy underworld.

Maybe it was just my mind; heightened by my research into this shameless district.

It was chaotic, prime business hour here despite it being late evening.

What struck me first, was the filth. Everywhere I looked, people, cars, noise, shop fronts spilling out onto the dirty rubbish laden street.

So, this was the infamous Garstin Bastion Road.

Buildings and shanty like structures piled upon one other, built high into the sky, old and decrepit, looking like they could collapse at any minute.

Did I dare?

I took a deep breath, summonsing the courage to leave the safety of my taxi.

'Lady Aanya, please, you not go alone here.' Madhav seemed anxious, almost pleading with me to stay in the car. 'No good place for the likes of you. Bad men everywhere.'

'I am okay, thank you. I will be careful; I know what I am doing. I must look for my sister, Jiera.'

That was a lie.

'No no Aanya, very dangerous place. You need chaperone.

Nothing good happen at night time like this. Not good.' He sounded convincing. But I had come this far. Again, I lied.

'Bina said it was okay Madhav. Can you wait for me? Wait here? Just give me one hour. I will pay well I promise.'

He glanced at the street ahead of us, then back to me.

'Okay, okay, one hour. You meet me here Aanya. If you not come, I return to Missionary, tell Bina. I cannot wait longer; I must attend another job.'

Stepping onto the sidewalk, I took a moment to gather my bearings. Shop fronts dominated the sidewalk, each packed with merchandise and food. Securing my backpack tightly around my waist, I shoved my phone further into the pocket of my jean shorts. Did I have a plan? Not really. But I was here, safe or not, I intended to investigate the street for any possible sign of my sister. She was running out of time.

At my request, Madhav had dropped me at the beginning of the infamous red-light district, Ajmeri Gate. I knew the street was long, ending at the junction of Lahori Gate. I'd read GB Road contained several hundred, multi-storeyed brothels. This was the home of over 4000 sex workers. Somehow, I had to ensure Jiera didn't become one of them.

I thought of Tilly. She would know what to do, she was my strength. Tilly had been so supportive over the last few weeks. Researching with me, listening to me ramble on, making me shower and eat. Tilly had been the one reading out loud to me, tears in her eyes about the brutal statistics.

But now I stood alone, in amongst it all. Surrounding me, just behind the shabby shopfronts were victims. Young women. I shuddered at this confronting reality. I was close enough to touch the girls now. The very same precious humans I had read about. I knew many were kept in slave like conditions, all of their earnings taken until they could repay their bought price. That process could take 4-8 years. I was so close, yet powerless to help them.

At first glance, the street looked like many other of the market streets I had seen since my arrival. But looking more closely, as I walked through the crowds, I could see the pimps and prostitutes oozing out of the buildings, trying to lure passerbys. Amongst the constant stream of people which were mostly men, young children played and ran about in the filthy gutters and side alleys.

Who did they belong to? Where were their parents?

Those poor girls. It was all I could focus on. Many were so young, so beautiful, their lives different in every way to mine now, yet surely, they had dreams and ambitions just as I did. What little chance so many would have of escaping this notorious world. Forced into a life that was not their choosing, their bodies and minds being violated. I was so stupid, to have thought this would not become personal to me. I knew this now. I'd been here around 20 minutes, yet would be affected by this forever.

How could this be the same world I live in? This was only one small part of India's child trafficking reality, yet far more of a problem than I'd ever dared imagine. I thought of LJ and my parents. The things they must have been exposed to. Question was, why was this darkness not exposed to our world? Was every country blinded by their own problems? GB Road was nothing short of pure evil. I felt sad a country as beautiful as India, filled with such diversity and culture, was also home to this adversity for so many.

As I walked, I was mindful not to seem as unsure as I felt. Trying not to stare too long at anyone in particular was hard, as the scene was gob smacking. Men called to me, gesturing for me to follow them into their shops or bars. Both men and women were keen to engage with me. They shoved phones in my face, with pictures of young girls. Despite them speaking in a foreign tongue, I knew exactly what they were offering. Trying to appear polite and confident, I smiled but shook my head. Doing as Madhav had instructed, and not stopping still for too long but all the while looking for any sign of either someone who looked like me, or a local who seemed to recognise my face.

The smells felt familiar. Tobacco, sewage, incense, perfume, spicy foods boiling in large pots or being fried up on the street carts. I stood, back up against the wall, just for a moment. The smoky swirls of the burning camphor were both comforting and alarming in unison. The bombardment of my every sense, caused me to feel woozy. Present time began to abate as my mind returned to the shadows.

Slipping into a side alley, only just off the main strip, I crouched despite the sediment. A rat startled me, scurrying past further into the darkness and excrement. *Please, not now,* I willed. Now was not the time for me to slip away into my shadows.

The dust storm surrounded the little girls.

Despite viewing this scene in my mind's eye, as I hovered above, suddenly my chest felt constricted and wheezy. Where the hell was I this time? Where had my mind returned me to?

Jiera held my hand, as we wandered slowly toward the group ahead. Squinting and trying to wipe the grime from our eyes, we were met by a tall man with a red headscarf. He poked us with his wooden stick, pointing to the family working nearby. There were so many bricks, some being stacked, many being carried toward the working kilns. All around I could see children, some younger than us, carrying the bricks on their heads. Everyone was shrouded in clay dust, feet bare, clothes covered in filth.

Suddenly Rahul appeared behind us, talking rapidly with the man in the red scarf before hitting us roughly on the back of the head, pushing us forward. A woman in a group beyond, called for us to join her. Begrudgingly we went.

In the background, smoke billowed from the looming brick kilns. The air was thick, dense with mixed pollution; the kilns themselves causing the sky to appear foggy and blackened.

As I hovered above, I realised this place was all too familiar. We had spent much of our time here. I was witnessing one of India's most dangerous child labor trades. Yet another thing I had survived, it seemed. Many Indian slave groups, often entire families worked in these outdoor kiln factories, 9-12 hours a day. Young children too, were forced to work in these dangerous conditions, with little food and pay. Sleeping the nights in the rubble with little shelter, their young bodies exposed to the harsh elements. Poverty stricken families often chose this type of work instead of remaining in the slums. They worked together, just to survive. Children were not given the opportunities to be educated, but instead carried out work tasks even adults found challenging.

I wondered now, how often I had worked here. My bet was, we had spent many a day, moulding, drying and stacking endless bricks from clay. This industry was big business in India, exploitation at its best.

As Jiera and I cowered in the outer edges of the group, a woman chastised us, clearly insisting we start work. Constantly looking over our little shoulders to see where Rahul was, we began moving the bricks. Dragging them along the ground on an old hessian bag, we added them to the pile the family had assembled. Rahul walked the perimeter liaising with the men posted on each corner, assigned to keep an eye on the workers. His tone was animated and aggressive; he eyed the workers with contempt.

We both wore head scarves. I wondered had Ami covered us to help protect our skin from the harsh sun? Bare feet and clothed in pants and shirts that were already soiled, I carried a small knapsack and water flask. It appeared I was guarding it with my life.

I could see myself scanning the perimeter, whispering something to Jiera. Surely, I was not thinking of escape? Rahul was gone, but another man, a guard was heading our way. We began frantically stacking bricks, heads down and no doubt desperate he would pass us by.

The guard was approaching. My anxiety heightened within my dream like trance, helpless to assist the situation from above. I knew his intention was brutal. Without warning he whipped the girls on the back, the cracking sound penetrating through the compound. We cried out like injured animals, almost primal in our sound.

Despite seeing some of the surrounding workers flinch, no one looked up. No one came to our defence, each too scared for their own lives no doubt. Knocked forward, into the dusty bricks and rough ground we desperately covered our heads, as again his whip cracked across our tiny backs. Jiera reached for my hand; our faces buried in deep rubble.

Why was he doing this? What had we done to incur such wrath?

The guard yelled at us to turn and face him. Reluctantly we did, I pushed Jiera slightly behind me, wanting to protect her from further abuse. The thin lines of blood were obvious now, seeping through the back of our thin shirts. Shaking in terror, our tears silently fell onto the dirt. Then, from the blackness, the outer edges of my vision, I could see another figure approaching.

A large woman.

She stood between the guard and our tiny bodies as we cowered on the ground. She gestured wildly, and appeared to be negotiating with the guard.

Was she helping us?

The guard spat at us before abruptly turning, heading back toward his post. The woman, whom I had seen earlier working with her family, helped us up, beckoning us to follow quickly. She led us toward one of the tiny brick shelters on the edge of the compound. The small room had mats on the floor, and a burnt-out fire pit in one corner. Washing hung from a rope. A crate like table was set with small pots containing flour and salt. Leaving us clothed she washed the lesions on our backs with a single bucket of water. Blood trickled onto the ground from under our clothes. We held onto one another tightly, the stinging of our wounds clearly evident on our faces.

Were we safe now? The reality was, we were not. I watched in horror as she picked up my backpack. Jiera gripped it as long as she could, before the woman slapped her fiercely across the face. The impact sent her reeling back across the small room. The woman's children appeared from the doorway, eagerly pulling at the bag now. They fought amongst themselves for the food parcels inside. I had no doubt, Ami would have hidden these for us before we left Rahul's house.

So, this was the woman's motive in helping.

All along, her intention was to steal from us.

These people were perhaps more desperate than we were. It was hard to blame them. Once again, we were in the wrong place at the wrong time. The story of our lives so it seemed.

The woman grabbed at Jiera and me, roughly pushing us toward the thousands of bricks awaiting us in the hot sun. Clearly, we had served our purpose.

'No, no' I was yelling. 'I'm not going out there. Leave us alone.'

Her strength was well beyond the little girls. They had no choice but to succumb.

Being dragged backwards, the darkness began closing in, I reached desperately for Jiera, but could no longer see her.

I felt a shift in my mindset. My dream was beginning to fade back into the shadows; a familiar rush of relief followed.

But it was to be short lived. Something felt wrong.

No longer was I crouched in the darkened alley of GB Road as I remembered. My dream had become a reality and I was being dragged into the street. I could hear the muddle of male voices but could not turn to see who was manhandling me. Trying to rub my eyes, I was desperate to get my bearings.

Fear swept through my body.

This was exactly what I had been warned against.

'Hey! Put me down right now, arsehole!'

Blinded by the bright lights suddenly all around me. I thrashed about as someone swiftly carried me through a shop entrance and up a narrow flight of stairs. But I was tightly restrained, being gripped under each arm and leg. People were everywhere; they moved aside as we passed.

What the hell was happening? Did this scene not alarm anyone? Could no one see my personal rights were being violated?

Obviously, they could. What dawned on me as even more concerning, was that no one seemed to care.

Being carried backwards like an animal to the slaughter, I continued to fight for my freedom. The strangers, all men, laughed and joked amongst one another, smirking down at me.

I screamed.

'Put me down, you bastards. I don't belong here. I don't work here. You have made a mistake.'

My voice was strong, adrenaline was surging through my veins. How the hell had I let this happen?

'No mistake, girly, you very pretty and fresh. We need something exotic like yourself. You come to the right place girly. Good work conditions here. We have pretty dress for you.'

A large man in a white shirt and too many gold chains followed behind us. He combed back his greasy dark hair as he walked. A cigarette dangled from his mouth.

My heart beat even more wildly.

I was forced into another crowded room. The filthy space was humid and cramped. The mixture of smells, perfume, body odour and cigarettes made me instantly nauseous. The airless space was filled with girls, all shapes and sizes and mixed nationalities. All of them, heavily made up and dressed to impress. Everyone vied for my attention. I was placed on a bench seat and told to sit.

'Don't move. We need to have a little talk.'

I stared up at the man in the white shirt; he was the epitome of disgusting. He turned and started yelling across the room.

'Ishita, Ishita. Come. Come.'

An older woman rushed in from a side door. She was large, and dressed in a sparkly green dress. Sweat beaded around her face, threatening to smudge her makeup. As directed, she sat next to me, grabbing at my wrist.

'Yes Sir, I keep her, Sir. I will not lose her for you Sir.'

Keep me?

What the hell?

'Move her Ishita, prepare her. Wait for me to return.' He grabbed at my chin, lifting my face roughly towards his. 'You don't go causing any trouble now girl, and I will look after you. You have come to the right place. Best place in town. My kingdom!' He gestured around the room, smiling as if I was looking at a palace of wealth and prestige.

Without warning, Ishita stood, keeping a firm grip on my wrist and pulled me forward. Again, the crowd seemed to part as we climbed yet another flight of stairs, these even thinner and more decrepit than the last. Many rooms led off the rancid hallway. The small entrances had no doors, instead covered in makeshift curtains and blankets. I could hear many people behind them. I knew where I was, yet no amount of research could have prepared me for this.

What the hell had I done? I was in a brothel on GB Road.

❦

'Ishita, please, you have to help me. Please, you have it wrong. I don't want to work here. I am just a tourist. This is a misunderstanding.' The desperation in my voice was real. I was terrified. Ishita knelt before me, her eyes wide and her tone adamant.

'Girl, listen to Ishita now, for your own good. Sit and stay quiet. It is for the best.'

She had placed me on a chair in a small room. Unfortunately, this room did have a door which was locked carefully behind me by Ishita. I had to assume she had done this before.

'We wait. We stay here until my next instructions. What is your name?'

Ishita sat heavily on the small bed beside me. Her stare was intense, but not mean. She was puffing and panting, using a fan to cool her body. Her strong perfume still failed to mask her body odour. My head swirled with fear, confusion, and anger.

How could I have been so stupid?

I had to think. I needed to focus and either try to talk my way out of here, or escape. I knew with certainty the longer I remained, the less chance I had.

My backpack was still on my back. Thank God for that. Tucked carefully into the waistline of my shorts was my phone. At least I'd had the smarts to do that in the alley, before my repressed memory had taken hold.

Somehow, I needed to call for help.

But who?

Stupidly, the only person who even knew I was here was Madhav. Would he alert Bina if I didn't return? Or simply move on to his next job?

Ishita handed me a cup of water. It was warm and had a brownish tinge, but my throat was so dry I found myself gulping the liquid down without thought. It wasn't until I was done did the realisation hit me.

What if I had just been drugged? It happened all too often from what my research had told me over the last few weeks.

I needed information. The more I could learn from Ishita, the better my chances were of escape. If I could just win her over somehow, maybe then she would help me. Surely, she could see I didn't belong here.

'Ishita, please help me understand. I don't want to cause you any trouble. So maybe you could explain? What am I doing here? Is this your place of work?'

I forced myself to look calm and smile at her. My stomach was churning. It felt as though I had fire ants crawling through my veins. My phone was so close, yet I dared not risk it being confiscated.

She looked at me for the longest time without reply.

'Where have you come from, child?'

'Australia. On holiday with my family. I'm just lost. I promise it wasn't my intention to bother anyone here. I was stupid. My family will be wondering where I am. Please help me.'

I was rambling, talking fast, lying, but had little other choice.

'We are all lost on GB Road, child. I was once like you, too. Young, full of hope and dreams. But this is who I am now. We become one with this place after a while. It's a matter of accepting this is your destiny and get on with it. This is my identity now.'

A single tear escaped her blackened eyes; tiny crack in her otherwise expressionless façade. This was a woman who had been through a lot, no doubt. I just had to pray I could touch the compassion in her.

'How old were you when you first came to live here, Ishita, if you don't mind be asking?'

'Actually, child, it's nice to talk to a fresh face. Saves me being in other places. But you don't go causing me trouble, okay? I don't need trouble today. So, you do me a favour too, and keep me company. I was only 15, a long time ago. I knew nothing. I'm 35 now. What is your name anyway?'

This poor woman had been working on GB Road for 20 years. She had been beautiful once, now all I could see was her gaunt face, shadows beneath her eyes that were now almost void of expression. She looked so tired and defeated. I wonder what had led her here in the first place. How many like me had she seen come through? And how many had never left, instead promised a life that would never be realised.

'I'm Aanya, I'm 19. I was actually born in Nepal, before living in India. I was adopted young by my Australian parents as I was an orphan.'

'That is very lucky, Miss Aanya. Very lucky indeed. Makes me wonder why you would return.'

She had a point. I wasn't ready to give up that information right now. She could use it against me at any time. I had no doubt Ishita had good survival instincts.

'Just a family holiday. That's why I need to get back to my family now. They will be worried about me, expecting me home. I don't want any trouble for your place here'

Again, Ishita seemed deep in thought, studying my features. She smiled sadly before she spoke.

'You are lucky to have someone who worries about you Aanya. You should never have come here. Now I am afraid it is all too late.'

Ishita

GB Road, India, 2018

Quietly, Ishita closed the door behind her, turning the key in the lock to ensure Aanya stayed put. She dared not let her boss down; the punishment for that she had seen before. For some time Ishita stood, leaning back on the door, eyes shut and a million miles away despite the present chaos. It was unlike her to become rattled so easily, but this unexpected visitor had certainly unsettled her nerves.

These days, she was good at blocking out the screams, the arguments, the injustice and the filth. Ishita was well seasoned at being able to shut out her reality when it all got too much. She had been swift in learning that came with the territory, all those years ago. From the beginning of her new life here, Ishita had realised if she were to survive, she would need to be thick skinned. To be devoid of emotion, detached. Ishita had made a personal pack to do this for her daughter, ensure she had opportunities that Ishita would never experience herself.

But today, the girl behind the door had complicated and challenged this mindset.

As soon as Ishita had laid eyes on Aanya, she had been reminded of her younger self. Not that she often dared let her memory return to her life before GB Road. That only brought heartache.

Never had Ishita wished for a life such as hers. Never had she wanted this existence to be forever. But these days, she'd accepted that GB Road was perhaps her final destination.

At a glance, it was obvious Aanya was full of life. A strong spirit, no doubt filled with hopes and dreams of impacting the world. Ishita remembered being exactly the same.

A sadness swept over her. She wished Aanya had never arrived here tonight on GB Road.

Had she known the dangers? Why would a young girl of her substance be here at this time of night, alone, no less?

Silently Ishita whispered a prayer out to the universe. Her wish was for Aanya to somehow get away. But Ishita knew, if things went according to plan for her boss, and most often they did, she would have little chance of escaping now.

Stupid, stupid girl, Ishita thought.

Such a waste of a good life.

For a fleeting moment, Ishita considered helping Aanya, but fear brought her quickly back to her senses. Remembering her own overwhelming terror when she had first arrived here on GB Road, Ishita recalled the grief and shame, her confusion and absolute disbelief that this was to be her new home. At this time Ishita had desperately needed work, and despite never being a victim of child trafficking like so many, she certainly had been a child herself, no less.

This job, she had vowed, would never be a permanent thing.

At just 15, Ishita had already been widowed. Her older husband had left her with much debt and their small baby to feed. Ishita had been a child bride, arranged by her family to marry, to ease the debt they too had faced. She had refused contact with them from that day, furious at the time her family had forced her into a marriage. At 15 Ishita was abandoned, a mother with no income, unskilled and illiterate.

Her mother-in-law had lived with her throughout her marriage in a tiny rented house on the outskirts of Delhi. To this day, Ishita could hear the venom in her mother-in-law's tone, feel the sting as she'd slapped her across the cheek. They'd never seen eye to eye. As soon as her son had passed, she had demanded Ishita find work, insisting the baby would remain in her care. Ishita had fought tirelessly to obtain work close by, desperate to be the mother her baby needed. She never trusted her mother-in-law; she was cruel, and in her eyes not capable of caring for her child. But after months of searching for work, Ishita had resorted to stealing food and supplies wherever she could, just to keep them from starving. The rent was long overdue and eviction was pending. She had little choice. It would only be for a short time, Ishita had promised her daughter. A pain stabbed through Ishita's heart now as she remembered this unkept promise.

Ishita's landlord, Sai, offered her a deal. Ishita shuddered at the thought of him even now. He was a sleazy, corrupt man. Her husband had warned her to stay away from him, look at the ground should he try to engage in conversation, and whatever she did, never, ever, follow him back to his home. Ishita didn't have to be told twice.

Sai's husky laugh was too loud to be an honest one, and his character told the truth of the type of person he was. Even the mere sight of him made her skin crawl every time he came around to collect his rent. Ishita had always been able to sense a person by looking into their eyes. She had remembered doing this from a very little girl, like it was her secret super power. Eyes, she believed, reflected a person's moral compass, their values and their honesty.

It was one of the reasons she had needed to step out of the small room holding Aanya captive today. To remove herself from Aanya's eyes. They were powerful, truthful, hopeful, pleading with Ishita. Their glistening depth was seemingly endless, almost magical. Ishita had a strong sense, from locking eyes with Aanya, there was far more to her story.

Something was different and purposeful about that girl. It took bravery coming to this hell on earth. But why?

Ishita felt it imperative Aanya get away from this world as soon as she could. Question was, could she be brave enough to help her do that?

Ishita suddenly longed to see her daughter. She would be a similar age to Aanya now. It had been so long now since they had connected. Would her daughter even want to see her again?

It was 20 long years ago that Sai had offered to give her a job. His friend, Ishita's now boss, had been hiring. Sai promised to take care of the rent should she take him up on his offer. Her baby would be safe. He even said he would make sure her family was fed, clothed, and had everything they needed while she was away. His cut in her salary was a steep 40%. The more she earned, the better off her family would be, he had reminded her.

Bastard.

She was left with little choice.

Until the day she had arrived on GB Road, never ever had she considered such a trade. Leaving her young child behind was the toughest moment in Ishita's life. She doubted to this day the anguish swirling inside her at that moment would ever be matched. As she tried to breathe a little deeper now in the crowded hallway, Ishita fought the tears recalling the past. It was just too painful to go back there in her mind. She had only seen her daughter a handful of times since her arrival here. Time was a thief and already her baby was 21 years old. Ishita was proud of the fact her daughter now attended University, lived in a good area of India and held a respectable job. Unlike her mother, Ishita thought. She would never ever disclose to her she worked on GB Road. That was a shame Ishita could not bear. She would rather die. It was a sacrifice, however, Ishita was proud she had made, for the sake of her daughter's wellbeing. Who knows what may have happened had she not.

Many times over the years, Ishita had considered going to the police. If the world became aware of the young innocent girls trafficked through here, surely justice would prevail. In a way,

Ishita knew by keeping quiet she was also to blame. Guilty by association. Plenty of the things that happened behind these walls were cruel and abusive. Many of the young victims were captives, ruled by their owners. Nothing much shocked her these days. But what would she say? The one thing always stopping her from going to the authorities was her daughter. After all, she was here on her own free will at the end of the day. Truth be told, part of her didn't want to leave. It was all she knew.

Ishita had witnessed over the years many police raids. There was certainly a police presence on GB Road. Some of them were good men and women, but many were not. It was not uncommon for the police to be regular customers themselves, but never would they pay. The non-corrupt ones would search the premises, yet rarely find what they were looking for. Ishita's boss and his band of loyal men were very good at hiding the young illegal girls and keeping them quiet when the need arose. Hidden behind the walls was a warren of tiny hallways and lockable cells, inhumane and airless. In them, young girls would be drugged and detained for hours, sometimes days.

She wondered, if the walls could talk, would the world even help us?

Aanya

GB Road India, 2018

What had I done?

I cursed my stupidity under my breath. 'Idiot Aanya.'

Without moving off the bed, I scanned my surroundings, every sense on alert. I wished this situation was one of my repressed memories, something I would soon wake from. But I knew it was not. The small room seemed to close in around me. My sweat was making me clammy and the unrelenting stench in the repressive air, nauseous. My heart was beating so rapidly, I was shaking with the surge of adrenaline it caused. Unknowingly, I had been hugging my body, subconsciously protecting myself from what was to come. I stood, willing myself to think. Determined to get out of here, I knew the only way was to keep a level head. Not easy to do when I was more frightened than I could ever remember.

Silently, I reminded myself, *I've been in worse situations than this. I escaped before. I can do it again.*

No windows, just a locked door. The old wire bed was laced with dirty crumpled sheets. A small rust-stained sink in one corner. A tall cupboard sat opposite the bed. Its wooden doors were stained with what looked like splatters of blood. Moving silently, I crept over to look inside. To my surprise, the cupboard was filled with dresses and colourful traditional Indian outfits. A shelf inside held makeup, brushes, hair clips and perfume. A full-length mirror, cracked down the middle, was attached to the back of one of the doors. Holy shit, was this where they prepared new victims?

Movement and voices remained consistent outside my locked door. Some laughed, others were abusive and harsh. There was music somewhere close, dulled by the white noise. I wondered just how many people were actually up here in this building?

For certain, not one of them cared that I was locked up.

Reaching for my phone, I knew it was my only hope. Fumbling, I dropped it on the wooden floor. I froze, praying no one had heard.

Please, please, please, have reception.

I felt certain I wouldn't be left alone for long.

Would Ishita return again, or one of the men?

Then what?

I dreaded to learn their plan.

Holding my breath, I entered my pin. I let out a slow breath of relief. One bar, one little bar indicating reception; my lifeline to the outside world. Crouching down beside the cupboard, I tried to focus on who to call. The police? What the hell was the emergency number for police here anyway? My parents? That would be a last resort; it would freak them out. Tilly? Maybe.

Madhav. I searched for his number, dialling it as soon as it appeared. Thank goodness Bina had made me save it in my phone. I couldn't even remember the number of the missionary centre.

'Bloody idiot, Aanya,' I cursed again.

The ringtone seemed endless. Why wasn't he picking up? I hung up and dialled again. Nothing.

Too late. They have got you now. Welcome home. Remember, some people count, and some don't.

For once, I could almost ignore his vile voice.

Bina? Did I have her number? No, I had meant to get it. Why had I been so impatient? I was screwed now. My mind was racing at a fast pace and I grappled for ideas.

A text message. Yes, that could work. It was worth a shot.

I was in enough trouble already, I had to risk it. The last thing

I wanted to do was hurt my parents further. The worry I would cause them and Tilly would be dire, but what choice did I have?

Frantically, I typed. Sending my plea for help to them and Madhav.

'Please, Universe,' I whispered, 'let my message reach someone who could help me.'

I kissed my phone for luck, pressing it to my heart.

Help me please. I am being kept in a brothel on GB Road. Not far from Aimeri Gate Road, on the left. The shopfront is dark red. Alley beside it. I am upstairs. I'm so sorry. Help me.

I was such an idiot. My poor parents would be mortified receiving my text like this.

Snapchat! I could share my location. Yes, now I was thinking. Tilly would think to look for that.

The time was 8.35pm, well over an hour since Madhav had dropped me off. Would he keep his promise and alert Bina when I failed to return? That would mean it was around 1pm in Melbourne. I felt hopeful.

My phone vibrated in my hand, pulling me from my prayers.

Tilly's image lit up the screen. Tears of relief spilled down my cheeks. My finger was shaking as I swiped to answer her call.

'Aanya! What the hell is going on? I got your text. Tell me what to do. Who should I call? What's going on? I'm freaking out'

'Tilly, stop!' Even as I whispered into the phone, it felt too loud. I had no clue if anyone was listening outside the door. 'Tilly, I am in—'

I froze, the abrasive noise beyond was too close, alerting me into silence. Something or someone was smashing the very wall I crouched behind. A man was yelling abuse and a woman screaming. Was it aimed at Ishita?

I could hear Tilly still desperately calling my name through the phone. I had to risk a reply.

'Tilly, get help, I need help, look for my location on Snapchat.'

Hastily, I disconnected from the one lifeline I had, as the door was being unlocked. Slipping my phone back inside my shorts, I quickly scrambled back onto the bed where I had been told to stay. The arguing in the thin hallway continued. I drew a sharp breath as the door was opened roughly, banging against the thin wall. Time had run out.

Ishita appeared, red and flustered.

'My boss not happy I left you alone, I hope you did not do anything stupid. We will both pay dearly if this doesn't go his way.'

'Ishita, please,' I was begging now. 'Please, can you help me?'

'I cannot, Aanya. I am sorry, but I cannot. Listen to me. Look at me.'

Ishita pulled me up from the bed, holding my hands firmly. She had turned me away from the door leading to the hallway. She stood so close I could smell her breath, feel her trembling.

'Look at me, do not resist now. Everything will be easier if you do not cause trouble.'

It was then I smelt that familiar aroma. A chilling fear surged through my body. I tried to turn toward the door, to fight her grip, but Ishita held me tightly. Then, in an instant, I was being smothered. Someone behind me placed a bag over my head, a cloth was being forcibly held against my mouth and nose. A familiar fogginess enveloped my consciousness.

Chloroform.

I felt myself quickly slipping away. I felt my body falling into darkness until the overpowering chemical triumphed.

꙰

My head pounded. Confusion loomed as I drifted between the past and the present as the memories swirled within the shadows of my mind.

Images raced, some distorted, some clear. They mixed together, then stood alone; Jiera, Ami, Bina, Tilly, the brothel, LJ, my parents.

Pain coursed through my body. I could feel a spasmodic tremor randomly causing me to twitch. An invisible weight seemed to push my body down. I tried in vain to manoeuvre my tingling limbs.

I was falling, spinning, my surroundings turbulent. I needed this confounded addling to stop. Let me sleep, please, let me go. I wanted the blackness to return; it was peaceful there.

Aanya. Aanya, come back. I need you. You are my strength, my only hope. Sister, please.

Despite their heaviness, my eyes suddenly burst open. I remained still, willing this new voice in my head to speak again. A dared not even breathe in case I missed the sound.

Aanya. You are close. So close now. Don't give up. I need you.

I was not imagining it. I felt her. The static current caused by the electricity of our connection was undeniable. I was not dreaming her soft voice, nor was this a hallucination.

I was sure.

Nor was it the evil tone of Rahul, the voice that had dominated my head for so long.

'Jiera, sister, I can hear you. I am going to find you, I promise.' I whispered into the darkened room, desperately trying to get my bearings.

Hurry Aanya. My time is running out. Sister, we will be together again.

Tears escaped me now. A swirl of emotions poured out with them. Relief, overwhelming grief, then a calmness. I knew it was Jiera.

Just like Bina had said, if I could feel her, she could feel me. We just had to learn to be still and connect in the subconscious mind.

'I'm coming Jiera, I promise I am coming.'

The blackness engulfed me again, as the distended images in my mind began to fade away to dust. A deep need to sleep dominated, one I could fight no longer. The density of emotions and the fallout of being drugged were taking their toll.

રેટ

'Aanya… Aanya, darling girl. Wake up now.'

The bright sunlight peeking through the window was both startling yet strangely reassuring. I rubbed my eyes and the first thing which came into focus was the eagle. Then Bina. I sat up gingerly. I was lightheaded, my mouth dry from dehydration no doubt. I didn't understand. How was I back in my bedroom, in the Missionary Centre?

Pulling my knees to my chest on the bed, I managed a weak smile as I set my eyes on Bina. She was beaming at me.

I was safe.

'You gave us quite the fright, Miss Aanya. If I didn't love you so much, I would be somewhat cross.'

Bina's voice was both scolding and comforting at the same time. She was sitting on the edge of my bed, gently patting my hand. My head still pounded and the grogginess had yet to subside. I was so parched.

'What happened? How did I get here? I'm so sorry. I never should have been that bloody stupid. I was so scared Bina. I don't understand? How did I get here? I think I was drugged. I was locked in a room with a lady called Ishita. They locked me in. I'm an idiot. What was I thinking!'

'Enough, child. Take a breath, you have had quite a night. First things first. Eat, you must eat to regain some strength.'

Bina handed me a bowl of a steaming mixture I didn't recognise. I knew better that to argue with her at this point. Truth be told, I needed to give myself a few minutes to find balance.

'This is my Mulligatawny soup. I fed you this many moons ago to restore your health. It will do the trick, you watch. It has miraculous healing powers, I tell you.'

Without questioning, I began to spoon the spicy broth into my mouth. It was delicious. Suddenly I found myself famished.

She was right, with every mouthful I felt better. It felt like liquid gold spreading through my being. As the minutes passed, my head was beginning to clear and my focus regaining. I was still wearing the clothes I had left the missionary in last night; my backpack and phone rested on the bedside table. Silently, apart from Bina's humming, we sat in the tiny room.

Sandalwood drifted into the air from an oil burner in the corner. Beyond my room I could hear the noise of the street, Indian music and laughter coming from the common room below. A sharp knock on my bedroom door broke the comfortable silence. Swiftly the door was opened revealing a large figure looming in the entrance.

LJ!

This, I had not seen coming.

I gulped the last mouthful of soup. It was impossible to swallow with the tightness that had formed suddenly in my throat. I felt the colour drain from my face as I met his dark, angry eyes.

He looked far from pleased to see me.

I barely noticed Bina quickly exiting the room, bustling past LJ awkwardly in the thin doorway.

'I will leave you both to talk. I will be back a little later, Aanya.'

I did not break LJ's stare as I nodded in Bina's direction. I wished she would stay.

'What the hell were you thinking, Aanya. You take the cake, girl. Hands down one of *the* most stupid moves I've seen in my time, and I've seen a lot girl. You are seriously messed up, bloody young minded and stupid.'

Like flicking a switch, his tone and the way he was spitting his abuse regained my spirit instantly. I glared back at him, furious he dared speak to me with such malice and disdain.

I raised my chin slightly and sat up a little straighter.

'Is that why you came all this way, LJ? To make me feel like shit? I don't need your judgement right now. You have no right.'

LJ crossed the room and sat heavily on a chair, pulling it

closer to my bed. I could smell the cigarettes on him, feel him seething. He was trembling his face red and the veins in his neck bulging. I pulled my knees back to my chest defensively. But then I remembered. I was the one who had begged him to come. Had I been me in his shoes right now, I too would be pissed off.

'Aanya. If this is going to work, you do what I say from here. I've come a long way, and let me tell you, I didn't want to. So, it's my way or I catch the next plane out of here. Your bullshit stunts end now. You will end up getting yourself in deep trouble, lost to a world you know nothing about. Or worse, killed. And in the meantime, you'll give your family a heart attack. They were sick with worry.'

'Is that your way of saying you will help me? If it is, I am very grateful. I mean it, I'm sorry. I have learnt a very harsh lesson in the last 24hours. Mostly, that obviously I am very naïve. I am sorry.'

'Yep girl, you have a few apologies to make, that's for sure. But not to me. You are bloody lucky, I will tell you that much.'

I felt so ashamed. But at the same time, would I do it again? Probably. I had to find her. Jiera was close, I could feel it.

'Your family and Tilly know you are safe and that I am here. I have assured them from now on you will be doing things my way, or I will detain you and put you straight back on a plane to Australia.'

I laughed, mostly in disbelief at what was coming out of his mouth.

'I am an adult, you can't do that. That's bullshit, against the law.'

LJ looked me up and down, shook his head, then smirked. It irritated me to my core.

'Girl, I can, and I will. You have no idea what I am capable of. If I can bust into that brothel and get you out within an inch of your life, I think I can handle a weak, little know-it-all, annoying upstart like yourself.'

'Full of compliments today, I see. You are wrong. I'm far from weak. Maybe I do have a lot to learn, but I'm determined, and I will find Jiera. I've never wanted anything more in my life.'

'We will see, Aanya. We will see.'

LJ looked as washed out and dishevelled as I felt. I wondered how long he had been in India. How on earth had he found me in that brothel? I needed to calm the storm between us. After all, he was here for me.

'I am sorry. I agree, I will do whatever you say. I am really, really grateful you are here. I'm shocked, but so happy to see you. Thank you.'

'You can thank me when we find Jiera.'

LJ stood, crossing the room to leave. His back to me now.

'LJ? He stilled. 'I'm glad to see you are beginning to believe in yourself again. Obviously, you are a very capable man. I can tell you are kind also, so thanks. I hope we can be friends.'

I saw him physically stiffen, then exhale audibly. He did not turn to face me when he spoke, instead fumbled with the door handle.

'You did a good job leaving us clues to find you. Your quick thinking was smart, but hell, you're bloody lucky. Thousands of girls have been in your position and have never been found again. Don't leave the missionary centre again till I say, right?'

I nodded for a second time, not that he could see. The shock of my reality, and just how easily things could have turned out so very differently, began setting in. I could all but stare at his tall frame as he left me to ponder alone.

Rahul

India, 2018

Rahul clenched his fists, his face was contorted with agitation; he could barely control the fury burning from within. Despite the coolness of the room, his navy shirt clung to his frame with sweat. Rahul paced the vast space of the spotless kitchen like a tiger awaiting its prey. It was a room he rarely frequented in his extensive home. He had staff to take care of such things. According to Rahul, preparing food and the likes was beneath him.

Some people mattered and some people didn't

Rahul would never apologise for living a life many could only dream of. Why shouldn't he live like a king? Had he not worked hard to gain his wealth? Rahul believed he deserved it all. No one had ever helped him on his way. He had built his empire alone, therefore deserved every luxury. Things had not always been easy. Never once had Rahul questioned himself on the ethical and moral questions raised by the way he made his money. Never would he admit blame. His victims were weak from the start. Life was all about survival of the fittest. As a young boy, Rahul's dad had told him to study the book 'On the Origin of Species' by British naturalist Charles Darwin. It was the one and only kind gesture his father had ever done for him. The rest had involved abuse or neglect. The message behind Darwin's theory had changed his life. Rahul had become obsessed with the notion and believed it was his key to success. In Rahul's mind, he could easily justify his actions and continued to turn a blind eye to the ruined lives and the devastation he caused.

Some people matter and some people don't.

Tonight, Rahul was seething. His famous temper was completely out of control. He was furious his advisors had failed to inform him Aanya had returned to India.

They were so incompetent, he ranted.

And Aanya, bitch.

How was she not dead?

This time, he would make sure.

Drink in one hand, cigarette in the other, his tirade continued as he stormed around in a violent rage.

Yet all the while, he worked on his plan of attack. He always worked best when pushed into a corner, where he fought harder. He had learnt this as a kid. That's why he had killed his father.

He knew exactly where Aanya was, and soon he would come for her. Stilling momentarily, an evil smile formed on his lips.

Then there was LJ. He was back too.

LJ didn't scare him. Without question, he once was a man to fear. Plenty of times in the past LJ had foiled some big operations. Rahul had lost a lot of money because of LJ's investigations and pestering ways. Not these days. From what he had heard, he was nothing more than a washed up, drunken has been. Easy pickings.

Rahul kicked a chair across the room, throwing his now empty glass against the tiled wall. Ami stood defenseless, only centimetres from where the glass shattered. She knew better than to scream as the shards of glass hit her hands. She had instinctively and protectively covered her face. She hated when Rahul had these episodes. From experience, she knew it would be many hours until the ferocity passed. Most often, it only ended because he passed out somewhere.

Like many times before, she wished he would die, then she too would be free.

'What are you just standing there for? Clean up this mess, Ami.

You need to earn your keep here. Bloody lucky I have put up with you this long. You are not getting any younger Ami, easily replaceable, remember. Get me another drink. I want the bottle this time. Move it.'

'Yes Sir. I will fetch your bottle from the study. Then I clean up. Why don't you come into the den, try to relax?'

Ami kept her eyes to the ground as she spoke.

'Relax! You of all people should know I cannot relax. How is it even possible she is here? Tell me something Ami, did you know she was alive before now?'

Rahul stood over her small frame, pinning Ami against the wall. Still, she did not meet his venomous stare.

Ami panicked, yet did not dare let on. Did he suspect her actions? Could he possibly know she had contacted Aanya?'

Ami held onto her calm exterior.

'Of course not, Sir. I would not betray you master. I heard whispers at the market only today. Some of the hired help from around were talking. The word is, she has returned with LJ in order to find Jiera. That is all I know Sir, and of course I came straight to you with the news.'

Rahul grabbed Ami's chin and forced her to look at him.

'Is that right?' Rahul laughed, throwing his head back in madness. The menacing sound soon turned into a scream of sheer agitation and mania. Ami was terrified and remained still. 'Move, woman, get me a drink now.'

Ami fled, not daring to look at her master of 15 years.

Rahul cursed under his breath. He vowed to find Aanya again. And this time, she would not escape him. Nor would her sister. A quick death would be too easy for those girls. He would make sure they lived out their days just close enough to him to pay the price for their betrayal.

Their final days on this earth would be worse than anything they had experienced before, and this would cause him great pleasure.

No one got away with leaving Rahul. Least of all, Aanya.

She had always been such a strong spirit, from the start she'd defied him, causing trouble. Aanya really believed she deserved better, even as a little kid.

Who did she think she was?

Some people matter and some people don't.

Ami never made it to bed that night. Nor did she rise at dawn the next morning.

Aanya
India, 2018

'Tilly please, just listen, this is a two-way convo you know.'

'I am listening Aanya, but you are forgetting I know you too well, and I can see it written all over your face.'

I smiled at my beautiful friend, wishing again she were here. We had been regularly talking over Facetime the last few days; she was as always, my rock.

'Tilly, I've been doing the right thing. I haven't left the missionary without either Bina or LJ since, well since my little episode. I am being patient, but it is so hard. Each day I feel like a ticking time bomb. Helpless. I can hear her Tilly, like Jiera is talking to me. I believe she knows I am here. Makes it even harder to wait.'

'She knows you are close, I agree. And your time will come to be with her. I really believe that. But we also both know how head strong and irrational you can be. I love that about you, but hey, you are out of your depth a little in India.'

'But am I Tilly? I lived here most of my life, remember!'

'Yes, but do you? How is the memory thing going, anyway? Are you still having times you can remember stuff?'

'Nothing Tilly, not a thing since I came back here. It's pissing me off. Dr Belshar said being here would ramp up the process most likely. It seems to have gone the other way, no memories and no random pains at all!'

'Hmmm, strange. They will come at the right time. I know it Aanya, Super Heroes always get their super powers just at the right moment. And what about LJ? Is he still being a pig to you?'

I smiled broadly at Tilly through the phone. Never did she fail to bring me the positive energy I needed. My smile faded. I could see the nurses in the background hovering. Tilly was in hospital again, having a new treatment.

'I'm sorry I'm not there with you Tilly. I hope this hospital stay really turns your health around. You deserve the best.'

'I'm actually not sorry, I'm reading an awesome book and no offence, but you do tend to talk a lot, and I'd get distracted. So, LJ, tell me, how's that going?'

Tilly coughed heavily and settled further down onto her pillows as we talked. I could tell she was wearier than she let on. I also knew without question she would much prefer I was there. She was the most unselfish person I knew. I loved her so much.

'Well? Hello Aanya, I'm still here remember'

We both laughed.

'Sorry, I was miles away. It is interesting with LJ. A lot has changed in only a few days between us. He is actually pretty awesome. Not entirely the prick I thought he was. There is a lot to that man.'

'Well, as we thought, just a little beaten down by the shit he has been through. I can't imagine.'

'LJ is letting his guard down with me slowly. Clearly, he was very damaged last he was in India. He blames himself for the girls in the brothel dying before he could get to them. He has suffered PTSD and turned to the bottle ever since to try to forget. I am really hoping by being here again, coming back to India, he will heal a little. Finding Jiera will regain his sense of worth, you know what I mean?'

Tilly was nodding but yawning at the same time. Some of the pre-med drugs the nurses had given her were kicking in.

'Aanya that's so awesome. Sounds like LJ needed you just as much as you needed him.'

'Yeh, under that gruff front he puts on, he is a kind, brave man. I am really grateful he chose to help me. It was a huge ask. I even think he is starting to like me a little. We have had some nice moments. He really listened when I told him what I knew of my story.'

Tilly had to go, as she was heading into surgery. It made my heart constrict, being so far away from her right now.

'Be strong Aanya. Listen to the voice within. That's all you need. I can't wait to meet Jiera. See you on the other side.'

※

So much had happened in the last few days. Yet at the same time, I was frustrated as we seemed no closer, in my mind, to the one thing I wanted the most. LJ assured me I was wrong. He was one mysterious man, I will give him that. For the last three nights he had left after dinner, and I was unsure when he returned. 'Research' he called it. Touching base with people he hadn't seen in a long time, letting them know he was back.

He never commented much on his role in India before he had left, but it was not hard to see the truth about him. In the past few days, he had let me tag along to pay a few people, including the police, a visit. Each time we entered a room a hush came over the space. People stared before almost greeting him with a bow of respect. This LJ was a far cry from the drunken mess I'd seen in his apartment the very first time we had met.

He was calmer here, that was for certain. An emotion I think he least expected (after all it had been almost 20 years) Maybe he felt more at home. I knew the nights still caused him pain. I watched as he snuck his poison of choice into his room. But hey, who was I to judge. He was doing the best he could, and I was so grateful he was even here.

The best thing about spending time with him over the last few days was his attitude towards me. No longer did he hurl insults and criticise my very existence. Instead, he was genuinely interested in my story and what I had to offer. I'd overheard Bina filling him in on my time here after my escape from Rahul one afternoon. He was keeping her company in the kitchen as she prepared food for the guests at the missionary. Innocently I'd wandered in, looking for her famous sugar biscuits myself. I'd halted in the hallway, just outside the door. A lump formed in my throat as I listened to her recollection of that time. She was the most amazing woman, Bina. Again, it struck me that until this trip, I had no knowledge of the huge impact she'd had in my life. But what caused me to hold my breath in that moment was LJ. He had told Bina how wrong he had been about me, how much he admired my courage and determination, and how I had helped him too. He told her he was beginning to care for me very much. Silently I wept in the hallway that day, before tiptoeing back to the common room. It was hard not to be overwhelmed by all the uncertainty and fear this situation brought. But LJ was here, and I was beginning to really care for him, too.

My parents Facetimed me daily. They were incredibly supportive. I knew they were talking to LJ also, and most likely Bina as well. My team was strong. Everybody was in my corner. Eager to find Jiera before it was too late.

So why did I still feel so alone?

I started to see the reality too clearly. Unless we were to get a strong lead from one of LJ's contacts or receive information from one of the organizations set up in India which worked to find girls just like Jiera, finding her would be a sheer miracle.

I tried not to feel down, but sometimes it was near impossible. The slowness of time, the heat, the frantic pace of India, the overwhelming feeling I was running out of time was getting to me. But most of all, it was the guilt. This was all my fault. If Jiera dies, or cannot be found and is forced into a life of further trauma, it will be all my fault. I was the one who ran away. Ran from my master's home and left my twin sister alone.

Why?

Why, if I was the strong, loyal, determined person people said I was, would I choose to leave her behind?

Because you are a coward, Aanya. You are a selfish, evil girl.

No. There had to be another reason.

LJ
India, 2018

Slumping onto his bed, LJ was exhausted, both physically and emotionally. He welcomed the solace of his small room on the third floor of the missionary centre. Here he could lock out the world, be alone to think. These days, people often were too much for him. It was the silence LJ cherished the most. He needed solitude to regain his composure, have the strength to pretend he was good enough to take up space in the world.

Again, LJ questioned whether it had been the right thing coming here? This same query he had repetitively asked himself over the last five days. That, and was he actually strong enough anymore to succeed? Physically, he knew he was, but mentally? LJ knew his mental health was fragile. He had been unwillingly stripped of the man he knew before.

Would coming back here to India help? Truthfully, time would tell.

LJ reached for the bottle. The brown liquid slipped down his throat too easily. It was both his comfort and his curse. Just one, he told himself, just one to calm the nerves.

Tonight had been the toughest so far. The way Aanya had looked into his soul. She was so full of belief and hope in him. She had hugged him earlier like he was her most favourite person on earth. Truth be told, LJ had relished the affection. In that moment, he began to sense he belonged again, not like all was lost.

Then there was the letter. LJ had placed it in his shirt pocket.

He felt like it was burning a hole in his soul. He promised himself he would read it after the drink. LJ didn't want to. He knew who the sender was. Someone had hand delivered it to the missionary centre today. Why did they not hand it to him personally?

LJ was being swallowed up in self-doubt and hate. LJ's greatest fears swirled continuously in his already addled mind.

What if he couldn't live up to Aanya's expectations?

What if his mental health battles stopped him from being the person he once was?

If panic and anxiety set in, would he be endangering Aanya's life?

Did he still have the courage?

He had failed before; what if history repeated itself?

Did the right people still respect him in India?

What if it all became too much? Where would he run?

Could he stay sober long enough to find Jiera?

What if they were too late?

LJ sat back up, attempting to push his racing thoughts aside. Looking at the familiar bottle next to his bed, his mouth salivated at the sight, and even without a drop reaching his lips, he could taste its magic. LJ shook his head in an act of defiance, but its pull was strong. Standing, LJ felt a little light headed. The heat in his room was stifling. At the tiny wash basin in the corner, he splashed warm water onto his face and neck, hoping to alleviate the beads of sweat. Catching his reflection in the mirror, LJ froze. The image made him reel. He hardly recognised the stranger intently staring back. The black circles under his bloodshot eyes seemed to be magnified against his dull, grey dehydrated skin. Was he really this old? Where had the years gone? Looking deeper into his eyes, LJ could see the congestion caused by grief, fear and torment. Yet for the first time in many long years, he noticed something else. Determination and hope.

LJ began to cry, small whimpers at first, yet soon his whole body shook. He gripped the sink to keep from falling to the ground; the sudden outpouring of anguish and regret all consuming. He was overwhelmed with the responsibility that lay ahead. Panic set in. Reaching for his saviour, he hastily unscrewed the bottle top with shaking hands.

LJ willed the familiar and comforting blackness to come. He lay back and waited for the liquor to wash away his reality.

Aanya

India, 2018

I held my photos of Jiera tightly; their treasured existence was like the breath in my lungs. Like every other night since I had received them, I found myself tracing her face and staring into the eyes of the little girl I did not know.

Where are you, Jiera?

Can you feel me, sister? Just give me a sign, please I need your help in this.

Tucked away in my small room, I felt home sick, wishing for the comfort of my family and my own bed. Had I taken them for granted back in Australia? Did they know how much I loved them? What were Rhubarb and Tabitha doing right now? Were they missing me too? Did animals work that way? I smiled at the thought of Tabby, all warm and curled up in my doona.

LJ had promised he would let me tag along tomorrow while he investigated out on the streets. He had a plan, he had said. LJ was always saying that, but did he really? Impatience was getting the better of me again tonight. I had little choice but to trust him. Bina had reminded me of this earlier. She was one incredibly calm woman to be around, often reminding me everyone was in charge of creating their own inner energy and peace. Masala chai tea was becoming a favourite of mine, and over a steaming mug and Bina's delicious Maida biscuits, tonight I had sat contently in the kitchen, listening to her stories of LJ. His reputation certainly preceded him, not that he would ever let on. LJ was as respected as he was feared, by all accounts. I felt sad he couldn't see this about himself anymore.

But that was not what was really bothering me right now. It was what Bina had hinted at, before quickly shutting the conversation down, just a few hours earlier. I still felt stunned by her partial revelation.

Lying on my bed felt hot and uncomfortable. My physical reaction no doubt exacerbated by my restless state of mind. To the outsider, I simply existed in the silence of my own company, yet internally my thoughts were far from quiet. What Bina had indicated left me completely perplexed and questioning everything.

Sleep would not be possible tonight.

Why would Bina start to tell me something, then bale on the conversation? I was irritated as much as intrigued.

Before bustling out of the kitchen, clearly flustered, she had said too much, Bina had implied LJ had known Ami. And not just 'known her' in a fleeting, distant way. Bina had said they were once very close, as in a secret relationship.

Could this possibly be true?

How could I not ask LJ about it now?

And if it were correct, why hadn't he contacted her since our arrival?

Why had he not gone straight to the source?

Then I had a sickening thought: Maybe he had.

Was there more he was not telling me?

Were we too late?

Getting up, I stared into the night sky through my little window, the only respite from the four walls. I visualised the framed eagle on the wall opposite flying free, embracing the bombardment of what was to come. The surrounding noise was constant, even though it was after 1am. The glow of lights, cars screeching and people still moving in a constant stream below. A mixture of laughter and conversation, horns blaring, and music distantly evident. Despite the darkness above it all, I could see the red tinges around the half moon, and an eerie yellow staining the clouds. Bina had said the pollution was so thick at times, even at night it was evident. There were no stars tonight. I wished there were.

My body began to tremble and without warning the familiar tunnel vision set in. The bustling street outside became blurry, and my present world was silenced. I stumbled to reach my bed, feeling heavy and suddenly exhausted.

I knew what was coming. Question was, which memory would escape the shadows this time.

The young girl couldn't run any further. Despite being only an onlooker to my younger self below, I could feel my chest stinging and a wheezing had consumed my lungs. My heart was beating wildly and my ears ringing.

Where was I this time?

Somehow, I knew without question, I was searching for Jiera. I began feeling desperate. Had I lost her?

I watched the scene beneath me. She had stilled. Bent over on all fours, the young girl was clearly weakened.

Just how far had I run that day? And from where?

Surrounding the girl, I could see the shadowy night, filled with narrow streets and back alleys weaving through a jumble of housing. Despite breathing heavily and coughing harshly, she tried to get up, stumbling a few metres before falling again. All the while her desperate eyes darted around, searching the twilight, but for what? Or for whom?

The young girl looked like she was in her early teens. A much older me than in any visual memories I had witnessed thus far. Still, she looked emaciated and sickly.

Was this presenting memory close to the time I had actually escaped?

The young girl began to call out. Her voice was but a whisper, faint and raspy.

'Jiera, Jiera, come back. Wait for me, please. Where are you, sister?'

There was no reply to her plea.

Again, she scrambled to her feet. Using the alley wall to stabilise her slight frame for a moment she wiped tears from her eyes, and took in a deep breath, pushing her shoulders back. Hovering above her, I knew exactly what she was doing. She attempted to ground and energise herself. To this day, I still use this ritual when faced with a challenge.

'Jiera, Jiera!' louder this time.

'Aanya.'

She froze.

Across the empty street was bushland and a river. The voice had come from there. Without hesitation the young girl crossed over, never taking her eyes off the spot she willed her sister to be hiding. Silently, an equally skeletal frame appeared, checking the area around her. Jiera stood, knee thick in a small bush.

'What are you doing, Jiera? Why did you leave me?'

The girls sat closely, hidden from the world in the bracken and thick trees lining the Yamuna River. How exactly had Jiera made it from their masters home, was unknown. Aanya had clearly given chase until she found Jiera.

'Aanya. I had to run. Tonight was our only chance. I knew Rahul was in a meeting with his horrible men. Ami left the gate unlocked, I'm sure by accident. But I saw it as our miracle, Aanya, my only chance to get out.'

Hovering above, I almost felt like I was eavesdropping on a private conversation, an unwanted intruder viewing this past encounter. But as foreign as the scene was to me in this moment, I was watching myself.

'Jiera, we do things together, remember? To be safe, and never be lost from one another. We promised. You were coming back for me, right?'

'Sister, how could you ask me that? Of course, I was coming

back. Listen to me, I found out about someone who I know could help us. The other day, when I was at the market with Ami, you were in the boiler room working. Do you remember?

The girls sat only inches apart. So close, they could almost be one. Their foreheads joined. Aanya was nodding as she gripped Jiera's hands.

'What about it?'

'Well, I tried not to be nosey, so to seem preoccupied I began picking the freshest fruit in order to please Rahul. But how could I not be curious about the man Ami was talking to?'

'What man Jiera? A stranger?'

'No Aanya, that's just it. He was known to her. I could tell by the way they looked at one another. When he touched her hand, she pulled away looking around to see if anyone had noticed. He was begging her to let him save her, to save us. You and me. He told her we would be safe with him.'

As I witnessed this long-hidden memory unfold, a chill furtively ran through my body. Not enough to pull me back into the present time, but powerful enough for me to understand.

This was a very pivotal moment in time.

'He was asking her for details of who we were, how old we were, how long we had been captive, all sorts of things. She wouldn't tell. She kept saying, not here LJ, not here. We will meet at our spot and maybe then we can discuss a plan. I could tell Ami was terrified. Not of him you see Aanya, but of getting caught. Then without another word, Ami grabbed me and we fled. When I looked back, LJ was standing, watching us go; he looked confused and frustrated. Shock swept into every inch of my being.

LJ!

A volt of electricity surged through me. The memory vanished without warning, the vision in my mind's eye vanishing as I crashed back into the reality of the present.

Only this time, everything had changed.

LJ had known Ami.

The revelation was monumental.

Bina had been right.

As quickly as I came to, again the memory took hold, clearly not done with me yet. I was aware I was shaking, and had curled into a ball on my bed. Hovering above the young girls for a second time, something felt amiss.

I knew something was very wrong.

'Jiera, that may be, but why did you leave me behind tonight? You should have taken me'

'Don't you see? It was now or never. Ami was not brave enough to do it. You have always protected me, Aanya, done so much to keep me alive. I wanted to do something to make you proud. I left to find LJ. I did it for us. Imagine we could finally be free and live the life we always talked about. You are my world. I was coming back for you, I promise you that.'

Silence surrounded the girls as they sat, content in the moment, taking comfort in one another.

'This is so dangerous Jiera. Rahul will kill us for sure this time if he finds us.'

'Well, we are free now, so let's make sure he doesn't. Our new life, the one we deserve Aanya, starts now. All we have to do is get somewhere safe. It's now or never Aanya.'

The girls embraced, quietly sobbing. All I could think about was how overwhelming that moment must have been. But more than that, I saw the immense love Jiera had for me.

Suddenly, from the blackened edges of this unfolding nightmare, a dark figure loomed. He was making a direct path toward his prey. The young victims stood not a chance.

Why hadn't they noticed him?

I was powerless to stop the unfolding terror.

Their screaming broke the silence. Followed by the most evil laughter I'd ever heard. Rahul had found them.

Inner turmoil again ripped me from the memory. I felt so physically sick I stumbled to the basin, dry retching as I shook.

Confused and terrified, my tears were uncontrollable. I could do little as my body convulsed and spasmed, evidence of its state of shock. For so long, I had blamed myself. I'd been driven by the guilt of believing I had left my sister behind on that final night. Then there was the repetitive voice of Rahul in my head, making me believe I was a coward, selfish in my actions.

None of it was true.

I had been chasing Jiera that night. She had left me behind. I felt no malice toward her for that. I understood that without question, her actions were true.

The reality was undeniable; our plan never came to be.

Sadness enveloped me like a heavy fog.

We never did get away that night. Well, Jiera didn't, anyway. I knew with certainty; I was only left at the riverbank because Rahul believed I was dead.

'You are going to wish I was dead, you bastard. I can promise you that.'

I spat the words, as they sliced through the silence of the night, poisoning the air.

⁂

I stormed toward LJ's room, barely noticing my surroundings, my mind fixated.

Maybe it was too late in the evening, but I sure as hell wasn't going to make that my problem.

Tilly is always telling me not to do things in anger. She knows me well enough to know that I didn't react rationally when I was pissed off. Again, I didn't care. I felt confident Tilly would give me a pass on that tonight. She would do the same given the situation, I was sure of it.

LJ owed me some explanations.

Some bloody big ones, and tonight, whether he agreed or not, was a good time for him to start talking.

I felt stupid for trusting him.

Popping my knuckles as I walked, my jaw was clenched and my nostrils flared. I was so bloody angry.

Are you surprised, Aanya? Some people matter and some don't, remember? You don't!

I thought I'd come to know LJ. To be honest, I was a little stunned he would be untruthful to me. He was a lot of things, and I'd really thought despite his gruff exterior, authentic was one of them.

My episode tonight had left me weak and exhausted, yet those emotions had soon turned to resentment. I felt betrayed by LJ.

Was it possible he knew of me before?

Why would he hide that?

And if he knew where Ami was right now, I wanted to know.

I'll demand he take me there.

Shoving my hurt aside, like I witnessed in my last memory, I pushed my shoulders back and took in a big breath. Pissed off or not, I needed the facts, as these would help lead me to Jiera.

Nothing else mattered.

Knocking abruptly on his door, I waited. I thought back to only a few weeks earlier, a complete stranger then, I had tracked LJ down to his apartment. Now we were friends, or so I'd thought. Shaking my head, I tried to consider why, perhaps make allowances for the fact he had kept this from me. Maybe I had it all wrong. LJ had come all this way to help me, after all. I needed to calm down a little and give him a chance to explain.

LJ's room was on the floor below mine. The hallway was stilled and darkened, the late evening shadows reaching very few pockets of the space. The smell of incense and spicy foods drifted through from below. The building was quiet. Again, I knocked.

'LJ, it's Aanya. Hey, I know it's late, but I really need to talk to you about something. Can I come in?'

Maybe he wasn't even here? He had been venturing out at night quite often. I hesitated, but quietly tried his door. To my surprise, it was unlocked. My irritation provided me with just enough confidence to see this as an invitation. I slipped inside the room, shutting the hallway out behind me. Remaining with my back against the door, I could all but stare.

Manila folders, notebooks, a backpack and a dictaphone were strewn across the single bed under the window. Something else small was wrapped in black cloth beside the bag. I wondered what the files contained? He certainly had been busy. Had LJ collected information on me or Jiera? What could it possibly be? Should I look? Despite the room being as small as mine, it was hard to focus in the dark. The dimness was exasperated by moving clouds covering the moon, my only source of light coming from the little window.

LJ wasn't here after all.

Fumbling for my phone torch, finally I gave light to the room. To my horror I realised I had been wrong. I was not alone.

In the far corner, crumpled under the sink, was LJ. He looked terrible, his skin ashen, his mouth slightly open and his body was covered in sweat. I stared at him, unable to detect any movement and not sure what to do next. LJ was completely passed out, an empty whisky bottle on the floor beside his chest.

'LJ, hey, LJ, are you okay? It's Aanya, I just came to talk to you. Hey, LJ?'

Should I go and wake Bina?

Was he dead?

Then I remembered some of my nursing studies. I just needed to check his breathing, make sure it was just alcohol causing him to be in this state. Kneeling down beside LJ, I could see his chest rising and falling. His raspy breath was consistent enough, and he reeked of booze.

'Bloody hell, LJ, what the heck are you doing? I need you sober.

What the hell is this binge about?'

He had no reaction to my presence at all, completely oblivious to the world. I gritted my teeth. If this was how it was, why did he bother to come at all?

I felt a stab of guilt; I was being a bitch. This man had been amazing since his arrival. His personal wounds were deep and his demons ever present. Returning to India was incredibly brave. Still, I couldn't help but feel let down tonight.

This is who is helping you, Aanya? He is not the man he once was.

Shaking my head, I walked back over to his bed, with every intention of leaving. Snooping was not my thing. But curiosity was calling, and it was loud. I began flicking through the folders of information. From what I could see, the papers were filled with contacts, dates, times, brothel locations etc. Nothing I could find on Jiera or me. I wondered how he had gotten all this information. The police had given me nothing.

Did I dare look inside his backpack? Intrigued, my eyes fell on the small object wrapped in black partially hidden beneath the bag. Picking it up, I was surprised at its weight as I unwrapped it carefully.

'Holy shit, oh bloody hell.'

I flung the half-wrapped object on the bed, staring in disbelief.

LJ had a gun.

Looking back at him, lying rumpled and paralytic on the floor, I was perplexed. Did I really know him at all? Or was I just plain stupid not to expect he would need a weapon? This reality was far more dangerous than I could have ever envisaged. Truth be told, I had only just scratched the surface of this perilous underworld.

I did a double take as I spied the envelope tucked into LJ's shirt pocket. It was none of my business, sure, I knew that. It was probably nothing anyway. Yet I was drawn to it like bees to honey. I felt an overwhelming need to see what it was. I stared for some time before finally gaining the courage to move and take a look.

I was not particularly proud of myself in this moment, yet the pull towards the envelope was undeniable. Maybe Bina was right, perhaps I was more connected with my intuition than I knew.

I tiptoed across the room. This time trying to be as quiet as possible, not that it seemed to matter. Had LJ been able to be roused, it most certainly would have happened with my outburst over the gun. Did Bina know he possessed a weapon? Crouching beside him for a second time, I reached silently for his shirt pocket, sliding the letter out with two fingers. Breathing a sigh of relief, I clasped my prize and moved swiftly backwards. Turning the letter over to its front, I was met with scrawly writing in black ink. No postage stamps.

This letter had been hand delivered.

As my brain registered the familiarity, my breath was swept from my lungs, making me unsteady on my feet. I knew this handwriting. I felt confident I would be able to identify it anywhere. I'd read and re read my own letter a thousand times, possibly more.

This had come from Ami.

It was identical.

Why hadn't LJ opened it?

Why had she written to him?

Maybe the letter was meant for me?

This would mean she must know we were here. Did Rahul?

A wave of fear and excitement hit me in the same moment. *Slow down Aanya. Slow down.* I recited the command in my head, forcing my breathing to slow.

I shook my head in disbelief and confusion, trying to quieten the questions shooting off like fire crackers, one after another. I had to know. Carefully, I began tearing the edges of the envelope. I glanced up at LJ. In that moment, I honestly didn't care if he was enraged at me when he came too.

Liar.

Traitor.

'You are the one with all the secrets LJ, I knew this woman too. You have no right to keep this from me.' I didn't bother to keep my voice down this time. Still, he didn't stir.

Ami would help me. I was sure of it. We had history.

Sitting in the opposite corner to LJ, my back against the door, I unfolded the letter. Tingling inside was a swirling mixture of excitement, fear, and intrigue. It roamed through my being, causing my skin to feel almost electric.

Monday August 20th 2018

Dear LJ,

Forgive me for the time we have been apart. I deeply regret not contacting you sooner.

Please understand I had good reason.

I was so pleased to learn you had returned to India, and my Aanya has accompanied you. I understand you are looking for Jiera. I will help you. I know where she is being kept and can help her to freedom.

For me, it is too late.

Please trust me now, LJ, for the sake of the girls. You must follow my exact instructions. Two nights from now, Jiera and I will meet you at our spot. You can take her to safety from there. I trust you remember the Yamuna Bank Forest Area. East Delhi, near the Yamuna Rail Bridge. It will be our only chance, as Jiera will be moved to a safe house after this time before her final destination in a brothel.

I long to see Aanya. I ask you to bring her with you, for me to say my final goodbye.

It is imperative you both come alone.

Yours in love and faith,

Ami.

The black inked words almost jumped from the thin paper as I read them. My tears cascaded down my cheeks. The many emotions attached to this message, and the chance to be with my sister again, was all too much. Leaning back against the wall, I felt in a state of shock. I needed my mum, or Tilly. I needed someone.

Was this letter real? It almost seemed too good to be true.

This was a godsend, the miracle we had longed for.

Ami had always loved us. I wanted to take her away from this life too, show her how much she meant to us.

How long had LJ had it?

Was he ever intending to open it?

Trying to wipe the gush of tears away, I read and reread the letter. Joy surged through my tears. Holding my hands up in the air, praising the universe, I felt incredibly grateful.

I was so close now. Soon Jiera would be with me, I could feel it.

'Ami. Thank you dear Ami, how will I ever repay you?' I whispered into the darkness, my voice choked with affection.

I felt invincible in that moment, filled with courage and determination. I could do this. But as I rose to my feet, sudden sickening thoughts darkened my mood. What if I was too late?

When did LJ get this letter? Had he actually seen Ami?

I scanned the single page, noticing the date on the top. What the hell was the date today? I prayed I was in time. Frantically checking my phone, I drew a sharp breath.

It was tonight.

The letter stated it had to be tonight. Two nights from Monday. It was already 9pm on Wednesday. I felt beyond desperate, shaking with the reality I could already be too late.

One chance, the letter had said.

'LJ, LJ, wake up, I need you, LJ!'

I shook him as violently as I could, screaming only inches from his face.

He stirred briefly, giving me hope, yet just as quickly fell back into his comatose state.

'Screw you. How could you do this. LJ? bloody hell, how could you not have read this letter? I don't understand you.' Violently, I pushed his body away from me, the sight of his pathetic state making me physically sick. 'I will never forgive you if I don't get to her. Never.'

Focus, Aanya. Forget him, I told myself.

I photographed the letter. LJ would need it when he came too. Hopefully, he would figure out I'd been in his room tonight and follow. I made a mental note to text him in the Uber on my way. Enough time had been wasted.

Without looking back, I slammed his door on my way out.

No, no Aanya. Do not come back, please sister.

Flying up the stairs to get my backpack, I pushed her voice away. Nothing would stop me now.

You are not strong enough, Aanya. I own Jiera. I will make sure you fail, then you will both be sorry.

Aanya, please sister, stay away. We are in danger.

What the hell?

I stopped in my tracks momentarily, for the first time noting the speed at which my heart was beating. Bringing my hands to my temples, I tried to calm the chaos within. A headache had formed. In my mind, both voices battled for my attention. Rahul's was far more dominant over the soft whisper of Jiera.

Maybe my own fears or longings were creating them?

Was this insanity?

I shook off the negativity. I didn't have the time nor the energy to waste on doubt. I know it has to be Jiera, I can feel her. I simply must have heard her wrong?

Concentrate, I told myself, focus my energy in this moment. I forced my inner voice to be louder than theirs.

I wasn't proud of myself, a little disgusted actually, at how easily the deception had rolled off my tongue.

I felt like a different person lately. Kind of ugly on the inside.

Is that what desperation did to people?

The thought had even crossed my mind that I should have grabbed LJ's gun. I wasn't ugly, I reassured myself, just frenzied. I know people do things they never thought themselves capable of when backed into a corner. I just never thought it would be me.

But then again, speeding along the highway towards Jiera in this critical moment, I wondered, how many times in my past I had done things I wouldn't have thought myself capable of?

I was a fighter, I knew that much.

Should I have taken his gun?

As I sat in the back of the Uber, I felt crushingly ashamed of lying to Madhav once again. I would lose his trust completely this time, and I knew better. He was a good man, and still clearly shaken from leaving me on GB Road last time as he talked about it often. I still didn't care what LJ thought. Like Madhav, I knew Bina would be disappointed when she discovered the truth.

I couldn't fix that now. All I could do was make them proud. I could only hope it will be forgotten when I return with Jiera.

Earlier tonight when I had phoned him, Madhav had been only 10 minutes away from the Missionary Centre, having just dropped a client at his hotel. I managed to convince Madhav that LJ had asked me to meet him at the park. I cringed at the thought of how I'd made up such an elaborate story. I'd convinced Madhav about LJ being sure that's where my body had been discovered all those years ago. That LJ was confident if I returned here at a similar time of night, my memories would also reappear.

Madhav was reluctant to agree and insisted he phone LJ. I had little choice but to nod and hold my breath while he dialled. When LJ didn't pick up, I knew it was now or never. I followed on with a further lie, telling Madhav LJ had said his phone would most likely be out of range at the park, but I would see him at the rotunda.

As we drove in silence, the trip seemed endless. Each second, I was closer to retrieving my sister. In reality, Madhav had said it would take about 20 minutes, depending on traffic. He knew of the popular tourist spot.

'I am coming, Jiera, very soon we will be together,' I whispered softly into the darkened night as we sped closer.

No. No, Aanya. Do not come, please, sister.

Before I could question her sweet voice, sudden agony took hold of my left knee. I desperately tried to stifle my scream, gripping at my leg. I couldn't let on to Madhav, or he would make me return to Bina. As the car travelled I frantically pulled my long skirt above my knee, searching for the source of the pain. What had started as a sudden intense tingle, quickly escalated into what seemed like a severe electric shock. Breathing shallowly, I bit through my lip and could soon taste my blood. Sweat poured from my body, the anguish didn't let up. Despite not remembering my pain when being stabbed, I would bet this burning, punctured sensation was how it felt. As I leaned forward in the back of the speeding Uber, trying to keep pressure on my invisible injury, a startling image presented in my mind. Jiera was on the ground, gripping at her own leg, blood pouring from her open wound. The scene was clear as day.

I was feeling Jiera's pain again. Someone had hurt her. Was this another repressed memory? Or was this happening now, tonight?

Breathe sister. Jiera, I am coming, hang on.

No, No Aanya. Do not come.

What? Jiera, why are you saying this to me?

Madhav interrupted my thoughts. 'It is just down here, Miss Aanya. Just through these trees, by the river. Very dark down here tonight, I can't see a car?'

We both scanned the area. He was right, it was eerily dim; a thick mist seemed to be spreading inland from the river.

I tried to make my voice sound as even as possible. The pain was not subsiding.

'It's okay Madhav, I've just spoken to LJ through text. Someone has borrowed his car for a short while and will be returning it soon to us. Just drop me here by the rotunda. He won't be far. All is good. Okay?'

'Miss Aanya, this not feel all good, it feels all wrong. Are you sure?'

'Totally Madhav, you know how big and tough LJ is. I'm in safe hands that's for sure, you know that. I will get a lift back with him.'

He nodded reluctantly, releasing a loud sigh. I reached over and patted him on the shoulder. I felt a flood of relief. I didn't have the strength to argue further, nor the time, and my lies were getting deeper by the minute. I loathed myself for this.

As soon as his car halted in the gravel carpark, I began to exit, nearly falling in pain as my leg touched the ground. Without exchanging further words, bravely I waved him off. As I stood in near darkness, only a dim light above the rotunda gave reprieve from the lurking shadows. My brave façade was fake. I had never felt so terrified in my life.

Without moving, I strained to listen for even the slightest noise or movement. All I could hear was the gentle lapping of the water as it reached the edge of the river, spilling across the ground only metres away. Some night birds quietly cackled in the trees beyond. The bush surrounding me was thick and vast. No one would hear my cry for help out here. From a distance, I could see a train approaching the station about a kilometre away. The carriages clattered over the thin bridge as it made its way over the Yamuna River to East Delhi.

Looking at my phone again, I reread the message from Ami. This was the spot all right. I prayed I had not missed them. Filled with nervous anticipation, I could barely stand still. Finally, I would get to take my sister to safety. The pain in my left knee had all but subsided, I hoped that meant Jiera's had too. I had little choice but to wait now. Turning toward the empty rotunda, I saw it. Tucked into the right-hand corner of the small covered area, just bright enough to almost shine in the shadows.

Ami's yellow bag.

I moved toward it. Bending down to pick it up, I could smell her sweet scent. A familiar aroma I was not aware I knew, yet instantly it brought me such comfort. On the broken wooden table in the centre of the rotunda was a thermos and small China cups. Typical Ami, always making sure we were hydrated and fed. I couldn't help but smile. Hugging the bag to my chest, I was startled by her voice, causing my body to jump in fright. Spinning around, I dropped the bag to the ground. Forgetting it existed, I stared at the woman standing ahead.

'Hello my dear Aanya. You are a good girl coming to us.'

'Ami. Hello. Where is Jiera?'

I felt as nervous and as out of place as she looked. Ami fiddled with her clasped hands held tightly over her chest. I had not a clue what to say or how to act in this moment. So much time, and so many memories had been lost between us. I felt like a statue, unable to move. I stared at her, crying and smiling. My overwhelming tension, mixed with relief, heightened the swirling trepidation as it poured out of my soul. She looked so much older, worn, tired. Were they bruises along her jawline? Stitches above her eye? It was hard to tell, as our only source of light came from behind her now, shadowing her features.

Ami covered the distance between us, pulling me into her warm and inviting embrace. It was then I noticed her heavily bandaged hand. She too was crying. Ami felt frail, yet her grip was tight. As she pulled away abruptly, her hands remained on my shoulders. Ami's eyes were intense; they flashed fear and almost warning before returning to reflect the kindness I knew I had once received from her.

Run. Run now, or it will be too late, sister.

'Ami, where is Jiera? Can you take me to her? Ami, thank you. Thank you for caring for us all those years. Thank you for contacting me and saving Jiera. How do I ever repay you?'

I knew I was talking too fast.

Ami sobbed now, pulling her eyes from mine, unable to look anywhere but the dirt on the ground. It was then I noticed how much she was shaking. Without meeting my eyes, Ami moved over to the table and began pouring tea from the small thermos. Handing me a cup, she insisted I drink.

'We have a walk ahead, Aanya, and it is a hot night, so drink my tea now child. YYou will need its strength as you are dealing with much emotion.'

I swallowed the smooth liquid. She had always taken good care of us. Ami took the cup from me almost instantly, yet could not seem to meet my eyes. She stared at the ground, poking at the dirt with her sandal.

'Ami, it's all going to be okay. Can you take me to Jiera now? She is here, right?'

Ami looked up intently, and a strange feeling swept over me; I was looking into the soul of a stranger, not the woman I had once trusted.

'Yes Aanya, of course child, she is waiting for us where I knew it would be safest, further down along the river. Come, follow me now, she is eager to see you too, of course.'

After retrieving her bag, Ami took my hand and led me out of the rotunda and further toward the misty river's edge. I had little choice but to follow. Pushing my doubts down, I shook my head to clear my mind. As I walked behind Ami, who was quick in her step as always, I strained to see a glimpse of the girl who was my twin. I longed for her.

As I walked, I began to stumble. The earth below me seemed to move in the dark. Feeling lightheaded, I was dazed. My dizziness was becoming overpowering and stronger by the second. I fell roughly onto all fours, an undeniable heaviness dominating my limbs now. It felt like an effort to gasp but a single breath.

'Ami, Ami, what is happening?'

My voice sounded weak, far away, as I fell onto my side. Struggling to keep my eyes open, my vision blurred. It felt good to rest my head on the dirt. I strained to hear her reply, but it didn't come. In the darkness, she remained silent, standing over me. I felt adhered to the damp gravel path. Momentarily, I was aware of the lapping water, then the rushing of feet on the path ahead. Was it Jiera?

Too late. The blackness washed over me, like a wave in the ocean. I could fight it no longer.

Jiera
India, 2017

It had been many years since Jiera had been with her sister, yet not one day had passed she hadn't thought of her. This morning as she sat cold and alone with her thoughts, she stroked the tattoo on her forearm. Jiera would never forget the day she and Aanya had been branded so brutally. On Jiera's forearm was the numeral one, and Aanya had the numeral two. Rahul had laughed as he inflicted the pain. Pinning each girl down he had poked an old needle into their skin, injecting a concoction of liquid pigment made up of lamp soot and tannin from the bark of local trees. Rahul had educated them on this traditional method of tattoo as he worked, reminding them his dad had done the same to him. Despite only being nine years old, much of their innocence was lost in that moment. Their skin had raged with infection for days, the pain had been like fire under their young skin.

How she hated him.

Never would she allow herself to let her memory go of Aanya. Days, then months, followed by years, had all rolled into one long road of heartache and torment for Jiera. Now, nothing much Rahul could do to her mattered. Jiera lived in the flesh, but inside she felt little other than numbness. Jiera knew nothing would ease her inner pain. Her detachment from the world was too far gone now. Her spirit had died with Aanya that night.

Today marked the day of Aanya's death. Despite it being four long years ago, the sounds of Aanya screaming, the gasps of her last breaths and the image of her broken, unmoving body, tossed aside on the dirt, still haunted Jiera. She wished it had been her, convinced it should have been. Jiera had been all consumed by the relentless guilt ever since, believing Aanya had died because of her.

Jiera knew the anniversary of Aanya's death would conclude tonight the same way it always had each year. It would be a long day ahead. Somehow Rahul always found a way to make her pay. He would end up in a drunken rage, and Ami and Jiera would be locked in cages like animals.

Was this because he felt remorse? Or regret? Jiera doubted it.

He was a filthy, disgusting excuse for a human.

But Jiera thought worse of herself. She had ultimately been responsible for killing the person that mattered the most, her only family. Truth be told, she would have ended her life long ago.

But there was one thing, always stopping her from taking her own life and that was the pleasurable thought of one day actioning the ultimate revenge on Rahul. She had planned it in her mind for years. Tonight, she visualised it once again. One day, she told herself. One day.

It was the only thing keeping her heart beating.

Rahul sickened both Ami and Jiera to the core. They had been trapped and abused for so long now it was hard to imagine a different existence. Earlier tonight, like clockwork, a lavish meal had been set down before them. Rahul had made a big deal of ensuring Jiera remembered it was all her fault. Each year it was part of his speech, he gloated in front of his loyal staff. He smiled, recalling how Aanya had died a slow, brutal death. Aanya's last dying thoughts, according to Rahul, were she paid the price, all because Jiera had been stupid, traitorous.

Bastard.

༟

Later that night, as Jiera ran her fingers along the inside of her human cage, she wept. Jiera hardly ever let herself cry anymore. Although the barbed wire on its edge had cut through her fingers, she felt nothing. Her blood seeped from the small puncture wounds, and she watched the dark liquid slowly drying in the heat, sticking to her pale skin. Despite the years apart, Jiera was sure she could still feel her sister's presence. There were so many times Aanya's voice seemed almost audible, stopping her in her tracks. Many nights, Jiera had sworn she could still feel her warm body pressed up against hers.

Tonight, Aanya's nearness in spirit seemed almost overwhelming.

Jiera could still remember the very first day they had arrived at Rahul's property. They were so young, so naïve to what was happening. How could a nine-year-old possibly know any different, she thought. The twins had been stolen so easily off the streets near their home.

Had anyone ever looked for them since?

They were taken like strays, sent to hell to be groomed for their new life. Annya and Jiera had never once had a say in their journey thus far.

Jiera's life was one she would wish upon no other.

Jiera hugged her knees to her chest. Hoping and praying they would be let out of their cages tomorrow. She was hungry, but had refused even a mouthful of dinner. That would be dishonouring her sister. Ami had begged her to eat. She was smart, always keeping the peace and remaining on good terms with Rahul. Jiera often wondered why Ami stayed. She was a grown woman, and it would have been far easier for her to escape the tight grip of Rahul than it had been for the twins. But when Jiera and Aanya had questioned Ami on this, her answer was always the same. Ami knew Rahul had ears and eyes all over the city. His power and wealth influenced all the right people, and his wrath spread far and wide. Ami knew, attempting escape was pointless. Rahul had made sure they understood this.

Everything always depended on Rahul's mood. His state of mind would dictate exactly how long Jiera would again remain caged after tonight's rampage. Throughout the years, Jiera and Aanya had quickly learnt his temperament imposed whether they were fed, washed, whipped or bashed. Whether they were granted sleep, or sent to work in the many harsh places both had become accustomed to. Rahul's mental state was very connected with his business deals and transactions. But one thing would always remain the same: If he'd had a bad day, the girls would pay.

Jiera tried to call out for Ami. Was she alright? She couldn't see her cage from hers. Ami had tried to block Rahul's path tonight, as he had aimed his rage at Jiera. Ami was the closest person she had to a mother. Ami had been good to the girls over the years, always trying her best to sneak them extra food, water, medicine or clothing. Ami had often accompanied the twins to the various worksites Rahul had sent them to. They were dangerous places, and where she could, Ami would try to look out for them. That was not always feasible. Jiera had many scars and frightening memories to prove it. But Ami was clever. She also knew it was important to self-preserve, and there were times, she could do nothing to help. Ami educated the sisters in secret. She always encouraged Aanya and Jiera to value education. She knew, being literate and gaining knowledge everywhere they could, would be their best chance of a better life.

Jiera wasn't sure she believed that anymore.

Despite trying many times, Jiera couldn't remember her parents at all. They had died when she and Aanya were only two years old. Exactly how, was never clearly revealed to the girls. The orphanage was vague when questioned, telling them it was a car accident of some kind. She did, however, have fond memories of their life in the orphanage. Much of Aanya and Jiera's time there was happy. They always had food, a warm bed, and many children to play with. But best of all, they always had each other. Never once were Aanya and Jiera apart. They liked it that way. From a very young age, they became aware of their inner connection. The girls could read each other's thoughts, feel one another's emotions. They had the ability to communicate on every level without words.

Tonight, Jiera was close to giving up. Rats scurried around her feet, but she didn't have the will to push them away. The rough slab of concrete beneath her wasted frame, caused her body to hurt. But the pain was nothing compared to the ache in her heart. He could beat her as much as he wanted; it mattered little to Jiera. The physical pain was better than her broken heart, and it helped her to forget. Rahul had all but choked her tonight. The bastard was always clever enough to take her almost to the point of death, but then refrain. Rahul wanted her alive. He needed her, as he always said, as a reminder of Aanya. Rahul would keep Jiera breathing, and under his control as living proof; some people mattered and some people don't.

Silently, Jiera grieved, longing for Aanya, languishing for freedom, and a different life.

Normally, Jiera did not allow fear to control her, but tonight her despair was relentless. A few days earlier, Ami had confessed to Jiera that she had overheard some startling news. Rahul was discussing with a colleague his plans to sell Jiera. He wanted a younger girl. She was coming of age at 18, and Jiera knew exactly what that meant. Surely, it was better to end her own life rather than to face that reality. Even without taking the revenge on Rahul he deserved, death was better than GB Road.

At least she would be with Aanya once more.

Tilly

Australia, 2018

Something was wrong. She could feel it.

Tilly had dialled and redialled continuously for the last hour.

Why wasn't Aanya picking up?

It was 4am in Melbourne. Apart from the beeping of machines and the low hum of the central heating system, the hospital ward was relatively quiet. Tilly should have been asleep, but was unable to settle. Aanya had missed their scheduled phone call earlier.

Every second day, they spoke. Facetime mostly. They had a permanent arrangement to touch base at 10pm Melbourne time, which was 4.30pm in Delhi. The rule was, if for some reason it couldn't happen, a text must be sent to explain why. But tonight, nothing had come. Tilly had called Aanya's phone, almost on the hour, ever since.

Something was amiss.

Tilly knew Aanya would never break her trust.

Tilly had become more alarmed when she'd investigated further. Aanya's location on Snapchat, or any presence on social media, was null and void. Her phone appeared to be out of range or switched off.

Tilly couldn't let it go. The last time this happened, Aanya had been in trouble. And tonight, she couldn't shake the feeling somehow her situation was dire again.

Tilly debated her next move, feeling frustrated with her containment. Why couldn't the hospital just release her now? She was due to go home later today anyway. All her latest results were good. Tilly's feisty approach to life and her determination to beat her illness was again proving to be just the remedy to tame her beast.

She picked up her phone again, in case she had somehow missed a message. Nothing. Aanya's parents would be rattled, receiving her phone call at this hour. Especially if it turned out to be fruitless.

But what if it wasn't?

Tonight was curry dinner at Aanya's folk's house. Tilly had continued the ritual despite Aanya being away. Jeff and Nancy had thought it a wonderful idea, enabling them to stay connected and share anything they had heard from Aanya or their contacts in India. Tilly wondered, should she wait till tonight to see it they had spoken with Aanya?

No. Somehow Tilly knew this was more urgent than that. Last week she had convinced Aanya to give her LJ's number, as well as the Missionary Centre. There was not to be a repeat of last time on GB Road, Tilly had insisted. Knowing LJ would not take kindly to receiving calls from Tilly for no good reason, she had promised to only contact him as a last resort.

Tilly dialled Aanya's phone one last time. She scanned through social media yet again, just in case. Aanya had all but disappeared.

This was not their deal. Momentarily, Tilly felt an annoyance toward Aanya creep in, despite her concern.

Without further hesitation, she dialled LJ's number.

Sitting up a little straighter, clearing her throat, Tilly hoped. As the phone connected and the ring tone began, Tilly rehearsed silently what she would say to him. But just like Aanya, LJ failed to pick up. Sighing, she left a short message, asking he contact her as soon as possible.

Not easily defeated, Tilly immediately dialled the Missionary Centre's office number. Someone would surely pick up there, despite it being 10.30pm in Delhi. After all, it was the city that never stopped, right?

Tilly tapped her fingers against the armrest of her wheelchair.

'Good evening, Delhi Missionary, Bina speaking. How may I help?'

Tilly fist pumped the air as she whispered a 'thank you,' to the universe. The connection was crystal clear, and despite the woman's thick accent, Tilly had heard her perfectly. She had made it through to Bina. Relief swept over Tilly in her darkened hospital room. For the first time in a few hours, she breathed a little deeper.

'Hello Bina. It's Tilly, I'm Aanya's best friend. I am ringing from Australia, trying to locate Aanya. I'm a little worried, she's not answering her phone.'

'Take a breath, my dear. I am sure all is well. I know all about you Tilly; it is my honour to finally speak with you, dear child. Aanya speaks so very fondly of you.'

'Thank you, and you too, of course. But is she there? She didn't answer my phone call tonight, nor any since. It is unlike her. I also tried LJ, he did not answer either.'

'Yes. I understand. Can you wait on the line for me? As far as I am aware, they are both retired to their rooms for the night. I haven't seen them for many hours now, but that is not unusual. How about I go upstairs and check for you. I am sure all is well.'

'Absolutely, yes, thank you, that would be so great.'

'Hold on child, bless you for caring. She is a wonder our Aanya. I will be right back, okay? Sit tight.'

Tilly heard the phone clank down as the line fell silent.

Time seemed to move all too slowly and Tilly grew impatient. The unease she had felt earlier, returned. Again, she knew. Something was not right. Tilly began to begrudge her tiny space. She stared out at the starry night, feeling like the distance between her and Aanya was greater than ever before.

Finally, Bina returned.

'I'm afraid I cannot locate Aanya. That is not ideal, as she has promised not to leave the premises alone again. No one here has seen her in many hours.'

'Well, what about LJ? Is he there?'

Tilly blinked profusely. Tears of despair were ready to burst forth. Her breathing reflected her unease, causing her chesty cough to return. Bina was hesitating in her response, Tilly could tell.

'Bina, are you there?'

'Yes, child. LJ is here, but, unfortunately, he is incapacitated. He is in his room.'

'You mean drunk, right? Passed out drunk?'

'Yes. Dear child, please try not to worry. I must go now, and try to locate Aanya, then sort out LJ. There will be an explanation, I am sure.'

Tilly already knew the explanation, feeling the weight of the pending threat press upon her. Aanya was in real jeopardy in this very moment. She had never been so sure of anything.

Tilly began to scream out, crying in terror. Pulling herself into a ball, she hugged into her pillows.

Aanya was her world, she could not bear the thought of losing her.

Tilly knew unless the situation was absolutely imperative, Aanya would not have broken her promise by leaving the missionary alone. There was only one reason why she would defy them.

If she had discovered where Jiera was.

Tilly felt powerless, knowing right now there was nothing more she could do about this situation. Her anguish could be heard throughout the hospital wards, her raw emotions unable to be suppressed. Tilly was only vaguely aware when the nurses began swarming into her hospital room.

She tried to push them away, as they fussed and insisted she go back onto her oxygen machine. Tilly's emotion had magnified her rattling chest and rasping cough. She cared very little.

Medical intervention could not help her now. Tilly just wanted to get out.

LJ
India, 2018

LJ could hear a voice trying to lure his mind back into consciousness.

Someone was poking at his stiff body, pinching his skin on his arm. Without opening his eyes he tried to fend them off, waving spasmodically into the space around him. LJ just wanted to be alone. The blackness was his friend.

Becoming acutely aware of his pounding head, LJ tried to open his drowsy eyes. Even the slightest movement caused his disorientation to worsen.

Without warning, a potent smell under his nose caused him to reel backwards, hitting his head on the wall. LJ attempted to sit up.

'What the heck? Where am I?' Sensing someone was close, he had not as yet been able to register who.

'It's alright. It is just me, Bina. You are in your room, remember?'

LJ sat up further, leaning against the wall. He rubbed his temples.

'What the hell was that smell?'

Bina smirked. Her mix of rosemary, ginger, and spices did the trick every time.

'Just a little helper when I need to wake someone up, LJ. Been using it for years. Don't worry, it's harmless'

'Well, it bloody stinks.'

LJ began to remember. He knew exactly why he was feeling he'd been hit by a steam train. In a sense, he had.

Bina remained beside him, crouched on the floor, her concern obvious.

'LJ, we have a problem. Aanya is missing. No one seems to know where she is. I was hoping she was with you when Tilly called.

'Tilly?'

Bina had LJ's full attention now. He gulped down the warm tea she had brought with her. It tasted vile. He could only assume it was another of her remedies designed to wake him further. Surprisingly, LJ thought, the elixir seemed to do the trick.

As if on a mission, Bina took the drained cup from LJ, handing him a different steaming liquid, insisting he drink. Again, LJ did as he was told. This time, the thick, bitter syrup almost made him gag. It was the strongest coffee he had ever tasted, almost like tar.

Alert now, LJ stood splashing water on his face from the sink; he dared not look in the mirror.

'Thanks. Now, tell me everything.'

She silently handed him the letter. Bina had found it on the floor and read it earlier.

The colour once again drained from LJ's face as his world once again came crashing down.

LJ stumbled to the bed, his panic returning with vengeance. Fleeting thoughts of the girls he had been too late to save swirled. Their faces were still so clear to him, their cries so loud.

Surely, he thought, this world could not be cruel enough to have it all happen again. Not to Aanya.

'Breathe LJ, this is not like last time.'

Bina was close enough to his face to feel his gasping breaths. Again, she crouched in front of him, clasping his shoulders.

'Look at me. You are here for a reason. I know it, you are not too late. You must believe. This is as much about your healing as it is saving Aanya. She will be okay. Ami will make sure. She is a woman with a kind heart. You of all people should know that.'

LJ stared back at Bina's blackened eyes, which all but pleaded with him to find his strength.

'Stand in your power. Go to her. It is time to finish this.'

LJ wasn't so sure.

Could he really trust Ami?

Maybe this was her way of making amends. After all, things had ended badly between them.

LJ stared up at Bina, suddenly needing her to understand.

'I didn't know. Bina, I swear I hadn't read this letter till now. It was here when I arrived tonight. I had my suspicions it may have been from Ami, but typical of the coward I am, I chose to drown myself instead'

Bina cupped his face, LJ's bloodshot eyes glistened with tears.

'Go. I believe in you, we all do. It is not too late. Aanya must have gone ahead. Bring them back safely. God speed.'

He could feel her faith in him. It almost beamed from her body, straight into his soul. In that moment, the energy in the room ignited something in LJ that had long laid dormant. Aanya's letter had done the same.

He began to remember who he had once been. He began to feel a determination to once again prove to himself he, too, was worthy of a second chance.

Question was, would his courage be enough?

Could he beat the demons which had dominated his mind for so long?

Aanya

India, 2018

Children's laughter and music filled the air. The afternoon was warm and peaceful. I felt so beautifully calm and safe in this moment. I looked around at my friends. My family was so big, I had brothers and sisters of all ages. Mumma Parul watched us play, clapping for us, sitting in her old cane chair under the shade of the apple tree. She too smiled and laughed, instructing us to keep trying. Her encouragement always meant the world.

Jiera squealed with delight. Like me, she was trying to master the tricky skill of hula hooping. Until this day, we had never seen such a toy, let alone attempt to spin one around our tiny waists. One of the younger carers in our home, Miss M was showing us what to do. I wondered had I ever felt this happy before.

The Hula Hoops were a gift we had all received from the local church. They came with new skipping ropes, chalk and soccer balls. My heart sang in this moment, I loved Tihar festival. It was the celebration we all looked forward to the most, every year. And right now, we were in the middle of festivities. I felt so loved, so valued right now, I could almost cry. I loved my family, different as we were.

As Mumma Parul always said, the world is made up of all types of tribes. There was no right or wrong. She was forever saying, 'The village raises the child.' Maybe we were not blood related, but I knew Jiera and I were cherished.

All week we had learnt about Tihar at school. The people of India celebrated the same thing, except they called it Diwali. Both meant *The Festival of Lights*. It was the most important national festival in both Nepal and India. I felt so empowered to be joining in the festivity which my people believed marked our victory of good over evil. All week Jiera and I had joined in making decorations. Our grade had filled the halls with brightly coloured lanterns and fairy lights. Even though Jiera and I were only 7, we certainly understood the significance of today.

Tonight, everyone in our home, all 53 of us, were outside. The carers, cooks, teachers and nurses, and of course, all of my brothers and sisters. The night had begun with the age old tradition of lighting diyas. We all had one, and the glow from their small flames instantly created a magical effect in the early evening light.

After this, we had been allowed to play and run free. The warm night air was sweetly scented. Incense was burning in pots and the pit fire had been lit in the garden. I glanced around again with delight at the intricate mandalas hanging from trees and buildings. I was so proud of the work we had done crafting them using coloured rice flour.

Looking about, I could hardly imagine a more beautiful place. Feeling so lucky, I grabbed Jiera's hand, twirling her around. I knew she could feel it too. We felt so safe, so loved. We belonged here.

It hadn't always been so easy for us, but that was in the past now. And even at just 7 years old, I had the strong sense to only look forward, never did we dwell on the past. We had much in the future to look forward to. That is what my teachers always instilled here. We could be whatever we wanted, as long as we always took learning opportunities and studied hard in school.

The Nepal orphanage was the only home we could remember. We had been living here for 5 years now. I wished and hoped I could remain forever. My people were kind and loving and never could I wish for a better home. We had plenty of food, clothes, and a bed. I knew many other children in Nepal did not.

Each year, to close the ceremony, we released a private wish into *the magic air of Tihar. Tonight, I would wish for Jiera and I to never have to leave our family, to always feel the acceptance we did here.*

But this evening, I felt strongly about something else. I needed to make two wishes. I wondered if that were allowed? No one need know, I thought. I would make a wish for change. When I grew up, I wanted to be a powerful woman who could save many children of Nepal. I'd educate them and provide a home and love for children just like us. I felt very driven in this moment to be the voice of change in our future.

Jiera was laughing at me.

'Aanya, you are always deep in your thinking. You are standing in the middle of our party, yet your mind is many miles away. You are not going to learn to hula with your hoop around your ankles.'

I smiled back at her, my clone, my most important other. I loved her fiercely.

'Okay, I am ready. Let's go, let's hula.'

'Try this, Aanya. Close your eyes and feel the rhythm. Miss M said that was how she started.'

I frowned but smiled at Jiera, nodding my agreement.

'Okay, if you say so. Ready, set, go'

I took in a deep breath, planting my feet firmly on the lawn, digging my bare toes into the damp earth. Gripping tightly, closing my eyes, I again attempted to twirl the plastic hula hoop around my waist. The festival noise seemed suddenly extra loud around me, causing a feeling of slight disorientation. I felt my body falling off balance and onto the soft ground. Laughing giddily, I opened my eyes.

Taking a sharp breath in, I scanned my surroundings.

Instantly bewildered, I knew nothing was the same.

Although the lights of the festival remained, creating a soft glow around the back garden, I could no longer hear even the faintest of music. Where had everyone gone? Instead of laughter and squealing and chatter, the field we were playing in was deadly silent. Scrambling to my feet, I realised I couldn't see the orphanage building. Blinking and staring harder, I tried to focus in the dim lighting. It was gone. My home was not there. I looked in every direction. The landscape had changed dramatically. I was all alone, the nightscape around me stretched on forever. Small diyas as far as my eyes would travel were my only companions, their shadowy light revealing the night's sparseness.

I didn't understand, suddenly feeling very frightened.

Nothing was the same as only minutes earlier. How could that be possible?

'Jiera. Jiera. Where are you? Where have you gone?'

My voice seemed to echo. Nothing, not a sound, returned to me.

'Jiera!' I screamed as I turned in every direction, straining to see any movement, desperate to hear the slightest noise. I fell to my knees, hugging them into my chest.

'Aanya. Quiet. You must be quiet. I am here. You are okay.'

I thrashed as someone pressed into me, hugging me from behind. My eyes were heavy, fighting their sedated state.

'Jiera? What's happening? I don't understand.'

'Hush. I am here. You must be quiet, sister, or they will hear us. Aanya, I need you to try and wake up now. We have very little time.'

I didn't understand. Heightened confusion consumed me.

Time? Time for what?

Where was I? What was happening?

What was wrong with my body? It felt strangely detached from my mind.

Why did I feel so heavy and sluggish?

༄

As my eyes adjusted, my senses were becoming more alert and responding to my sister's pleading. I looked around me once again. This confined space was dark, the smell putrid with mould and stagnant water. I was sweating in the stifling heat; someone was gripping me tightly from behind. I was lying in their arms. How long had I been like this?

Suddenly, frightened of the stranger I was yet to see, pulling away and began crawling forward. My body shook uncontrollably. I was overcome with dizziness and fell back down on the muddy wet ground. I was desperate to try to understand. Where was I? Obviously, I wasn't alone. Was that a good or bad thing? Through blurred vision, I turned reluctantly to face the figure in the shadows. Despite the semi-darkness, her slight frame, huge smile and big dark eyes identical to mine, brought instant calm.

She took my breath away, silenced every voice of doubt.

Did I dare reach out to touch her?

This was no stranger, my body tingled from head to toe. A wave of realization followed by relief washed over me.

I began to sob. I barely recognised my heaving cry, clearly exposing the years of deep grief in their outpour.

I had found my sister.

Our eyes locked and Jiera scurried toward me. This time, I did nothing to resist. She held me firmly in her arms and swept my dampened hair back from my eyes. She was crying too.

I knew I was still slow in my responses, and my head felt foggy and unhinged. Yet nothing mattered in this moment. What could be more important than being beside my sister again? She continued to smile at me, yet even in the dim light of the small room, her sadness and fear was unmistakable. Holding her hand, I placed it on my heart. Not once did our eyes leave each other.

'Jiera, what is happening? Where are we?' I searched around for clues of my whereabouts. 'Was I dreaming? It was all so real. Jiera, you were with me, at the orphanage, just now. Except... we were younger. We felt so happy, playing with our Hula hoops. Do you remember? I'm confused.'

Jiera hugged me tighter before releasing me so she could again look into my eyes.

'There is so much to tell you, and I will, I promise. But for now, I need you to listen to me very carefully. Can you do that for me, sister?'

I nodded, still bewildered.

'The orphanage feels like another lifetime. But yes, I do remember that day. We were so happy then. You must have been having a dream. Do you remember coming to meet Ami tonight? It was a trick, Aanya. Her letter was written to lure you here. Ami drugged you. That's why you are feeling so strange.'

I sat up further. The fog was retreating from my mind quickly and a reality I didn't want to face was flooding back with vengeance.

I thought about my letter, the one Ami had sent to me in Australia, and then the one I found with LJ.

Why would Ami betray me?

'We are locked in an old water pumping station by the river's edge. It's not far from the rotunda where you met Ami, nearly 2 hours ago now. It was all in Rahul's plan, Aanya. That's why I tried to reach you with my mind. I wanted for you to stay away. It was so hard for me to understand you were back, and alive. I wanted to be with you more than anything in the world, but not like this.'

Jiera's smile had vanished. She was crying harder than me now, moving a little further back from my touch. Looking at her in distress caused my senses to sharpen even further, adrenaline fuelling me. And so was my fury.

'What the hell Jiera, who did this to us? Not Ami, surely? Why would she do it?'

My stare was intense. I reached for Jiera but she refused to meet my eyes.

Surely, I thought, I had not been captured for a second time. Did I not learn? How could I be this stupid? LJ was going to kill me, if I ever got us out of here.

'Jiera, tell me. What is going on? Why have we been locked in here?'

Jiera was in a weakened state. She was half my size, frail and jittery. She was also injured, I could see now. Despite her knee being bandaged roughly, blood seeped through the cotton from a fresh wound. Instantly I knew, Jiera had been stabbed earlier tonight. I'd felt her excruciating pain in the Uber.

Who had done that to her?

Finally, Jiera looked up at me.

'I am so sorry, Aanya. I am confused too. So much I didn't know, until today. Rahul discovered that Ami had betrayed him by sending the letter to you in Australia a few weeks back. She tried Aanya, she does love us, but her own fear... it was just too great. He was so angry knowing you and LJ would dare return for me. He never really got over you after you left. We all thought you were dead; Rahul gloated about it for weeks. So, you can imagine my shock when Ami admitted the truth to me. I still can't believe it is true, that you are alive, that we are together again.'

'I can't imagine what you have been through. I am so sorry. For years I have had no memory of you, our lives, or what happened. Only recently has my memory started to return. I promise I would have come for you earlier had I known. I need you to believe that Jiera. But what exactly has that to do with us being locked in here?'

Jiera reached for both my hands again, kissing them softly. Her smile was wavering, yet her eyes told me she believed.

'Do you remember Rahul?' I nodded. He had rarely left my mind over the last few months. 'Well, once he learnt you were back in India, he ordered that Ami lure you here tonight. He knew his plan was fool proof, using me as bait. Rahul has no intention of letting us go Aanya, ever. He told me he has organised for both of us to be sold on to brothel owners on GB Road. Rahul has the power and connections. I'm very afraid this is the end for us. I know him well. There is little point in fighting anything further. Ami knew it too; she didn't want to betray us.'

Jiera turned away from me now, almost seeming shameful. Surely she wasn't blaming herself? The sight of my sister, all but believing we were defeated, only fueled my inner fire and determination.

'No Jiera, you're wrong. This is not the end for us, not by a long shot. Rahul has messed with our lives long enough; I intend for that to end today. You have to believe there is still hope, we are not giving up. I am here for a reason. This is our chance, I know it.'

Jiera looked at the ground, pulling away from me again. I watched as her shoulders slumped further toward the ground. She shook with silent emotion, her hands covering her face as she rocked.

This is not how I envisaged my reunion with Jiera.

LJ
India, 2018

'I am coming with you. You must allow me to assist you.'

LJ shook his head at Bina, not thinking about the repercussions of his body movement. He had sobered up fast enough, yet his head pounded and now a sharp pain pierced through his soupy brain. He felt ashamed, angry at himself for letting the bottle win again tonight. He silently prayed his actions would not lead to a deadly outcome for those he cared so much about. LJ could not bear that again.

'Not a chance. I need you here. There is much you need to do. Firstly, contact Aanya's family. Update them, without alarming. Tell them I am on the way out to the Yamuna Bank Forest area after receiving news from Ami. Tell them not to worry, I am confident I will be returning Aanya and Jiera safely home.'

Bina eyeballed him as they stood face to face. Reaching out to grasp his shaky hands, LJ flinched. He dared not let emotion cloud his judgement, and this woman, he knew all too well was a tough negotiator.

'This is the big break we have been waiting for Bina, I know it. But I am better alone. Less complications that way. And just in case the girls get here before I return for some reason, I need you to get them to *the* safe place. You know where I mean right? You are the only one I can count on.'

Bina stepped back slightly, giving him some air, he didn't look so good. She nodded.

'Prepare the room while I am away, with food, clothes and bedding and,' he glanced at Bina's pale face, 'medical supplies. Who knows what state the girls will return in, especially Jiera. We need to be ready to get the girls into hiding. Even if they needed it, a hospital visit would be out of the question at this stage. Rahul has contacts everywhere; they will be all too willing to assist him should the need arise.'

LJ turned to look out the window at the bustling street, life beyond the missionary. Bina knew she must stay, despite what her heart wanted. LJ was right. Her mind was reeling as she remembered the very first time Aanya had arrived at the mission, all those years ago. She had been so ill, so broken, both physically and mentally. The situation tonight may very well be the same all over again.

Many years ago, a well-hidden, underground secure room was built below the missionary building. Very few people knew about it, not even the authorities. It had temporarily provided a safe refuge for many children, women and families over time. Victims remained here until arrangements could be made to relocate them. When individuals were removed from trafficking situations, most often the courts became involved. Paperwork within the system needed to be generated; this all took time. During this process, victims still remained very vulnerable. Traffickers do not take kindly to being raided and their prisoners rescued. To put it simply, it was bad for business and their reputations. In many instances, these organizations would stop at nothing to get their prize possessions returned.

'Should I contact the police? You might need some help.'

LJ stilled. He turned to face Bina, resting his hands on her shoulders this time. Smiling, he looked directly into her eyes. He aimed to comfort her with this gesture, give her the feeling like he had it all under control.

Someone had to believe he did.

Truth be told, LJ was far from calm. His well-practised false bravado, the mask he put on for the world, along with a rush of determination, disguised his inner turmoil.

'No Bina. This has to be done my way. Firstly, I need to ascertain whether this is a legitimate rescue or foul play. I'm really hoping Ami has the girls tucked away somewhere and is just sitting tight, waiting for me to come and get them all to safety. The police, however well meaning, will only draw attention to their whereabouts. If Rahul is looking for them, which I suspect he will be, their involvement will unintentionally hinder me. I know Rahul operates using inside intel. Without question, part of his vast arsenal will be police scanners.'

LJ gathered up his backpack. He didn't attempt to hide the gun as he tucked it into the belt of his jeans. Although Bina stared, she remained silent. She had been in this environment long enough to understand. LJ was encroaching on the dark side of India. Without question, he would be risking his own life tonight.

LJ's inner turmoil raged. This situation encapsulated everything he had vowed never to return to. Briefly, he let his mind drift to Ami. He had loved her once. Surely, she had loved him too? Could he trust her now? LJ had trouble accepting anyone was genuine these days. But Ami? She had meant the world to him. He would have done anything to save her and the twins. But she had simply vanished and never had he been able to contact her again. Right up to this very moment, he wondered why.

Had she intentionally disappeared?

Gruffly, LJ stood a little straighter, annoyed at himself for letting the past rule his head again. Pushing his shoulders back, he exhaled loudly. He knew, if he had any chance of getting the girls to safety tonight, there was no room for self-doubt or hesitation. His focus and actions needed to be precise.

Without meaning to, LJ glanced in the small mirror above the sink.

He could all but stare. The man looking back was almost unrecognizable.

But then he saw something else, causing a shot of adrenaline to surge through his body.

Under his aged appearance, the unshaven blotchy face and bloodshot eyes, LJ saw the man he once was.

Tonight, he vowed he would be that hero again.

It didn't matter should he live or die. His focus was on finding the girls. Removing them from Rahul's world would allow them the chance to live safe and full lives.

That was what they deserved.

LJ ran his fingers through his thinning hair, standing taller still. He smiled at Bina, squeezing her hand as he passed without saying a word.

Bina watched hopefully, all but holding her breath as he strode out the door.

Never once did he look back.

Aanya
India, 2018

I paced the small room, desperately searching for a way out and any object that would help me to be free. I felt claustrophobic, as the old pump station had a low roof and damp slimy walls. The only way in or out was through a heavy steel door. The old key lock refused to budge, no matter the force I used. I shoved a piece of rusty wire in its tiny hole, trying to achieve what I had seen in the movies many times, but to no avail.

Scattered in my movements, I forced myself to slow down, allowing my mind to still. This way I would think more clearly. Time was running out. I sensed this accurately. Jiera had further withdrawn. Her tiny frame lay curled in the dirt, up against a far wall. I knew pain, exhaustion and most likely starvation were taking their toll on her. But it was imperative now I didn't let her give up. Lost in the moment, I stared at Jiera. Scanning her body, I could see so many scars, burns and bruises, some old, many very fresh. The bastard had even shaved her head. I wanted Rahul dead.

My backpack and phone had been taken from me. Who knew where they were now? Surely, LJ would wake soon, and when he did, I was confident he would come. We were going to be okay. Reaching into the pocket of my jean shorts, I felt the small package. I had forgotten all about it till now.

'Thank you, Bina,' I whispered.

She had given me a snack to take to my room earlier, in case I felt hungry in the night. Had she known I would need it for something else? I headed over to where Jiera lay, in her semi-conscious state. This was not good. Unwrapping the sweet sugar biscuits, I tried to rouse her. 'Come on, sister. I need you to fight. I am here now, and we are going to get out of here. Try to sit up a little. I need you to eat this.'

At first, she tried to push me away, delirious in her exhausted state. Sitting her up so she could rest her body on mine, I forced the food into her mouth. It broke my heart to see Jiera like this. So tiny and weak. Was she closer to death than I had thought? It was as if all the fight had left her.

'Jiera,' I tried again, this time my voice firmer, 'eat. You must listen to me.'

'Aanya? Is that you?'

Jiera seemed shocked at my presence all over again. I could see her confusion as to where we were. Her physical state was worse than I had thought or perhaps she had she been drugged, too. Just how much blood had she lost from her leg?

Again, I attempted to put a tiny amount of biscuit into her mouth. This time, she chewed and swallowed.

'Good Jiera, good. Now have some more.'

Like feeding a tiny sparrow, little by little I watched in hope as Jiera regained some energy and composure. She needed water also, but there was none. When I felt confident she could sit propped up on her own, I moved to look at her leg. I needed to see the extent of her injury, know what I was dealing with and how far she would be able to travel on our escape.

Staring at her knee, I knew better than to unwrap the bandages now, to risk further bleeding could be fatal. Whoever had treated this had done a good job stabilising the wound. I knew Jiera would be okay, as long as we could get her medical treatment soon. I was so absorbed in the task, it almost shocked me when Jiera reached for my hand.

'Thank you. I am okay, I promise. The last few days have been taxing, I just needed some food and a little rest. I've had little of either.'

For Jiera to voice this, after all she had been through in her life, I could only imagine it must have been horrendous.

Sitting beside her again, I tried to think of what we should do next. Strangely, I thought, I wasn't feeling the fear that perhaps I should.

'Jiera, we need to get out of here. Is there anything you can remember? Maybe Ami or Rahul let something slip that may help us now?'

She sat silently for some time, reflecting. I was grateful to see her regaining strength. She looked up at me suddenly.

'Aanya, the night you nearly died, I put you in such danger. I am so sorry. Can you ever forgive me?'

'Jiera, I came all the way back here for you as soon as I could. You are my world, all that matters to me now. I just want us to be together. You did what you truly believed was the right thing trying to get us away from Rahul. We both know I had attempted the same a few times, right? Never would I begrudge you for that.'

'Ami explained your trauma amnesia. You are lucky, that even for a little while, you got to forget. So many times, I wished I could have.'

'I don't know about lucky. I have missed so much, being without you.'

I knew it wasn't the time to be asking but in all the memories that had returned, one significant piece of the puzzle remained; continually plaguing my mind.

'Jiera, how did we become prisoners of Rahul?'

'Too easily, Aanya. And if I ever get out of here, I am going to dedicate my life to helping young girls, and children, not to fall victim the way we did.'

She was full of life now; Jiera had my complete attention. Her sudden energy and passion was contagious. And she was right.

That would be our cause. I would stand firmly beside her in that mission.

'We were only nine Aanya. We had lived happily for many years in the Nepal orphanage, the one you dreamt of. We had lived there since we were two. Our parents had already died by then.'

'Yes, I was told about where we had lived, and of the death of our parents in Nepal. I saw some photos Ami sent; we were just babies.'

Jiera smiled before continuing.

'They were such happy years for us. We had it all. A huge family, a safe home, we even started school when we were five. We were literate and quite well educated by the time Rahul got us. Luckily, Ami continued to teach us many things, as well as care for us the best she could.'

I stared in disbelief at Jiera. How could she still regard Ami so fondly? The woman betrayed us, and LJ too, so it seemed. I didn't understand her continued loyalty. We were trapped here right now because of Ami.

'I know what you are thinking, but it's not Ami's fault. She always cared for us as best she could. She was terrified when Rahul found out she had contacted you in Australia. He cut off two of her fingers Aanya, right before he made her write the second letter to LJ. Not once has Rahul let her out of his sight since.'

'Oh, hell Jiera. This guy is brutal. How can this possibly be real? It's like a horror movie. It seems impossible Rahul could get away with behaving like this in our world today. How many other young children are in similar situations?'

I didn't expect an answer, and I was already buried deeply in my own shame. Thinking of the comfortable life I had lived back in Australia made me cringe. I was ashamed at the thought of complaining about slow Wi-Fi or my coffee taking too long at a café, yet I knew no different. Not many in the western society would. People, just like me, needed to be educated in exactly what went on. I knew it was not just in India. Child trafficking was rife across the world.

I vowed, should I get out of here, that is exactly what I would do. Join Jiera in being a voice of change. I felt very passionate about beginning in Nepal.

'Aanya, although our carers at the orphanage had warned us of the dangers many times, on the day we were picked up by Rahul's men, we were careless. Naïve and stupid. In a split second, our lives changed forever. We were in the town, not far from our home, really. The same walk we did every day returning from school. I remember the warmth in the sun, the sparkle in your eyes, the way we were singing a song we had learnt.'

Jiera seemed agitated; her body jittery.

'Is this too hard for you to tell me Jiera? It's okay, I can wait.'

'No, I have relived it a million times. If only we had run, or fought. The street was quiet that day. A white van pulled up, two men got out and walked straight up to us. Intrigued but not frightened, we all but watched them approach. Our curiosity was soon replaced with terror. It was all so surreal. In a split second, one man scooped you up, the other me. Looking back, clearly the operation was pre-planned. That's all I remember of that bit. When I woke, you were still asleep. We had been drugged and tied up. I'm not sure how far we had travelled that day, but all I knew was one minute we were walking home from school mid-afternoon, the next, it was pitch black, sometime in the night. We were locked in some sort of container ship. Kept there for three days until we were moved again. The same men, in their dirty white van took us to Rahul's house. I knew we were no longer in Nepal. At some point, we had been smuggled across an unmarked point of the border into India. And just like that, our new lives, if you can call it living, had begun.'

It was a lot to process. I felt sick and saddened to my core. We remained quiet for some time, the reality of our past weighing heavily on our emotions. The only sound was dripping water and the distant rush of the Yamuna River. Never once did Jiera let go of my hand as we sat huddled close enough to feel each other breathing. I never wanted to let her go again. Being beside her felt surreal.

⚹

I'd had enough waiting. It was time for us to leave, take control.

I was so angry at Rahul and the organization he proudly worked within. As shocking as it was, I honestly thought in this moment I would be capable of killing him, should it come to that. I wasn't proud of this malice within, yet all the while was prepared to do whatever it took to ensure our freedom. We had been pushed into a corner and I intended to fight.

If I did kill him, would I go to jail?

Would I be exposed as a murderer? Or would it be self-defence?

Both Jiera and I were on our feet now, checking every inch of the tight space. I'd managed to pry a few pieces of old pipe free, placing some near the door. Maybe we would need them later to fight someone off. Using one piece of the rough steel to bash at the lock, I smashed it as hard as I could, until my arm could take no more. It was pointless, my frustration was heightening and I screamed in frustration.

We must have been here around three hours, including the time Jiera said I was knocked out. What the hell was Rahul waiting for? Bring it on, I fumed irrationally. I was past being scared of him, despite the monster he was. We had everything to lose now. Fighting was our only option, and exactly what I intended to do. Part of me even wished I had brought LJ's gun, not that I had a clue how to use one.

In the distance, I could hear voices. Hushed at first, then becoming more animated.

'No. No, ask him again. Please, you must let me go. Get your hands off me.'

A pleading female's voice was desperate, somewhat agitated. Scuffling became apparent as the voices became nearer.

'Rahul promised I would be set free after tonight. I did this for him, now I can leave. You have it all wrong. Ring him again, do it now. I tell you, I am not working for Rahul anymore. He gave me his word I would be allowed to go free.'

Jiera and I looked at each other intently. Barely daring to breathe, we stood only centimetres behind the door. The lock was being tampered with; someone was attempting to get inside. We stepped back silently into the shadows. The struggle outside was becoming far more vigorous. I could hear male voices now too, aggressive in their responses.

Jiera touched my arm. She silently mouthed it was Ami. Obviously, Rahul's men had captured her too. You'll never win, doing a deal with the devil.

As the door burst open, instinct saw us scurry back against the wall. A large framed man, dressed all in black, literally threw Ami inside. She fell heavily on the ground, landing on her back. Gasping, Ami cried out in pain. He spat in her direction. A second man, slightly finer in stature yet dressed identical to the first, followed closely behind. He had a cigarette in one hand and a large knife in the other. The first man grinned, his hands on his hips and legs wide apart. As he began speaking directly to us, I maintained my eye contact but noticed Jiera had faded into the shadows further still.

'Rahul said to pass on his regards to you all. He will be joining you shortly. Right now, however, he is enjoying a lavish dinner. You, Aanya, have caused quite the celebration.'

The man laughed, eyeing us all, before spitting on the ground again. Behind him, the other man flicked his cigarette at my head. It was his turn to gloat.

'Honestly, Ami, did you really think he would just let you go? You are one stupid old bitch. Tough break ladies, but like Rahul always says, some people matter and some don't.'

As abruptly as they came, the men left, slamming the door shut and turning the lock. Jiera wasted no time rushing over to comfort Ami. I watched through conflicted eyes as they hugged each other tightly. Ami was crying, Jiera whispering words of comfort and reassurance. I couldn't move, my limbs as heavy as lead. I stared, blinking as rapidly as my thoughts raced. Only a few hours earlier, the sight of Ami had brought me comfort and relief. Now my emotions churned, I felt compassion yet anger. Resentment and almost a jealousy watching them. Yet most prevalent of all, I felt fear consuming me.

Simultaneously, Jiera and Ami looked up at me. Both smiled weakly. Were they looking for my approval?

'My precious Aanya. I know how you must feel, but I beg your forgiveness.'

Ami buried her head into her hands, curling forward on the rough ground.

I tried to rationalise my anger, and my protectiveness of Jiera. But right now, I couldn't see past her betrayal.

'I am not *your* Aanya. Ami, you made that choice when you lured me here. You chose Rahul. I don't know you anymore, so don't pretend to know me, or assume you can judge how I feel right now.'

I could sense Jiera's stare, but refused to give in.

'Why Ami? Why would you do this to us? First you beg me to come to India and save Jiera, then trick me into coming here tonight. WHY?'

I knew my voice was abrasive and far too loud for the restricted space. Jiera, now standing beside me, rested her hand on my arm. She willed me to calm down. I shook her arm off.

Ami stood slowly, facing me head on. I admired this, yet raised my chin even further, glaring into her tear-filled eyes. I could tell she was in pain both physically and emotionally, yet at this point I refused to let compassion touch me.

'I have always loved you both, like daughters. You didn't deserve the life you were dealt. Nor did I. But every chance I had, I tried to make things the best they could be for you both. For many years I did whatever I could, just to keep you alive.'

I looked away from her, forcing a deep breath.

'Then why? Why would you betray us now? Surely you knew the consequences of bringing me here tonight'

Ami was weeping again. Jiera went to her. Was my own sister on her side?

'You must believe me. I would rather die than cause either of you harm. When Rahul found out about my letter to you in Australia, he made it very clear. Unless I helped him going forward, he would arrange to kill you, your family, LJ and then Jiera. Not me though, as he said he would enjoy watching me for the rest of time, watching my guilt and shame slowly take its toll.

I believed him. He has the connections and the power. He showed me evidence of both LJ's and your address and the work places of your parents. He even knew your best friend was a girl called Tilly. Still, I refused, trying to call his bluff. Then he broke one of my fingers off. The next day I refused again; he broke another. On the third day as he began to twist and crush my thumb, I just couldn't take it anymore. I am so sorry, I was weak, finally agreeing to help him.'

Ami fell to her knees. My eyes rested on her heavily bandaged hand. She stared at the ground.

'Please believe me, I could not bear to see you or your family hurt. I thought maybe, just maybe, if you came here with LJ, things would be okay. Somehow, that we would all be set free. LJ always promised me he would protect us.'

I continued to stare at her, feeling my anger slip away, but just as quickly taking hold again. Jiera stayed quiet, looking from Ami to me. She remained by Ami's side for a second time.

'How do I know this is not another trick? Why bother telling me the truth now?'

Ami shook her head. I noticed for the first time how old she looked, weary and defeated.

'Fair enough Aanya. I can't prove that what I say now is the truth. I wish to God I had not been part of luring you here tonight. I will gladly give up my life, should it come to that, in place of yours and Jiera's tonight. Rahul will be returning soon. He betrayed me. He promised I would go free, be able to leave his house, start a new job. I should have known better. So, I have nothing to live for now. I will prove it to you when he comes.

Jiera spoke for the first time now, directly at Ami, 'You betrayed LJ too, all those years ago. He loved you Ami, I saw it with my own eyes that day at the market. He wanted to help us, yet we never saw him again. Why? Did you love him?'

It was the same question I wanted to ask.

'Girls. It was so complicated. Yes, very much, I loved that dear man. Apart from you both, he was the one shining light in my life. We secretly met for years, when Rahul let me out to run errands or go to the market. It was near this very spot one night, he asked me to marry him. We planned to start a new life together. LJ made me believe I deserved more. He wanted to help you both, too.'

'Then why didn't it happen?'

I knew I sounded harsh, but still felt somewhat untrusting of this woman.

'That day at the market, you remember Jiera, you were with me. LJ turned up, wanting details of where we lived, how he could help get us out. We were careless and overheard by others. Rahul got wind of this. Never was I allowed to leave the house again. His punishment was the cruellest so far. It was then I was made to share Rahul's bed, as a punishment for my love for another. I hate that evil man to the core.'

I felt a rush of nausea. Ami had had little choice. I was being such a bitch. Deep down, I knew this situation was not her fault. Ami had been treated as harshly as us, maybe worse. I was being selfish. It was not right I punish her further.

Jamming my eyes shut, I rubbed at my temples. This was a lot to absorb, and my mind raced. So many emotions, mixing with memories and questions, all spasmodically moving within. Like a balloon in the wind, they jolted this way and that, up and down, fast and slow. When I finally opened my eyes to look directly at Ami again, something in me had shifted. It was like I really saw her, remembering the lady I had trusted and loved. Now my eyes were open to Ami's pain, her turmoil and self-loathing. Her body language reflected her defeated spirit.

I knelt beside her, noticing Jiera smiled broadly at me. She knew of my heart's revelations.

My resentment quickly washed away, and as vulnerable as I felt in that moment, the forgiveness I felt was incredibly calming. On the dirt floor, amongst the damp mould and filth, the three of us held each other in the dark. I let my guard down, relishing in the beauty and power of our embrace. I felt myself melting into the comfort of my family, realizing I had longed for this moment. No more words were needed. We understood what most of the world would never know. We had a bond that no man could break. No matter what happened next, we would be forever kindred spirits.

After some time, Jiera broke the silence.

'So, there is something I don't get. How did it come to pass that you know LJ? Where is he now, anyway? Does he know you came here tonight?'

'It's a long story, but I am hoping by now he knows I am here. He was drunk, passed out in his room at the mission when I left to come here tonight. It was a sheer miracle I found Ami's letter at all.'

I looked attentively at Ami, giving her a sad smile, squeezing her hand. 'LJ has suffered greatly over the years. Like us, he has his demons. He fights hard each day, but at times loses his personal battles. LJ is not the man you once knew, Ami, of that I am sure. But he is a good man. I practically forced him to return to India with me. He was a stranger at the time, but now I care for him very much. We have become close friends. I know he will come for us as soon as he is able. I would bet my life on it.'

Ami listened intently, tears now streaming down her cheeks. Her voice was but a whisper when she spoke.

'Well, I pray he does, Aanya. He will be our only chance.'

⁊⁊

'Aanya, Aanya, are you in there?'

I sat bolt upright from the damp wall I leaned against, as did Ami. Jiera remained sleeping with her head on my lap; she had weakened considerably over the last half hour, her pulse weak.

He was here.

I grinned at Ami. I would have recognised his gruff, gravelly voice anywhere. Ami was smiling too. My relief was instantaneous. Scrambling to my feet, rousing Jiera in the process, I raced to our saviour. I placed both hands on the door and pressed my ear into the cold metal.

'LJ. Thank God. Yes, I'm locked in here with Jiera and Ami. It was all a set up. Please don't be pissed off at me for coming, LJ. You would have done the same. Time was running out. Jiera is injured, but we are alright. Can you get us free?'

'Girl, I didn't come out in the middle of the night, feeling like a dog's breakfast for nothing. We are all getting out of here tonight. Mark my words.'

I loved this man.

Jiera and Ami had joined me, our sudden energy and excitement contagious. We hugged each other tightly. LJ's voice sounded so strong and commanding, I felt empowered by his reassurance. I could tell Jiera and Ami felt the same.

Just in time, too, I thought. Finally, we were getting out of this hell hole.

'Listen carefully, Aanya. I need you to find a safe spot, away from the door. I'm going to have to shoot the lock out. These old buildings are almost bomb proof, so it's the only way.'

Limited in choice, I spied the steel pump engine. Behind it was our best chance of protection against the gun fire. Wasting no time, we carefully avoided the rusty engine and sharp metal pieces threatening to slice open our skin. We were barely able to fit behind the old contraption.

'Okay LJ, we're out of the way. Go for it.'

Despite expecting it, the blasting of gun fire seemed ferociously loud. I instinctively covered my ears as it echoed around the room. Together we remained huddled, waiting for LJ. Seconds later, the door flew open. LJ's dominant frame stood tall in the open space, silhouetted by the restricted light of the moon.

Never had I been so pleased to see anyone in my life.

Carefully stepping over old piping and slippery parts of the ground, I rushed into LJ's arms. I was in no hurry to let go, as tears of solace came.

'Hey Aanya, nice to see you too. You are a bloody pain in the arse, you know that, right?' Through my tears, I smiled, looking up to see his smirking face. He kissed me on the forehead. 'But hey, so am I, right? I'm sorry, I should have been there for you earlier tonight. Let's get us all home.'

I squeezed him even harder, almost oblivious for a few seconds to the others in the room. Then I remembered he was yet to meet Jiera.

'LJ, I'm sure you remember Ami, right? And this is Jiera, my beautiful twin sister.'

I held his hand, pulling him further into the tiny room. He seemed reluctant to move, almost shy.

Again, I was reminded of just how confronting this must be for him.

LJ was a brave man. And in this moment, I knew what I had done was brave too.

'Hello Jiera, nice to finally meet you. And Ami, my dear Ami....'

His voice trailed off, and LJ covered his face with his hands. Overcome with emotion, he sobbed and dropped to his knees. Ami stepped forward, taking his hands, placing them firmly in hers. Jiera and I watched on, uncertain of what would happen next.

'LJ, my great man. I have never stopped loving you, despite my actions. There is much I need forgiveness from,, but I beg you now, please save the girls. I have no further concern for my life, but I beg you to take them away from here. Away from Rahul. He has terrible plans for them and they still have so much life to live, given the chance. My soul is finished; it simply doesn't matter anymore.'

LJ continued to weep, head in his hands, yet to face Ami. A tense silence filled the room again. Finally, as we held our breath awaiting his response, LJ slowly looked up into her eyes. Clearly distraught and broken, yet he managed a smile.

'Ami, your life matters very much. I have never stopped loving you either. We did the best we could back then. I believe we all have been given a second chance here tonight. The universe has brought us together. I won't leave you behind again Ami. You are coming with us now.'

⚜

'Oh bravo, what a gallant speech. You are most certainly my hero, LJ.'

Startled, we had not heard the intruder approach. Spinning around, we froze. Jiera grabbed me, almost pulling me over in her fright. Abruptly I felt the blood drain from my head, the breath exit my lungs. I was sure I would faint. Ami grabbed my arm, trying to hold me steady.

I would know the intruder's menacing, blunt voice anywhere. I'd heard it for months in my head.

Blocking the entrance, the man continued clapping, grinning from ear to ear, before taking a bow.

'Good luck with those plans LJ, hate to be the one to tell you, mate, but we will be doing things my way from here.'

Rahul had found us.

My world crashed down around me.

His vile laughter bounced off the walls. Leaning casually in the open doorway, Rahul gloated. Obviously pleased with himself. Ami, Jiera and I stood close together, daring not to speak, I was unable to take my eyes off him. He was as disgusting as my memory had served, pure poison. I briefly found myself wondering how he lived with himself.

A feeling of dread filled the space. We were so close to being set free, now I could hardly breathe at the thought of what was coming next.

What did he intend to do with us?

Rahul had a gun too, and waved it around carelessly as he circled us like a shark would its prey.

'Thanks for coming everyone. Our little reunion is certainly long overdue, Aanya. Never thought I'd see the day honestly, considering you are supposed to be dead. Did you think I wouldn't find out? You look good, much better than your sister, I must say. Oh, you are going to be a popular choice down on GB Road my friend.'

Rahul traced the outline of my face with his fingers. My mind had blocked his unescapable stench, but now the mixture of cigarettes, sweat and pure evil filled every sense, evoking memories best left behind . Feeling violated, my anger was surfacing. I pulled away before spitting in his face.

For a split second, he looked shocked, his eyes darkened, then Rahul burst into more laughter.

'Ahh yes, the same Aanya I remember. Headstrong, but so very stupid. Maybe you tricked me once, making me believe you were dead, but not again. This time I am going to make you wish you were.'

'Leave us the hell alone. You have no right. Screw you. It's over, arsehole. We are not going anywhere with you tonight, or ever. Get that through your thick skull. You are a low life.'

Rahul slapped me so hard I went reeling back into the wall. My wrist slammed into a metal pipe and pain instantly radiated through my body, enough to cause me to be nauseous.

'Leave her alone, Rahul. Just stop!' Ami shouted, trying to move toward him. LJ was holding her back with one hand and gripping Jiera with his other. They were desperately looking to see if I was okay. I nodded, silently determined to be brave and reassure them.

But was I?

The dream I had replayed again and again in my head over the last few weeks, the moment I was reunited with Jiera, was nothing like this. I was terrified, and pretty sure my arm was broken.

I watched on as LJ stepped forward, pushing Ami and Jiera towards me in the corner. We gripped each other tightly. I could only pray at this point that LJ had a plan.

'Rahul. I am willing to do a deal. What is it you would want in place of the girls?'

LJ sounded confident, sure of what he was doing. I hoped his bravado was real. He stood tall, eyeballing Rahul.

'Ahh, welcome back to my country LJ. I can't say I am pleased to see you, intrigued maybe, a little shocked at your stupidity, but not pleased. I don't need the hassle of the likes of you.'

Rahul had stepped closer to LJ now. A power play was taking place. Despite him being smaller in stature than LJ, he seemed none the less intimidated. Rahul practically spat his next venomous words. LJ did not break his stare, nor move a muscle. The only indication I had of LJ's trepidation was his fists now tightly balled by his side.

Where had LJ put his gun?

'Despite your stupidity and misplaced better judgement, I admire you for coming. I must say, I was satisfied to hear you have not been doing so well my friend. Last I heard you were nothing more than a 'has been', a washed up drunk. Pretty messed up in your head so they say. You never could get over losing those girls hey?'

I saw LJ's jaw tighten. The veins in his neck bulged, yet he remained solid in the battle.

'At least by you turning up LJ, it provides me a wider audience to enjoy the pleasures which will be unfolding. I have such grand plans for Jiera and Aanya. And as for Ami, well, she is returning with me to my home tonight. I don't expect you will see any of them again, so make sure you use your time well in the next few minutes. We will be departing shortly, and goodbyes are so important.'

LJ was at boiling point, unable to contain his composure a second longer. His bulky frame launched at Rahul. Grabbing him around the neck, choking Rahul, he pushed him toward the door. But Rahul held his own, wrestling to regain power, by scratching at LJ's eyes and face, punching him randomly. Both men were determined to gain control, as they had everything to lose. I screamed, frightened and shocked. Never, to my knowledge, had I witnessed such an aggressive brawl. Jiera and Ami were cowering behind me. I begged silently for this terrifying moment to end. I prayed LJ would be able to knock Rahul out. That would buy us some precious time.

I scrabbled for the bits of pipe I had placed near the door. I could help LJ. Could I possibly reach them with the men scuffling in my path? As I attempted to move toward the make shift weapons, a deafening blast sent me crouching in fright. A single gunshot ripped through the space. Simultaneously, the room lit up with orange and yellow, blinding me momentarily as I tried to adjust to the dark once more. I grabbed at my ears, shocked at the rush to my senses and filled with confusion. What had happened? As the room stilled and the dust settled in the dim surrounds, fear consumed me.

One of the men had been shot.

'Get the hell off me old man.'

Rahul pushed LJ back. He hit the ground hard, in arms reach of us. Reeling in pain now, LJ's face was contorted, he rolled around grabbing at his leg. Rahul had shot him in the foot.

Ami rushed to his aid, trying to stop the bleeding with her dress. Jiera and I huddled closely.

What the hell should we do now?

I stared up at Rahul, who was towering silently over us. He smirked in delight, then shook his head.

'Enough. Not another movement or sound from any of you, or I shoot you in the head. My men will be here soon. I have organised for you girls to have a nice little induced sleep. When you wake, you will be in one of my safe houses along the border. Just like you were 9 years ago. Funny how life can repeat itself, hey.' Again, Rahul laughed, spitting in our direction before reaching for his phone.

'We should take a selfie Aanya, I'm sure your parents would love to have it as a keepsake.'

Rahul crouched beside me and gripped my neck tightly, pulling my face toward his. I struggled as best I could, the mere touch of this revolting, shameless man sending my every sense into overdrive.

I managed to pull away, knocking his phone across the dirt.

'You stupid bitch. This is far from over, trust me. You are about to come across far worse than me. You should respect the mighty Rahul. Save that feisty spirit of yours, I guarantee you are going to need it.'

He turned, still on his knees, leaning forward to search for his phone in the rubble. Using all the strength I could muster, I launched both my legs at his back. My kick sending him face first into the ground.

He turned, thrusting his gun into my head without warning. Time stood still. The only sounds I could register were him loading his gun and the drumming of my incessant and furious heartbeat I stared in Rahul's eyes, everything else faded. We had so much history. I could see much of it flashing before me. Feeling like a little child again, I was helpless against such a monster. Rahul gripped me by the hair, twisting my head around to face Jiera.

'I want you to watch your sister die, Jiera. I will make sure she does this time. See you in hell, Aanya.'

I closed my eyes, needing to shut out the image of Jiera and Ami. Desperately they screamed, their eyes filled with sheer terror, their voices frenzied.

Everything that happened next came so fast. Yet at the same time, somehow, it felt like slow motion. My eyes flung open as I became aware of sudden movement. The air, which was once stagnant, was filled with a vortex of dust, making it hard to breathe. Jiera launched at Rahul, closely followed by Ami. They screamed, throwing themselves into the lion's den. Tussling, kicking, scratching, punching, in a final attempt to protect me. Rahul let go of my hair, and I fought to regain some air in my lungs. Next, over the top of them both, flew LJ. He knocked Rahul flat onto his back, fueled with angry power, his adrenaline masking the pain of his injury. I scrambled to join them. Barely feeling my own broken arm now.

This would be our only chance at freedom.

Another gunshot radiated across the room. Deafening and blinding us briefly, instinctively we backed away. Jiera, Ami and I crouched together once again, anxious to know what we faced next.

The instant I registered our new reality, my screaming began.

Screams of anguish, terror, shock, anger and pain.

LJ lay motionless on the ground. Blood pooled quickly below him. He had been shot right through the chest.

'No, no,' I cried in utter despair. Ami tried to get me to be quiet, Jiera too, knowing this would further enrage Rahul.

But in this moment of clarity, I didn't care. I needed to be with LJ.

I struggled to get them to let go of me. However irrational it was, I wanted to save LJ, then face this evil man, beat him at his own game. Crossing the room on my hands and knees, I began begging. Willing LJ to respond.

'LJ, LJ please. Please talk to me. Please LJ, we need you. Don't die, you can't leave us.'

'Shut up. He is on his way to hell.' Rahul kicked me away. 'Do you want to be next? What will your precious Jiera do then, hey? Bloody hell, I don't need this shit tonight. All of you, on your feet. Face the wall. I should have tied you up from the start. Dumb bitches. Look at me, I'm filthy.'

He waved his gun in my face again. This time, reluctantly, I submitted. I knew had I not, another one of us would die. LJ remained still and lifeless. For the first time, I felt defeated. I was sure he was dead, and it was all my fault.

'Like I said, Aanya, some people matter and some people don't.'

⅔

Cable ties tightly secured our wrists. Being almost sure my left wrist was broken, the force Rahul used was excruciating, yet I was almost numb to the pain. I had managed to detach again from the moment. I knew with certainty this was how I had survived as a child.

Ami, Jiera and I were separated. Left waiting, we dared not imagine what was coming next.

How could this be the end?

Nothing was supposed to turn out this way.

I was way out of my depth. Had I been too cocky thinking I would save Jiera?

LJ still had not moved. I could smell his blood now, see it trickling across the floor. The shock of seeing him lifeless for so long was unbearable. I forced myself to look away.

All I could do was try to focus on my sister. If I dared think about what was coming, I found myself hyperventilating; this was not going to help us. I needed to remain strong. Jiera had been tied up behind the pump engine. I couldn't see her and it was driving me crazy. Rahul knew this would be the case.

Unfortunately, I could still see Rahul. He paced relentlessly out the front of the building. He was animated, yelling instructions into his phone. Had his men been held up coming here to get us tonight? Had they had a change of plans? Rahul certainly wasn't pleased about something.

Aanya, can you hear me, sister?

I looked up, searching for a glimpse of Jiera. She remained out of sight. Although we dared not speak aloud, we had other ways of communicating. I remembered clearly now; this was another way Jiera and I had survived over time. We had shared a secret telepathy since young girls. I could now recall using it in the orphanage. Our secret weapon when it was us against the world.

How could my mind ever have blocked Jiera?

Was I a bad sister?

I shook it off. This moment was all that mattered.

Jiera, what can we do?

She was smart. I smiled proudly at her resilience and courage. Jiera would have needed these qualities, at the very least, to survive over the years. All that time, she believed I was dead. It broke my heart, then just as quickly, I became angry again. That man, he deserves to die.

While Rahul was only metres away, he was momentarily distracted by his rage. Barking orders at whoever was on the other end of his call, he kicked the dirt and continued to storm around.

Jiera, seeing this, instructed us to find something sharp to rub our cable ties on. She was right, we would have a better chance of escape once untied. Eagerly I set to work. For the first time in about ½ hour I felt a little hope. I edged closer to an exposed bit of metal to my left, my broken arm throbbing. Hardly daring to breathe for fear I would make a sound. I relentlessly worked at the plastic holding me captive. The ties were painful, their tightness causing pins and needles in my hands. I sweated profusely and a nasty headache, most likely from dehydration had set in. Yet never would I consider quitting.

Aanya, come closer to me when you are free. I cannot get loose. Ami is free of hers.

I am coming Jiera. Almost there.

Rahul continued to pace outside, oblivious to our plan. He was smoking one cigarette after another, taking swigs from his hip flask. I wish Ami had been able to put some of her tea in there. It had certainly knocked me for six earlier. Rahul remained on the phone, yet now he spoke in a more rational tone. This, I had to assume, was not good news for us.

As my eyes remained glued to Rahul, I steadily crept closer to Jiera. I stayed as low to the ground and as close to the wall as I could. Turning away from the door now, I faced Ami and Jiera. They were tucked behind the old engine. Ami was vigorously shaking her head at me, willing me not to move. I could see she was absolutely terrified. Assuming shock had consumed her, I tried to smile at her, let her know it was alright. But quickly, her eyes took my smile away. They became widened, and she began to scream. Within a split second, I was being dragged back by my hair.

'What do you think you are doing? Seriously, don't you ever learn?'

I cursed myself for not seeing him coming.

Rahul had stepped over LJ and was pinning me down. The tread of his boot covered most of my throat. I gasped as the air became more and more constricted. Despite still being tied, Jiera attempted to move toward us. Rahul easily pushed her away, prodding her chest with his gun to move her back. Ami sat motionless her eyes glassy.

'Rahul. Please. You can take me, do whatever you want. I am yours. But please, these girls, they have been through so much already. Isn't it time to let them go?'

Rahul's boot lifted slightly, allowing me to breathe precious air into my lungs.

'Do you think this is a fairytale, Ami? I thought you would have learnt. Surely, after I found out about your little romance with Mr dead boy over there, the famous LJ, you would have figured out, I am in charge of your destiny. Dreaming you can have better, it will never happen Ami. You should have never let the likes of LJ convince you of anything but the truth. You are worthless. My father taught me all I needed to know about real life. Do you think he ever gave me a chance? No, not once. These girls deserve what they are getting. So do you. Now back off.'

Rahul was distracted. This was my chance. I bit down hard into his ankle. Screaming out in pain, he pulled his leg free, then stomped down angrily on my throat again. This time I could get no air. His force was brutal. I knew I was in trouble, frantically pulling at his pants, anything I could to get free, but he was too strong. I started to see stars in my eyes, feel my body becoming weaker. Distantly aware of Jiera and Ami screaming, my heavy arms flopped beside me.

Yet another gunshot silenced the chaos. Rahul collapsed on top of me. In my half-conscious state I gasped for air, pulling at my throat. In my confusion, I couldn't grasp what had happened. I knew I had to fight. I could breathe now, yet was still weighed down by his body. Pushing Rahul off, I managed to roll over the other way, facing LJ again. To my shock, his eyes met mine.

Jiera and Ami were hovering close to LJ and me. Rahul was now motionless, face down in a pool of his own blood.

LJ slowly reached for me, trying to talk. His voice was weak and husky. I still didn't understand.

'LJ came to just long enough to shoot Rahul from behind Aanya. He saved your life.'

Jiera held my hand. Tears streamed down her cheeks. I looked from her, back to LJ.

'LJ, I can't believe it; you are alive. Thank you. I owe you everything. You were lifeless for so long. I was so scared I would lose you. You are my family now LJ'

Wrought with emotion, I attempted to lift him up to a sitting position. But he cried out in pain. His blood was everywhere. Shallow breathing, he gathered himself before speaking again, his voice barely a whisper.

'Leave me, Aanya. You need to go now, all of you. Take them to safety Aanya. You have got this. Run to the road, Madhav is waiting there for you. He brought me here tonight. He understands the situation. I have instructed him to take you back to Bina with or without me.'

That was not happening. I could never leave him, not now, not ever.

'No. No, LJ, I'm not going without you. We can carry you out. I know we can.'

I was begging now, pleading with him to listen. Despite my broken arm, Jiera's stab wound and Ami's age, I was more than willing to try.

'Aanya, do this for me. For Jiera. I have lost too much blood now. I have done what I came here to do. That is all that matters to me. Please, I need you to do this for me. You must understand, I can't fail again, Aanya. If you and Jiera are free, then I have been successful once more. I can hold my head high knowing I am still a worthwhile human. It is hard for me to explain. I need this success to heal me, live or die, I want to go out knowing I redeemed myself. Do it for me, for Jiera, for Ami, please. Don't let me die knowing I was a failure.

This was all too much. How could he ask this of me? I owed LJ for the very breath in my lungs. I wanted him in my life, our lives going forward. I looked to Jiera and Ami. Surely, they would back me.

'We can do this LJ, come on, I will carry you out.'

I shook him, trying to get him to look at me, to listen to my voice of reason, but he had fallen unconscious again. Truth be told, I knew the reality. He was too weak to move, his injuries too extensive. Movement without medical treatment could prove more harmful.

This was not fair, yet again I was backed into a corner. How was I possibly to choose? Either way I lost. Either way seemed selfish.

Maybe if I just got my sister to safety, I could come back for him? But I knew LJ's men wouldn't be far away.

The police or the ambulance, I could call them as soon as we were safe. But would they get to him in time?

'Aanya, look at me, please hear me. I know, LJ, and like you, I love him dearly. But he would want us to get to safety. To him, that means more than his own life. All he wanted was to be healed from within, escape his guilt and shame. I understand he is wrong, thinking he is worthless, yet it's what he truly feels. Knowing you and Jiera are safe, he will rest in peace, I assure you of this. But we cannot carry him all that way, it is a couple of kilometres, at least. He is gravely ill. We must go now, should we have any chance of returning to save him.'

Ami was right, but it felt so wrong. Jiera again pulled me to my feet. I could feel her confliction and torment as strongly as my own. I knew this was our one and only chance.

But could I live with myself, knowing I had left LJ behind?

Holding my hand, Jiera pulled me toward the exit. I turned back toward LJ one last time. He was motionless, pale, and uninhabited. I wished to God this could end differently.

'I love you, LJ. Thank you for everything. I will get help as soon as I can, I promise.'

I felt near breaking point.

Ami remained kneeling beside him. I looked at her, perplexed. Maybe she just needed a moment alone with LJ herself. She seemed to be reciting some sort of prayer, her hands carefully placed on his heart.

'We will wait outside for you, Ami.'

'Go. I am staying with LJ. I want to be with him now; it is my duty. Be safe, my girls, be smart. Stay close to the tree line and low to the ground. Trust no one but Madhav. He will know what to do. We will see you soon my loves.'

I did not see this coming. Gasping, my mouth fell open, yet no words came. Her face expressed that her decision was final. Her tone adamant.

With one last lingering goodbye, reluctantly Jiera and I stepped further into the darkness. It felt so frightening to be leaving the safety of the two people we loved so dearly.

We held hands tightly. It was up to us now. Like when we were young, two became one. Stronger together, we ran.

Fleeing into the unknown darkness, we decided there was no choice but to believe.

We were finally running toward our freedom.

Jiera

India, 2018

Some people matter Jiera, and some people don't.

As they escaped into the night, running for their lives, Jiera felt conflicted, unsettled in her spirit, yet unsure why. Her challenges were far more than physical. Without question, the pain from the knife wound was excruciating, slowing her movement. Jiera knew she was close to fainting. The light-headedness was becoming all-consuming. Feeling unsure of her surroundings in the dark added to her estrangement. Each breath Jiera took now was labored. A sharp burning sensation was ever present in her chest, and the tightness in her lungs was causing her to cough. But worst of all, was the deep onset of anxiety.

Jiera second guessed herself. After all the torment and torture, why would she be feeling like this now?

Wasn't this what she'd dreamt of all along?

They were free. Well, nearly.

You will never be free, don't you get it?

Jiera was stripped as physically bare as a human could be. Possessing nothing more in this world than the thin cotton dress that clung to her body, sweaty and stained with blood. Whose exactly, she didn't know.

Jiera had no other belongings; Rahul had never allowed such luxuries. No bag full of personal items, no clothes, no money, no passport.

Overwhelmed, Jiera's mind raced with all the unknowns.

Silently she struggled with many unanswered questions. How could she ever pay for the privileges of a new life? There was food and accommodation going forward. She was unskilled, messed up emotionally, frightened of just how she could ever fit into a new society. Did she even want to?

In reality, what possible use was she to Aanya?

Maybe it would have been better if Aanya hadn't bothered to return for her.

You are not worth it, Jiera.

She just needed a moment. Inner chaos was causing Jiera's step to become even more unsteady. Jiera gripped Aanya's arm, signalling her, willing her to stop. The girls had agreed to speak as little as possible while making their way out to Madhav. Every move and every decision they made tonight could make or break their success in escaping.

Although unspoken, both girls knew the reality of their situation. The dangers lurking all around them were ever present; the threat of recapture, far from over. Rahul worked with a team of equally brutal men. It was part of the plan they would come to collect and deliver the girls tonight to the pre-arranged destination. Jiera knew she and Aanya were nothing more than a business arrangement. They were the merchandise. Predators of this calibre did not like to lose. Once Rahul was discovered dead, they would still want their cut in the deal. The hunt for the girls would be relentless, as the risk of these men of being exposed was out of the question. Jiera knew if it was required, the men would not hesitate to kill them rather than endanger their empire.

Some people are better off dead. We will find you.

Jiera and Aanya took the moment to rest, huddling closely in the rough terrain. Jiera was exhausted, unsure she could go on. She watched silently as Aanya fussed around her, checking her wound. Jiera formed a weak smile, admiring her sister as she always had.

'No matter the consequence, you took such good care of me

over the years Aanya. I've missed you so much.'

Aanya stared at her for the longest time. Reassuring Jiera with
a gentle embrace. It must be hard, Jiera thought, not knowing so
much of what had happened. But maybe it was better that way.
Jiera knew, she would never be able to forget.

'This looks good for now, the bleeding is minimal, and the cut
stabilised. I want to get you to a doctor though, as soon as we are
safe.' Aanya winced as she spoke.

'Is your arm bad?'

'Don't you worry about that, it is fine.'

Jiera knew she was lying. She could feel Aanya's pain. But she
also knew how determined Aanya was. Jiera knew Aanya would
agree, their injuries were a small price to pay for their freedom. It
was so close now. Aanya smiled again.

'I can't wait to show you Jiera, just what life can be like.'

Jiera rested her head on her sister's shoulder.

Thank you, Aanya, for everything, she thought.

Aanya squeezed her hand. They needed no words.

Without Aanya's phone, the sisters were unaware of the time or just
how long they had been on the run. Their terrain was challenging and
their injuries prevented them from moving at speed. The girls took
shelter behind a thick mass of shrubs, exhaustion and intolerable
thirst, taking its toll. Their only chance tonight of reaching Madhav
was to remain as silent and invisible as humanly possible.

The night around them was humid and sticky. Insects ravaging
their skin caused their legs and arms to sting and itch. Despite not
seeing any night creatures thus far, the girls had been constantly
stilled by animal calls and the rustling of their distant movements.
Jiera knew this area was home to foxes, boars, jackals, even jungle
cats. The trees too were awake to the sounds of parakeets, seagulls
and crows. Although some could be dangerous to humans, she
also knew they were far safer to be around the bush animals than
Rahul's men.

Why had they not seen the men pass yet, Jiera wondered. The girls were travelling close enough to the road to see anyone coming either way. Not that Jiera expected anyone to be coming from the pump station. She was certain Rahul was dead, and LJ not far off. Poor Ami, what would happen to her then?

In barely audible voices, the girls whispered.

'Aanya, please let me rest a minute. I am not feeling strong enough to continue.'

'It's okay Jiera. By my calculations we are nearly at the entrance to the park. It shouldn't be long now before we see Madhav. He will be somewhere there on the main road.'

'Aanya ... I am scared.'

You are nothing, Jiera, you are not strong enough to escape. Why would you leave? What about Ami?

Jiera couldn't explain all she was feeling. Although she had longed for this moment, prayed for the taste of freedom, suddenly she questioned her courage to follow through.

Aanya hugged her sister tightly; this gesture easing some of Jiera's fear.

'Is it the pain in your leg? Do you want me to piggy back you? I used to do that, remember? We would take turns, depending on who was stronger on the day.'

'I remember Aanya. The pain I can get through, it's not that. I am worried for Ami. Maybe we should go back for her?'

'I promise you, as soon as we get to safety, I will organise for help to get to Ami, and LJ. I believe we still have time to help them. It seems odd we haven't seen Rahul's men return thus far. Maybe that's why Rahul was so mad on the phone. For some reason they have been held up? Who knows.'

'Aanya, what if I can't do it?'

'Do what Jiera? I will be here for you always, no matter what happens. You can Jiera, I know you can. You are not alone anymore, neither am I.'

Jiera began to cry. For so long now, she had been brainwashed into believing she would never be safe unless she was with Rahul. His cruel and twisted world, his rules and beliefs, had all but convinced her she would not survive without him.

How could she possibly explain this to Aanya?

She had risked her own life, and come half way around the world to save her.

But this sudden freedom, the unknown which lay ahead, all felt overwhelming, too much. Jiera had not anticipated these crippling emotions, nor did she understand them.

Without probing further, Aanya took Jiera's hands, pulling her to her feet.

'Jiera, everything you are feeling is normal and together we will work through it, I promise you that. You don't even have to elaborate, or try to understand it all now. I can feel your turmoil. I need you to trust me now, sister. We have to keep moving. Bina taught me to focus on the now; this moment in time is all that matters. We are together and we have a chance of a lifetime to begin again.'

Jiera stared at Aanya. Her sister, her twin, yet after so many years apart, she seemed like a stranger.

Jiera knew she should trust Aanya. She wanted to trust her, but the voices in her head dominated. They willed her to turn back, run to the safety of Ami. Tell Rahul she was sorry. His punishment would certainly be severe, but she had survived them all, and at least there, her surrounds would be familiar.

Jiera felt like she was a crazy person. Grabbing her head, she pounded at her skull, desperate for the confusion to depart.

'Stop Jiera. Stop it.'

Aanya gently pulled Jiera's hands away from her face, kissing them reassuringly.

'Jiera, listen to me. I need you to look at me now.'

Reluctantly, Jiera slowly opened her eyes.

'I am your sister. I am here to save you. The voices, they are just stories. Your mind is making them up. Rahul is dead. We can be free. But we need to keep moving.'

Stunned at her sister's strength, Jiera stared back into Aanya's pleading eyes. Aanya's words hit home. Jiera knew this was her time to be strong. Maybe, if they pulled this off, they would never have to fight for freedom again. Some of the fogginess began lifting in Jiera's mind. The voices, not yet ceasing, decreased to a mere whisper.

Jiera knew Aanya was right.

Rahul was dead. Rahul was actually dead. It was over. It was up to them now to get to Madhav.

Jiera forced herself to believe she was worth this chance at freedom.

Pushing her shoulders back, taking a few deep breaths, Jiera reminded herself just how tough she really was. She had out survived Rahul and she didn't intend to waste this moment.

Jiera curled her hand tightly into her twin's.

'Thank you, Aanya. I have missed your strength'

Jiera began to move forward through the rough terrain again. This time leading Aanya, she directed them toward their new life.

Just one step at a time, she repeated silently. Just one step at a time.

Aanya

India, 2018

Ahead, I could see the bush beginning to clear. Relief came so thick and fast, I burst into tears. I needed to remind myself to focus. We had a journey ahead yet, and it was not going to be easy. If the tree line was becoming sparser, then so was our cover.

I could hear the bustle of the constant traffic along the highway. For the first time since arriving in India, I took comfort in the harmony of the congestion. It really was the city that never slept. This had to be the right location, the main road I had entered on earlier tonight. Yet nothing looked familiar. I hoped to God it was. Madhav would most certainly be close but what if he had not waited?

What if LJ had been confused?

Trust no one, Ami had said, and she was right. If Madhav wasn't here, our dreams would be dashed.

I looked across at my sister. She stood silently resting against a tree. Jiera seemed vacant, appearing void of emotion, her pale skin lifeless, almost like a mannequin. Yet I knew inside the warrior remained; we were survivors. That bastard had inflicted all kinds of cruelty on Jiera, but I knew her inner strength. I just needed to help my sister hang on. I wondered what she was thinking? I knew whatever it was, Jiera was suffering more than I was right now. It was imperative therefore, to keep my own doubts at bay. I refused to acknowledge their negativity. I scanned the immediate area again before whispering to my sister.

'We are close now, Jiera. Madhav will be here somewhere.'

Not daring to leave the safety of the bushland, we looked at each other intently. I remembered now we had always gained strength this way. At least this had made Jiera smile; she continued to hold my hand. I gave her a reassuring squeeze. I imagined hugging Bina again. She was such a great source of comfort. I couldn't wait to taste her delicious spicy tea and biscuits and sleep in my comfortable bed. But more than that, I couldn't wait to see Jiera do the same.

'You will love Bina. She will look after us, I promise.'

'Then what, Aanya? What will happen to us then?'

I'd planned our future out a million times in my head. With Jiera's blessing, I intended to take her back to Australia as soon as I could organise her visa. She would have the full support of my family there. But now was not the time to discuss this.

'Remember Jiera, this is the moment that matters. When you are ready, we will decide on the next step, together. Okay?'

Jiera nodded, her face toward the ground, as she moved the dirt between her toes.

'I think you should wait here. I will go and check out ahead, try to spot Madhav first, so we know exactly where to go.'

'Don't leave me alone. Please.'

Car headlights veered onto the road to the right of us. This was the entrance to the forest and pump station. A white van travelled erratically at high speed. Although I couldn't be sure, something told me it was Rahul's men.

Roughly, I pulled Jiera down with me to a crouching position. My heart was beating so rapidly I felt the blood rush to my head. The ground was rough, the sticks and rocks grazing my legs but anything was better than risking capture.

Jiera faced the ground, tucked into a tiny ball. As I placed my arm over her protectively, I noticed the tremor running through her body. I felt my rising anger, sweeping through my veins. Just the thought of what had been done to Jiera over the years caused this physical reaction .

'Jiera, trust me now, we will be okay.'

I watched as the van sped closer toward us; I dared not turn away. All I could do was pray it would pass us by, oblivious to our close proximity. They wouldn't know Rahul was dead yet and would be following his instructions to meet at the pump station. The van continued past us rapidly. Despite straining to do so, it was impossible to see the driver or passengers through the darkened windows. I sat up, listening intently for what was to come. Nothing but silence followed. But my reprieve was short-lived. As Jiera sat up, looking directly into my eyes, I knew she was thinking exactly as I was.

We might be safe, but Ami and LJ were not and there was nothing we could do to help them.

The thought sickened me.

I forced Jiera up. We needed to get out of here, and it had to happen now. There was one thing I knew for certain. Rahul's men would be after us very soon. Gingerly, we crept closer to the final band of trees before the highway. Grateful the night was so dark, in one respect, I desperately searched for Madhav.

'There, is that him over there?'

Pointing to our left, I followed Jiera's gaze. Just to the side of a red bus stop was his car. The same old white Holden I had been in many times before. And leaning on the boot was the old man himself, nervously smoking a cigarette. Madhav was repetitively looking at the traffic in both directions, then back to the tree line. Obviously anxious, I imagined how keen he was for us to appear.

'That's him alright. Oh, thank God, Jiera. We have made it. I told you we would. Let's go. We need to do this quickly.'

Grabbing Jiera's hand, I didn't expect her sudden resistance pulling her forward. Turning back, I looked at her, confused.

'What if it's a trick? Are you sure we can trust him? What if Rahul's men are waiting inside the car? How can we know?'

'We have to go now. If LJ trusts Madhav, then I know we can too. He is a good man, I promise. I will call out to him as we approach. He will signal to me I am sure, if it's not safe. I'm not going without you. Let's move'

As we got closer, I called to Madhav.

He fell to the ground, yet rose his hands to the sky, crying out as if he had seen a miracle. Then just as quickly, he opened the back door, beckoning us to hurry. Without further hesitation, he jumped into the driver's seat. The engine was already running. We were in safe hands. In this moment, it was obvious Madhav had experienced a rescue like ours before. It would make sense, considering he too had worked for the missionary centre over many years and our case would not have been unique.

Satisfied he was alone, I pushed Jiera into the old car first, following her hastily into the back seat. I dared not look behind me. Before I had even shut the door, we were moving. Madhav drove like a madman, weaving in and out of the traffic, swerving around anyone in his path. Despite this, I felt safe. I hugged into Jiera, pulling her protectively into my grip. She continued to shake; tears freely flowing between us now.

I nodded my gratitude to Madhav through the rear-view mirror. His old, kind eyes were filled with tears also as he smiled back at us. He wiped them away rapidly, before refocusing on the road.

No words were spoken. For the entire trip, our private emotions seemingly all consuming. I desperately needed a few silent moments. I wrestled internally to regain composure, consume some energy and give my personal prayers of thanks. Today in itself would take a lot to process. Each of us, I am sure, was battling different dispositions as our car sped through the traffic, the outside world oblivious to our plight.

The big picture was all that mattered in the end. Jiera. She was safely tucked beside me now. I didn't know what the future would hold, it was too overwhelming to let the thoughts in. Instead, I chose to just sit, comforted by the feeling of Jiera's body pressed into mine.

I hope she knew. I'd give up my world, my life, to save hers. Today I nearly had.

Ami

India, 2018

As she watched the girls flee into the night, Ami sobbed. This was an expression of emotion in which she rarely let herself partake.

She wept for her girls, wondering had she done enough? She wept for the many wasted years endured in captivity. And she wept for LJ. He was such a great, selfless man. Ami knew she had let him down in the past.

Ami silently begged him to hang on, desperate for him to pull through.

That tyrant, Rahul, he had purposely ruined so many lives. The brute who now lay motionless, only about a metre away in the darkened room behind her. Ami spat at him.

Keeping one hand protectively on LJ, she placed the other over her heart. Her stare returned to the open door of the pump station. The silence encapsulating the dark night beyond reminded Ami she still had time to escape. Her own freedom lay just ahead, if she wanted it. But this option Ami would never consider, she would never leave him.

Not again.

Ami was shamed by her many mistakes. Over the years, she had done as best she could. Never would Ami have wished her life upon another. But Ami was a survivor. Even in this very moment, she had not given up hope.

Her heart bled for Aanya and Jiera. All she wished for was their safety. Ami would continue to pray over their journey in the next few hours. Aanya and Jiera deserved a chance at freedom. She hoped desperately Aanya had listened to her instructions. Aanya held the inner strength the girls needed tonight. Ami could see it. She was the one, always had been. That is why Ami had taken such a risk in contacting her back in Australia.

Ami knew time was running out.

'LJ, LJ, can you hear me?'

Feeling him stir, Ami began shaking him ever so gently in an attempt to regain his consciousness.

LJ's eyes fluttered open; he was startled and confused. LJ began searching the room, assessing his surroundings despite his groggy state.

'You did it. The girls are on their way to Madhav. They are going to make it. Because of you LJ, they will be free.'

Ami knew it was important her tone be animated. LJ needed some adrenaline, something to give him a will to fight.

LJ continued to stare at Ami. Slowly a smile formed on his lips. 'I did it?'

'Yes, my love, you did.'

Ami's simple statement seemed to breathe new life into LJ, and even if it was short-lived, Ami knew she had to use this moment to attempt to move him.

'Ami, why are you still here? I told you to go. It was important to me you be free too.'

Ami cupped LJ's face, smiling at him as tears coursed down her face.

'I left you once before, remember? My life is nothing without you. We have wasted enough years apart. Even if tonight is my last night on earth, at least I will be with you.'

'Then we had better make sure it is not.'

Ami was pleased to hear him say this, her aim being to get them out of the pump room as soon as LJ could comply. Ami knew they would have little time left before Rahul's men returned. She was surprised they had not done so already.

'I know this will be near impossible considering your state, but I want to get you out of here. There is a small well in the bush beyond. If we can just get to it before Rahul's men return, I think we might have a chance.'

LJ nodded. It was a long shot, both of them knew it. Ami also feared LJ might die in the process, but at least she had tried. She felt in her heart she owed her great love this, at the very least.

Ami was exhausted, barely able to keep her eyes open. Had she not been so amped with adrenaline and its temporary boost of strength, she too would most certainly have passed out.

LJ lay beside her, unconscious once more.

But they had done it. Ami had mostly all but dragged LJ to the safety of the old well. The round bricked structure, only a short distance from the pump station, was the best chance they had tonight to stay alive. At only a few metres deep, the narrow space barely held them.

Once Ami had LJ propped up against the wall of the well, she had climbed again to the top, retracing their steps to cover their tracks. These men were clever and Ami knew they would not be the first victims they had tracked and hunted down to kill over the years.

Only moments earlier, Ami had returned to the pump station, carefully orchestrating a false escape track. She had designed a path heading in the opposite direction from the well. She could do little more than hope the men had not found the girls and presumed them all still together in their attempted escape.

Using LJ's heavily stained jacket to smear tree branches and the ground with blood, Ami had broken bushes and created footprints leading toward the river. With any luck, the men would assume they had attempted to swim across to safety. Ami even threw LJ's jacket and Aanya's backpack into the river. They had caught in the bracken upstream, strengthening her plan to falsify the direction they had headed.

Returning to the well, Ami used her little remaining strength to push some old tin and bracken over its entrance. It was a long shot, but the best she could do. Ami knew the men would certainly be shocked to find Rahul dead. Hopefully this would rattle them enough into thinking less clearly and throwing them off their scent.

Ami rested her head gently on LJ's shoulder. He murmured something briefly before slumping further. She knew time was running out for him, perhaps for them both. She shivered. The well was damp and cold. The filthy water they sat in chilled her body. She had taken off her jacket in an attempt to wrap up LJ's wound. It wasn't ideal, but would have to suffice till help arrived.

If help was to arrive.

Again, Ami's thoughts returned to the girls. How far they had gotten? She begged silently they would find Madhav and reach the safety of the missionary. Suddenly, a beep in her pocket startled her. Cursing herself for not doing so earlier, Ami remembered. She still had Aanya's phone. Immediately filled with shame, Ami shuddered at the memory of what she had done only hours earlier. Drugging her dear, trusting Aanya was deplorable. Ami knew she could never forgive herself for this betrayal.

Reaching for the phone, Ami frantically thought about who to call. The beep had been a message from Aanya's friend Tilly. Ami hoped she would soon be able to return the phone to Aanya personally, so she could message everyone the good news of their safety. But first things first.

Bina. She could ring Bina, inform her of what had happened. Then she could get Madhav to return for them. It was a long shot, but could think of no better alternative.

Ami praised Aanya silently, finding Bina's number listed. Smart girl, that one, she thought. Bina picked up after the first ring. Both women instantly animated, were desperate in response to one another. Ami related their situation, explaining the girls had made it out and gone on ahead to meet Madhav. With the phone reception minimal and inconsistent, Ami could only hope Bina would be able to understand. Ami could hear herself rambling. A combination of shock caused by the events she had witnessed tonight and her shame at being involved was almost all too much for Ami to bear. The only thing keeping her going now was the chance to redeem her actions.

Alerted to the change in her surrounds, Ami was pulled from her thoughts. A loud engine approached, followed by skidding tyres and the slamming of doors. The noises pierced through the still night. The intrusion shattered the comforting silence, which had only moments earlier protected the well. Instinctively, Ami disconnected the call mid-sentence. With fumbling hands, she turned the phone onto silent. Hardly daring to breathe, Ami remained fixed and listened.

Rahul's men had arrived.

They were animated in their tone.

Within seconds, there was an explosion of chaos. The men had clearly discovered their dead boss. Ami and LJ had little choice but to remain still and silent, trapped in the tiny well. Their hiding spot was far from ideal, Ami knew, should they be discovered, it would serve as a death trap.

LJ stirred, alerted by the yelling and screaming. Pandemonium reigned. Ami covered LJ's mouth, pointing beyond the well. He nodded, understanding what was happening, despite barely being conscious.

Above them, birds screeched in protest of the unwelcome intrusion of the men. Ami could hear the heavy movement of the men's feet, as they thrashed around the nearby bushland. Clearly, their search for clues as to what had happened here tonight had begun. They spoke in urgent, agitated voices, with one man in particular barking orders at the rest. Ami wondered how many men were out there? It had to be at least four.

She knew her and LJ's survival was going to take a miracle.

Flashes of light spasmodically moved above them. Ami was sure the men were coming closer, torches in hand and no doubt armed. The crackle of their walkie talkies, the snapping of bracken and their animated voices seemingly were getting louder.

Ami gripped LJ's hand.

'I love you,' she mouthed without uttering a sound.

He managed a weak smile, returning her words silently. At least if we die tonight Ami thought, we have been able to voice our truth, and die with the hope Aanya and Jiera had made it to safety.

Ami closed her eyes, leaning into LJ. In doing so, she felt an unexpected peace wash over her. For the next few moments, she welcomed its solace, relished in its calm.

But Ami's peace would be shattered all too soon. Ready or not, fate had dealt her hand.

Aanya

India, 2018

The weeks preceding had been some of the toughest, yet without question, the most rewarding of my life.

As I rested my head back against the seat now, a sudden weariness was taking hold. I had not let myself unwind until this point, and even now it was only partial.

Unlike my plane journey here just over a month ago, today I was unfazed by the cramped space and stifling air. I had become accustomed to India, in such a short time learning and experiencing a great deal about what was in a sense, my other life. Allowing myself to zone out from the constant chatter, laughter and animated conversations consuming the compartment, I drifted into thoughts and memories of the last 23 days, my precious time reunited with Jiera. Then there were the weeks before I had found her. It was all going to take some processing. But I could feel the storm easing. The whirlwind was settling, this part of our journey nearly complete. Or so I hoped.

We were going home.

I smiled, knowing this would not be the last time Jiera and I set foot in India. In such a short period of time I'd developed strong feelings about this. I intended to find out how exactly my biological parents had died, discover the village we had been born into and revisit the orphanage. I knew without a shadow of a doubt my journey would involve making an impact here and in Nepal in our future.

All my plans could wait. There was only one thing now that mattered. The rehabilitation and healing of Jiera. I'd need a strong team around me to achieve this, and I knew I had one. My family would become hers.

I was so proud of Jiera's bravery. She had been a tower of strength in the last few weeks; we even had small glimpses of thinking toward the future. Yet I knew it was imperative firstly, she worked through her deep trauma. I would not let her ignore the damage within, as I had.

As I knew, the shadows reappear eventually

Today, the constant waves of emotion were crashing over me, making me feel unsteady. Although my body would appear still to the outsider, my mind was far from settled, my conflictions overpowering.

I felt saddened to be leaving the people of India. I had come to love and respect them so much. The missionary would always be my second home.

I felt heartache thinking about LJ and Ami. The unknown was unbearable, and in any idle moments, I found my mind returning to them.

I couldn't get past it, and I knew it was the guilt. I never should have left them behind. We had been left with no choice.

Yet I felt excited and relieved at the prospect of being reunited with Tilly and my family again in Australia. Over the past few weeks, I had talked daily with them. Tilly was still my rock, and I simply couldn't wait to see her smile, feel her hug again. I knew she was going to love Jiera and be a huge strength to her going forward.

I felt like a completely different person today, to the naïve girl who had charged over to India last month. Yet somehow, I had to slot back into the life I had left. Was this even possible?

Did I even want to?

This was both exciting and mind-boggling.

It was impossible to forget what we had witnessed over the last few weeks, not to mention a lifetime in captivity.

I felt overjoyed, of course, to be returning with Jiera, yet heavy with the responsibility of rehabilitating her. Would she ever be capable of a normal life? Now that my memories were returning rapidly, would I?

Without opening my eyes, I reached for Jiera's hand, and she entwined her fingers with mine. Our plane had not yet moved from the tarmac of Delhi airport, but at least we had boarded. An announcement had just informed us of a further delay in taking off. I wished we could just get moving.

We were one step closer to safety. Just a flight away from the freedom of our new life together in Australia. But I would not fully rest until our plane reached the air. Even in this very moment, we still were at risk of being recaptured by Rahul's men.

Everyone had warned us of this. Today was one of the only times we had dared leave the safety of the missionary centre.

My mind travelled back there again, reliving the night Madhav had delivered us to safety. Swiftly we had been taken underground, to their safehouse. It had to be seen to be believed. I was still amazed at how incredible this facility was. Clearly, the rooms had been used in many rescues. The small apartment like space had everything we had needed. It was purpose-built to provide the safety and security victims required during rehabilitation. Bina had told me there were many of these safehouses throughout India. She had been animated as she proudly shared stories of the many brave people working tirelessly, fighting daily against the child trafficking industry.

As we sat patiently now aboard our plane, the air was unbearably humid, causing my skin to itch relentlessly under my cast. I couldn't wait to rip it off. My broken arm and Jiera's wound had been swiftly taken care of by the medical staff working within the missionary centre. Bina had been there every step of the journey, ensuring we were comfortable and recovered as best we could.

Despite the trauma of the ordeal, I felt strong. For the first time in my life, I felt really proud. Everything I had endured was worth it, and I knew I would do it all over again to have Jiera by my side. In a very short time, my twin had again become my reason for living. I loved her fiercely and always would. Now I just had to allow her the space to recover in her own time, not be over protective.

Looking across at Jiera, she rested peacefully, her hand remaining in mine. Her hair had grown back slightly, dulling some of the scars on her skull. She had so much to learn and discover. After all, she had been in captivity since the age of 9. Jiera had never experienced being an experimental teenager, having friends, talking on the phone, going out to dinner or shopping or the movies. And then there was education, and health care and even having a bed or a safe place to live. My sister was not letting much escape her veiled façade, but she must be overwhelmed.

All had been surreal over the past few weeks, like we were characters in a thriller movie.

In reality, we were the lucky ones, many victims still remained. Never would I be the same again; how could I be? Exposure to the inhumane side of our world had altered my existence forever. I understood now why my mind had spent so many years shielding me from the truth.

Over the last few weeks, countless memories had come flooding back. I welcomed both the good and bad, feeling completely ready to embrace their fallout. I wanted to know who I was, and the journey I had travelled. Finally, the pieces of the puzzle were coming together. Spending time with Jiera had allowed them to gradually resurface. My past didn't scare me so much anymore, but instead inspired me.

But again, the all too familiar ache in my stomach returned.

Part of this story was still unresolved.

I would never rest until I discovered the fate of LJ and Ami.

Madhav had remained suspiciously quiet about them after

that night, despite my badgering. I had pressed him many times, begging he tell me what he had witnessed.

Had Madhav made it in time?

Did he get them to safety?

If so, are LJ and Ami alive?

Not even Bina knew the truth, so she said.

Madhav's silence infuriated me, yet I was careful not to let on. Surely, after all we had been through together, I had the right to know. Why did Madhav not trust us?

Thinking of Bina now calmed my spirit. She was simply one of the most beautiful and kind people you could meet. She brimmed with wisdom and intuition. I felt a little ashamed at how I had hounded her relentlessly over the last few weeks about LJ and Ami. Poor lady, I knew I could be forthright when I wanted to be. Undoubtedly, she could understand all the reasons why. She had sworn she knew nothing, Madhav had refused to tell her too. I believed Bina, but this made me question even further.

Either way, I just needed the truth. Once I had the facts, I would know whether to grieve or set about finding them. But now it was too late. I was on my way out of India. Silence on the subject had remained, although not in my mind.

There had been so much more to Madhav than I'd first thought. Although Madhav played it all down, insisting he was just a taxi driver, Bina had told us quite a different story. The truth was, Madhav had been quite an integral part of the rescue team over many years. He and LJ had worked together in many successful rescue cases. I'd had a strong feeling from the start there was more to him than met the eye. Like so many beautiful Indian people I'd come across, this team was certainly amazing. No wonder my parents were so captivated by India. The western world could learn so much from their traditions and spiritual beliefs, not to mention their cooking. Oh, how I was going to miss that about Bina.

My only solace in the whole LJ and Ami situation was the mystery itself. I wasn't stupid, and they knew that. I truly believed Bina knew nothing more than Jiera and I did. Obviously, Madhav was covering something up, and surely this meant they were not dead.

I knew he was suppressing information, but why?

The night after we had returned to the missionary centre, Madhav had shared dinner with us in our underground hideout. Relishing this opportunity, I was able to thank him for returning us safely. I also had needed to apologise for misleading him in the first place. Always priding myself on my honesty, I greatly regretted having to lie to Madhav, not once, but twice. He had been very gracious.

'Sometimes Aanya, we need to make hard decisions, take actions for the greater good.'

Was he cryptically referring to his decisions with LJ and Ami?

That first evening, when I had pressured him, begging Madhav to tell me everything he knew, he had all but warned me never to speak of it again. I cringed at my behaviour. Silently, Jiera had backed me as I refused to accept his secrecy. She wanted answers too, but was always the more reserved of us. As we had sat across the small table in the kitchenette, the air in the modest space had become thick and uncomfortable with unresolved tension. Bina had continued to ladle her soup from the steaming gold pot placed in the middle of the wooden table. I had tried to catch her eye, gain her support too, but she had refused to look up from her task. Crusty bread remained untouched on the chopping board. Spices sat in small jars, and steaming sweet tea brewed.

I could recall every detail of that night, down to the clothes we all wore. It's funny, the things you remember in pivotal moments. Well, those your mind allows you to, anyway.

I couldn't let it go.

'Surely Madhav, you can understand. We need to know. Jiera and I have the right to the truth.'

His words had been etched into my memory ever since, as was

the way he looked at me. Madhav's eyes had darkened. Reaching for my hands, he had spoken softly, with tears streaming down his wrinkled, leathery face.

'Dear girl. Aanya, you and Jiera, and Bina too, are all very precious to me. Please, you must forgive my silence. But I need you all to respect and trust I cannot tell you anything further for now. I promise you, I have good reason. You all remain in grave danger and some truths are safer left unknown.'

He was serious, and his warning certainly did make us consider he held a dangerous truth.

Never did I dare discuss it again with Madhav. It was something in his eyes. Normally calm and filled with patience and strength, that night his eyes had reflected very different emotions.

Their blackness haunted me to this very moment.

His eyes had swirled with alarm and apprehension, reflecting his own confliction.

He left me questioning and aggrieved, yet from then I was also wary.

⚛

As the air hostesses performed their routine safety drill, I opened my eyes, blinking at the sudden false lighting in the cabin. Forcing my mind back to the now, I looked across at Jiera. Still clasping my hand, she was dozing contently beside me. Transfixed with the tattoo on her forearm, I felt the bile rise in my throat remembering the day we had been branded like animals. Rahul had done it himself, pinning us down as he had engraved the number one on my arm and a number two on Jiera's. Bastard. I shook the memory off. I had more important things to focus on now.

My sister continued to need lots of rest; her health was still not up to par. Bina had said it would take many months, maybe even years, before she was back to the able-bodied young woman I knew she could be. Medical testing had revealed her deficient in many vital nutrients and vitamins. Still, I couldn't help but smile at her now. Physically, there was not a doubt in my mind she would regain her full potential. Thanks to the excellent care of Bina, even in the past few weeks I could see she had put on a little weight and gained some colour in her beautiful face. Her energy was improving too, she was sleeping less and able to concentrate for longer periods. I just needed to be patient; time would heal all.

My smile faded as my thoughts turned to Jiera's mental health. This battle was so much harder. I'd rather physical pain over emotional any day. This is something LJ and I had discussed at length one night. He had been so brutally honest about his personal battles, only making me love him the more. What if Jiera never recovered from the years of neglect and brutal torture? Sure, I had been there for much of it too, but still my mind sheltered me from some things, of that I was certain. And I had been given a second chance over the last six years; one Jiera had not. I knew on our return I would need to tread carefully. I tended to push too hard, be a little outspoken when I felt passionate about something, especially when it came to my family. Jiera had agreed to see Dr Belshar when the dust settled. This had brought me great relief. We would both need her expertise going forward.

In the nights we had spent together over the last few weeks, Jiera had told me many of her stories. They had strangled my heart again and again, as well as incredibly enraged me.

I will never understand how one human could treat another as such. I could see, it was her warped sense of self that would take the longest to rectify. Rahul had done a thorough job ensuring she was brainwashed, programming her mind meticulously over time. Jiera had a deep-seated conviction she was useless, mattered nothing, and to no one.

Being forced into servitude at a very young age was brutal on both of us. But Jiera was beaten into submission on a whole new level after my departure.

Would I ever get over the guilt of being the one that escaped?

Why hadn't I known about Jiera earlier?

I felt annoyed at myself even thinking about the time I had wasted. Had I been that caught up in shit that didn't matter back in Australia, I failed to really listen?

Deep down, I'd known all along those niggling feelings inside me needed to be addressed, yet I chose to detach.

I was more than aware my guilty emotions were useless, but I couldn't control them. It had helped me to share this with Bina, and she had worked tirelessly over the last few weeks in beginning to transform my mindset. She educated me in understanding the big picture. My body did the best it could. I was recovering myself. Bina taught me to visualise my body, healing from the inside out, reminding me of the strength it had needed to fight its silent battles. My soul was preparing me, in a whole sense, for this time. Bina insisted had I remembered Jiera before my mind was ready, I simply would have failed.

'Your soul always knows the answer, her timing forever perfect. You just have to be quiet enough to hear her and patient enough to listen.' I repeated her words in a whisper now. Bina had insisted I do this often, her tone serious and eyes wide at the time. 'Everyday, at least, recite this mantra, even back in Australia. Promise me you will.'

I intended to keep my word to Bina. I missed her already, despite not yet leaving India. She was a truly precious and wise human, who brought us such strength.

'I promise, Bina,' I breathed.

I recited more of her words in my head.

'Healing is not the absence of the storm. Healing is in the way we ride it. You are just like the eagle, Aanya. Remember, as long as you persevere and work hard, you will triumph. Eagles have a strong vision; they set their minds and eyes on their goals. Lock your wings in the face of adversity my dear girl and you will fly higher than your storm'

Jiera whispered into my ear unexpectantly, breaking my thoughts. I almost jumped at her gentle touch.

Turning to face her, I could see despite her eyes remaining shut, a smile had formed on her lips.

'Our wounds are the places the light enters us, Aanya. Rumi said that remember'

She was grinning at me now, well and truly awake. Her brown eyes seemed to shine. I couldn't help but laugh, easing some of my tension.

'More Bina sayings hey, she certainly left her mark, such a beautiful lady'

'We will see her again, Aanya. You know as well as I do, our time in India is far from over.'

I looked intently at my sister, admiring her insightful smile. Despite the minimal conversation between us regarding our future, we were on the same page.

Nothing could make me happier.

One thing I knew with certainty, having a purpose to indite change, was what I desired. It made me buzz inside just thinking about it. Maybe then, with this project in mind, I could begin to rationalise, why the hell all this had happened to us.

We didn't deserve it. No victim ever did.

We had done nothing wrong.

But we'd been blessed with a second chance. I knew this was for a reason.

As the minutes turned into an hour, it was hard not to become restless, contained on a plane yet to take off. Especially when everything prior was in the lead up to this moment. Time moved so slowly, it almost appeared to be stilted.

'Aanya, do you think Bina and Madhav are still waiting in the airport?'

'Yep, 100%. Bina will not leave us until she knows we are in the air.'

Earlier today, we had said our teary goodbyes. Bina had hugged me so tightly, part of me never wanted her to let go. Madhav had been very emotional too, promising us that everything was going to be alright. I was so tempted to ask him one last time about LJ and Ami, refraining at the last minute remembering my promise to him.

'Hey Aanya, I nearly forgot. Madhav gave me this. He told me not to show you until we were in the air, but I figure we are close enough.'

Jiera reached into her new backpack, pulling out books and ear phones, chewing gum and a water bottle, biscuits and chips before she found what she was searching for. I stared keenly, willing her to hurry up. This backpack contained more than Jiera had practically owned her whole life. No wonder she was in a fluster trying to find Madhav's gift.

'Come on Jiera, what did he give you? Show me. Why did you wait this long to tell me?'

Finally, Jiera pulled out a small package, wrapped in brown paper. It had been neatly encased, sticky tape binding it securely. I grabbed it from Jiera, a little too abruptly. She laughed at me, shaking her head.

'You always were so impatient.'

Silent for a moment, we both stared, somewhat perplexed at the mystery I held in my hand. What on earth could it be?

'Why didn't Madhav give it to me?'

Jiera giggled.

'He said you would ask me that.'

'Well?'

'He told me to tell you, had he given it to you, you would open it before instructed and we may not have flown out today.'

I swallowed a little harder, suddenly nervous. What the heck did that mean? My mouth was dry and my pulse raced. I felt a mixture of excitement and nerves. Somehow, I knew. Whatever this package contained was very important and would hold some answers.

Now it was Jiera's turn to be impatient.

'Well, open it, hurry up. Looks like a block of chocolate to me. I hope it is. I'm hungry again.'

I laughed, trying to relax the anxiety causing my stomach to churn.

'You are always hungry. Making up for lost time I reckon. That's why Bina packed so much into that backpack of yours. It is a long flight you know.'

I tore open the brown paper. Whoever had wrapped this certainly had done a thorough job.

I recognised the object immediately. Surely my eyes were not deceiving me? The realisation came quickly. Holding this in my hands now, without question, could mean two very different things. It was proof that Madhav knew what had happened to LJ and Ami. He had known all along if they were alive or dead.

Staring down at my phone, I knew the last person who had this was Ami. She had taken it from me just before I passed out. I remember laying on the ground, confused as to what was happening. She had pulled my phone from my grasp and slipped it into the front pocket of her apron. Part of her daily attire, Ami had often used this pocket to hide things from Rahul, storing food or medicine for us over the years.

I noticed a small note had also been placed in the brown paper, I looked across at Jiera before swiftly beginning to unfold it. She was as transfixed as me. Familiar scrawly handwriting met my eyes. Tears came from nowhere, blurring my vision.

'What, Aanya, what is it? Who is this note from? Do you know whose phone this is?'

'It's mine. Ami had it last, at the pump station.'

Jiera moved her hands to her mouth, as shocked as me. I pushed my shoulders back, taking in a long, slow breath. As I tried to contain the seemingly unstoppable tears coursing down my cheeks, I became oblivious to the commotion and congestion of movement in the plane cabin. Time stood still. I felt paralysed. Something stopped me. I just couldn't finish unfolding Ami's note, literally terrified at the truth it would reveal. I wanted so desperately for LJ and Ami to be alive and safe, but I had dared not dream it, as my rational side knew it was near impossible.

If the note revealed LJ was dead, could I survive this truth?

It would all be my fault.

As if reading my emotions, Jiera put one hand on my back, reaching for the note with the other.

I watched silently as she held the small piece of paper, scrutinising it before revealing to me its message. There were only a few lines of text. I closed my eyes, begging silently it revealed what I desperately needed to hear.

Dear Aanya,
Please turn on your phone. I have left a recorded video for you.
Ami.

What the hell?

I stared in disbelief.

'That's it? That's all it says?'

I leaned in closer, inspecting the note myself.

'Yep, that's it. Aanya, snap out of it, come on, we finally have the answers we have been waiting for. Turn on your phone. Hurry up.'

I stared back down at the untouched phone in my lap.

'What if it's bad?'

'Either way, we need to know. Together, we can face anything, remember? We always have and we will do it again now. You are not alone.'

Briefly, I looked up at my surrounds. The other passengers were seemingly oblivious to our existence. All deep in conversations, reading, on devices, or resting as we had earlier. Our plane remained grounded. My hands were shaking as I switched on my phone, waiting and praying it would come to life. I just could not bear the torture if it were flat or broken. To my relief, the apple symbol appeared before uploading all my apps. Quickly, I flicked the screen across and found the promised video. I turned the sound up as it started. A blackened screen met our eyes.

As the seconds passed and the video played, we sat fixated, hardly able to believe this was real. Jiera squealed in delight, jiggling up and down in her seat. I couldn't move, frozen in the moment, not even daring to blink. Both LJ and Ami smiled, waving into the camera. They looked relaxed, sitting closely, Ami had her arm resting over LJ's shoulders. Looking as though they could have been on holidays somewhere; their smiles were bright and faces relaxed.

Their images blurred again, as more tears washed down my face. I forced in a sharp breath, blinking rapidly but still not daring to look away, for fear they would disappear. Jiera grabbed my hand; she too was overcome with the emotion of actually seeing LJ and Ami's face. We had dreamed of this moment for so long. It was almost too good to be true.

I prayed it was real.

What if this was a ransom video?

Or worse.

No. Ami and LJ were alive. That was all that mattered, I thought, forcing myself to shake off the fear.

We sat devoid of movement except for our smiles and the tears trekking down our cheeks. We watched LJ and Ami's recorded video again and again until I could almost repeat their messages word for word.

Never would I forget this blessing, this incredible moment.

I tried to abate my mind, granting it comprehension. I could see Jiera's too was a million miles away, seeking to process it all. Perhaps Madhav was right. Had I seen this message before we had boarded our plane, I may have delayed our flight out of here. Then again, maybe not. Although I would have been torn in my decision, Jiera would always be my first priority.

'Play it again, Aanya, please. I love that bit when Ami laughs at herself for recording instead of writing a letter. It's hilarious how proud she is. They look okay Aanya, don't you think?'

I nodded. They really did. LJ lay on what looked like a hospital bed, with Ami tucked in by his side. They seemed calm and settled, a far cry from what I had last witnessed, the scene haunting me till now. I could see their shared love and closeness, which had obviously remained despite being separated for so long. I understood this connection. The years may have kept Jiera physically apart from me, time and memories lost, but in reuniting our bond was instantaneous.

Jiera spoke in all but a whisper, resting her head back on the seat. She was coughing more frequently and needing her Ventolin. The black circles were darkening around her eyes again, her skin paling. Although happy, I could see her exhaustion was returning. The emotional rollercoaster we were on was certainly taking its toll, but her bravery was undeniable.

Pulling Jiera closer, linking her arm in mine, I pressed play. Although we had to strain to hear the recording, LJ and Ami's faces said it all. Their smiles and animation brought us joy and a peace beyond words. When speaking into the camera, they constantly looked from one another back to us.

Tranquillity washed over me afresh. Everything was going to be okay.

With Ami recording herself first, both had taken the opportunity to share and leave us their heartfelt messages. Ami began.

Hello my beautiful girls,

Please forgive us for not contacting you immediately. We had to make this hard decision, knowing it was crucial for your safety. Madhav was the only one aware we were safe, as it was he who aided us in our escape. We instructed him not to tell you we were alive. LJ knew it would be far too dangerous for you or Bina to have this knowledge, should Rahul's men have found you. I know how your hearts must have been tortured waiting on news from us, and for that, I am truly sorry.

As you can see, we are alive and well. I thought you would get a smile seeing us using such modern technology to send a message. I am so grateful to know you are on your way back to Australia safely. That was everyone's priority and brings such joy to LJ and me.

I need you both to know just how much I love you. From the first moment I saw you, it was so.

I am immensely proud of your courage and resilience. Promise me you will do everything it takes to heal. It is important to me that you take every opportunity life presents. You are both deserving of nothing less. Despite the years lost, I know your strong spirits will lead you to a life of great purpose. Big things are coming for you both. But first, you must regain your health and stability.

Until we are together again, and we will be I promise, stay strong and brave. Never let the world hold you back again, my loves. Do not worry for me, I am now in the good company of LJ as you can see.

With that, Ami had handed the phone over to LJ. It kept recording as she fumbled, all the while instructing LJ to talk into the screen. LJ had whispered to her not to be bossy. The amusing scene brought a smile to us, relieving some of our mixed sentiment.

Ami had become very choked up at the end of her speech, and no matter how many times I had watched it over the last half hour, repetitively I became sentimental myself. By now I knew my face would be puffy and blotchy, yet why would I care?

LJ was gruffer and matter of fact in his speech, yet somehow I could tell this was just a façade. His words affected me deeply, even more than listening to Ami. I loved this man, he was my hero.

Hey Aanya, Hi Jiera,

Glad this is getting to you.

Excuse my outfit, as you can see, I am still recovering in hospital. Well, not a real hospital, but close enough. We are staying in another safehouse on the other side of Delhi. You might hate me for this, but Madhav and I thought it best we stay apart until we knew both of you were safe. I've seen your moods before, Aanya, and I know this would have annoyed you greatly.

I'm sorry I scared you girls. And I know it would have been bloody awful not knowing what had happened to us. Forgive me for that, too. But I can promise you now, I'm going to be just fine. Thanks to Ami. She saved my life, this girl did. Tough old bird this one, kind of pretty, too, don't you think?

Anyway, we will tell you the whole story when we see you.

Oh, I forgot that bit. I have pretty big news. Ami and I will be returning to Australia as soon as I get the all clear to fly. We have the authorities assisting us in getting out of the country safely when the time comes, so don't you worry your pretty head about that. The three of you, well, you gave me a reason to live again. Thanks for being such a pain in the butt, Aanya. Thanks for not giving up on me, and believing in me when I couldn't do it myself. You saved my life, girl, even though you got me shot.

Speaking of annoying, Ami is bossing me around like I am some sort of cripple. Boy this woman can talk! But I am going with it, turns out she is the love of my life and I'm bringing her home as my wife. So yeh, we all have got a bit of celebrating to do I reckon.

Oh, and it's all a bit early to talk about, but I've been thinking about the future. Maybe, if you girls are up for it, we could work on a plan to head back to Nepal or India at some point. I'd reckon we would make a pretty good team, the four of us. Stir the pot a bit. Anyway, Ami is poking me to shut up for now about the future and let you be. Too early to be talking about this stuff she is saying. Maybe so.

I miss you girl. I never thought I'd say it, Aanya, but I love you both. I intend to be in your lives going forward…that's if you will have me, of course.

See you soon girls. Travel safe.

I had no words.

My tears just kept flowing, and I had no intention of stopping them, so instead I smiled at their presence. I thought of Bina again. She always said tears were a gift. The way we cleanse our hearts and rejuvenate our spiritual selves. From the window of our souls, tears are the perfect expression of our purest emotions.

I realised in this moment something profound about my own healing. Over these past few weeks, I had grown immensely. No longer was I detaching from emotions but instead letting myself experience them, accepting who I was. I knew with certainty my past would certainly not define my future.

❀

'Aanya, earth to Aanya.'

Jiera was poking me back into the present, I smiled at her insistence.

'We are moving. Does this mean we are finally taking off? Is it scary flying?'

Looking out the small window, I could see she was right. Our plane was preparing for flight.

Holding Jiera's hand, taking a deep breath of relief, I smiled at the heavens.

Soon we would be safe.

'Yep, we are on our way. The plane trip is not to be feared. A new home awaits you Jiera.'

'But I'm feeling weird Aanya, something feels wrong. I'm dizzy and I think I'm going to vomit. Maybe I'm not ready.'

Suddenly Jiera unbuckled and tried to stand. She was frantically looking around her. Was she trying to leave?

'What are you doing Jiera?'

'Aanya, make it stop, I'm frightened, it is too noisy, I want to go back, I want to see Bina.'

I grabbed her hand in an attempt to still her, distantly aware of the people staring and the stewardess marching toward us.

'Girls, the captain has turned on the seatbelt sign, you must remain in your seats, we are preparing for take off. Is everything okay here?'

I glared at her. Did she really have to take that impatient tone? Jiera began to cry, she was shaking and disorientated, panic had gripped her tightly. I had to get rid of the stewardess.

'Sorry, my sister is a first-time flyer, I will take care of her now. We are fine, thanks and sorry for the trouble.'

The stewardess continued to hover and I could sense Jiera searching for a way out.

'I need you to leave us alone now, I appreciate your help, but you are making it worse'

The stewardess raised her eyebrows at me but backed away swiftly, my tone had been commanding.

'Jiera, look at me. Please. Jiera.'

I cupped her face, forcing it toward mine. We locked eyes, without breaking her stare I eased her gently back into her seat, remaining close.

'I can't even imagine how scary this is for you Jiera. But I can promise you, you are not in danger. I will be right beside you every step of the way. I'm not going to let anything happen to you I promise. Please Jiera, Breathe, you are safe with me.'

She continued to weep yet remained still, gripping me tightly. I pulled her shaking body close.

'Aanya, I don't know when I will be ready to go back to India, even though right now I don't want to leave. This is all so confusing. I heard you talking to Bina about coming back to work here as a missionary. Even though I know it would be the right thing to do, right now, the thought of returning is all too much. Please forgive me. I don't want to hold you back, it's just—'

I cut her off mid-sentence. Her tone had become almost urgent, I could feel her anxiety heightening again

'Jiera, none of that is important right now. I don't care about any of it. Breathe. There is nothing else you ever have to do except be my sister and let your new family show you how to be happy and content. You are more than enough right now, Jiera, all that matters. We will love you fiercely through whatever comes. You got that?'

She smiled weakly and closed her eyes, squeezing my hand harder. I was reminded again of just how fragile this dear girl was.

Soaring into the sky, leaving some of our past and pain behind, my mind drifted to the majestic eagle once more. Its metaphor was so relatable to our journey. I closed my eyes once again, letting a stillness wash over me as Bina had taught.

Intentionally or not, we had done what an eagle does best.

Endure and embrace a storm.

Our life squall had encapsulated the majority of our years, yet despite this, we had locked our spirits together, allowing our unity and hope to lift us above the trauma.

I had learnt as a little girl you either had to choose to run, or rise to survive. Again, in this moment I vowed to be brave, not only for myself, but for Jiera and for my families, both in Australia and India.

As I embraced the movement of the plane, I visualised myself as an eagle. Australia was our peace, our victory after challenging and embracing our storm. I knew I must look ridiculous in this moment, eyes shut, grinning from ear to ear, but I couldn't have cared less. It felt so good.

See you on your return, Aanya. We will meet again. I can promise you that. Remember, bitch, some people matter and some do not.

My eyes flew open, and suddenly I was gasping for breath, my pulse was drumming in my temples as I grabbed at my head, trying to get him to leave. I surged forwards in my seat, knocking Jiera in the process, stirring her abruptly from her sleep. In that split second intense fear reigned, knocking me back, its weight all suppressing.

No.

You actually thought you were rid of me, Aanya? Stupid girl.

No. This couldn't be possible. Rahul was dead, wasn't he?

Jiera looked at me intently, her eyes pleading. Had she heard him too?

Then over the loud speaker came the voice of the pilot. The interruption jolting me back out of my head.

'Ladies and gentleman, welcome aboard. We have now left India and are on route to beautiful Melbourne, Australia. Sit back and enjoy the flight. We will endeavour to make your journey as comfortable as possible.'

I looked across at Jiera, forcing a fake smile.

'Rahul has stolen enough from our lives, Aanya. It is up to us now.'

She was right. She understood.

A steely determination began surging through my body, superseding the fear of him. I could feel its force spreading rapidly. Bringing with it an intense realisation that this man, this monster, dead or alive, was not going to rule me any longer.

I would make certain of this.

I intended to be the author of my own life story from here.

My true purpose was just emerging. For the first time in my life, it was crystal clear.

Destiny is not a matter of chance; it is a matter of choice. You can create your own future.

I have chosen to live free from the shadows of my mind.

Aanya, you will never escape me.

I pushed Rahul's voice away. Acknowledging him, accepting his presence, yet this time knowing I was stronger.

Maybe our journey with Rahul wasn't over. If that be the case, this time it should be him who's afraid.

ॐ

As our plane touched down at Melbourne airport, I held Jiera for the longest time.

Never will I be able to explain the elation in that moment. We were free. We were safe.

Bina was right, I was like the Eagle. I, too, was a courageous, tenacious defender. I had faced the storm and flown high. My vision for the future would silence my shadows.

The eagle had landed.

Shawline Publishing Group Pty Ltd
www.shawlinepublishing.com.au

SHAWLINE
PUBLISHING
GROUP

Lightning Source UK Ltd.
Milton Keynes UK
UKHW020706251022
411061UK00016B/1168